Reign and Jahiem:

Luvin' on His New York Swag

Reign and Jahiem:

Luvin' on His New York Swag

D. Brown-Newton

www.urbanbooks.net

Urban Books, LLC
300 Farmingdale Road, NY-Route 109
Farmingdale, NY 11735

Reign and Jahiem: Luvin' on His New York Swag

ISBN 13: 978-1-64556-526-0

First Mass Market Printing October 2023
First Trade Paperback Printing August 2022
Printed in the United States of America

10 9 8 7 6 5 4 3 2 1

This is a work of fiction. Any references or similarities to actual events, real people, living or dead, or to real locales are intended to give the novel a sense of reality. Any similarity in other names, characters, places, and incidents is entirely coincidental.

Distributed by Kensington Publishing Corp.
Submit Orders to:
Customer Service
400 Hahn Road
Westminster, MD 21157-4627
Phone: 1-800-733-3000
Fax: 1-800-659-2436

Chapter One

Reign

"Mom, will you please just leave this man's store before you get arrested?" I pleaded with my mother. I was at the corner store of my block, trying to get my mother, who was heavily intoxicated, to leave because she was tearing this man's store up.

"You fat motherfucking bitch. I'm drunk, but I will never be drunk enough to suck your fucking dick," she cursed at the owner.

After she said that to him, my blood was boiling, because if he had violated my mother, I was about to help her destroy his store.

"Muhammad, I know you wasn't trying to get my mother to suck your nasty-ass dick," I spat at him.

"Yes, the fuck he did. All I asked this punk was to let me get a box of Newports until my check come on the first. He said if I suck his dick, he will give me two packs, but he got me fucked up."

"Take your mother and leave my store now before I call the cops," he yelled.

My mother was still throwing shit around, so I joined her, knocking down all the cans off the shelves. I even went into the freezer and broke a few forty ounces before telling my mother to haul ass.

"Call the cops and I promise you that I will have this motherfucking store burned to the ground, so play with it if you want," I told his ass before running behind my mother.

When we got inside our house, she burst out laughing at me because I was out of breath, bent over like I had just run a marathon.

"Mom, that shit not funny. I told you stay your ass from out of that store begging. I knew it was just a matter of time before his fat ass started treating you like one of those crackheads," I spat, but all she did was cackle.

"He better be grateful I didn't tell his pork-belly ass to pull that shit out, because as soon as he did, I would have cut off his little dick," she laughed, pulling the razor out of her dingy jeans.

"How you know that man dick is little?" I asked, giving her the side-eye so she knew I didn't think the shit was funny no more.

"You know what? Fuck you, Reign. Go to the store across the street from Muhammad and get me a box of Newports and a beer," she said, pulling out a crumpled-up $20 bill.

All I could do was shake my fucking head because now I knew that she had run game on that man, taking his money knowing she wasn't sucking no dick.

"You ain't shit," I said to her before taking the money and going out the door.

My mother had been drinking and partying for as long as I could remember, but she always took care of me by any means necessary. I would protect her at all costs whether she was right or wrong because she was my mother and I loved her. I wished anyone would disrespect the woman who gave me life. Any motherfucker who did must have a death wish. She was well known in the neighborhood because she had always been good to everyone, even on her drunken binges. She threw down in the kitchen, so she always fed me, my friends, and anyone else who was hungry.

"Yo, Reign, let me holla at you for a second," Jahiem demanded, knowing damn well he wasn't asking.

I already knew what he wanted, so I didn't even want to go over there because most likely we were going to end up getting into it.

"What's up?" I asked with a roll of my eyes.

"You have to get some control over your mom. She can't be coming to the block wilding, making shit hot for everybody."

I should have known Black, with his snitching ass, would call him, but I didn't give a fuck because I was always going to be ready for whatever when it came to my mother.

"Last time I checked, my mother was a grown fucking woman, so as far as me getting her in check, it's not going to happen. If you want to blame someone, blame that bitch-ass Muhammed for trying to violate her," I told his ass, walking off with an extra switch in my walk.

"That smart-ass mouth is going to get you fucked up one of these days," he barked, but I let that shit go in one ear and right out the other.

Jahiem knew that he wasn't going to do shit, and he wasn't going to allow no one to do shit to me, so I was far from worried. I knew that he had a thing for me, but I wasn't trying to give his ass no play because of the many bitches he entertained. Fucking with him meant fighting all those thirst buckets he fucked with who'd be claiming his ass.

After leaving the bodega with my mother's cigarettes and her beer, I walked out of the store expecting to see him, but he was gone. I was low-key feeling his ass, but I didn't have the time to be dealing with all the drama that came with him. I was cool with his sister Jamila, so whenever I was at their house, he was always trying to shoot his shot. I'd be trying to explain to him that I was not even fucking him, and his birds be flocking, so I wasn't interested.

After handing my mom her things, I went into my room to finish my assignment I had started before my neighbor called about my mom. My cell rang, causing me to suck my teeth. I was never going to get this assignment done.

"What's up, Jamila?" I answered.

"Jahiem just told me what happened at the corner store, so I was calling to see if Ms. Peggy was good."

"You know Mom is always going to be good. She had me in that store ready to go to war for her ass when she robbed that nigga of his twenty dollars. She told him she was going to suck his dick, then once she got the money, she flipped the script on his ass." I laughed, causing her ass to laugh too.

"Your mom be on that bullshit, but I admit that her ass got game."

"She know what the fuck she be doing. Now she in the kitchen cooking like nothing happened with her crazy ass. Anyway, I need to finish my accounting assignment, so I'll see you tomorrow at school. And tell your brother to stay up out of my business." I smiled at the thought of him.

"Girl, stop fronting." She laughed before ending the call.

After finally finishing my accounting assignment, I went into the kitchen to get something to eat because I was hungry. My mom was now sitting in the living room, talking shit to our neighbor, Ms. Trina. I knew that she only came over to be nosy about what happened up the street with her ugly ass. I always told my mother that ho be smiling in her face but talking about her behind her back, and I believed that she was creeping with Mr. Jimmy.

Mr. Jimmy was my mother's on-and-off-again fuck buddy. He wasn't shit. He stayed just as drunk as her ass. They both were functioning alcoholics, and because of that, you couldn't tell either of them that they had a problem.

You wouldn't believe that my mother held down a job for ten years before alcohol became her full-time job. Don't get me wrong. She always had a problem with alcohol in my eyes, but it had gotten worse when my dad passed away.

"How are you doing, Reign? I just stopped by to make sure that Ms. Peggy was doing okay. I heard what happened down at the corner store, so you know I got her back," she said.

I wanted so bad to pull her card, but I didn't say shit because it was only a matter of time before my mother got in her ass. She must have been coming down off her alcohol, because when she had enough drinks in her, she'd be cursing folks out. The next day, all would be forgiven like nothing happened because no one really took her seriously.

"Reign, make Trina's ass a plate so that she can take her nosy ass home," my mother spat, but all Ms. Trina did was shake her head.

"Mom, why you do that lady like that?" I laughed a while later after letting Ms. Trina out and locking the door.

"Didn't you tell me that bitch be talking about me behind my back? I know she didn't care about what happened down the street. She was probably here to see if Jimmy was here, but I'm on to both of their asses. I haven't seen it with my own eyes, but when I catch them, I'm putting my foot in his ass."

"Well, if you put your foot in his ass, you have to put your foot in her ass too, because she knows that you and Mr. Jimmy fool around." I snickered.

"I don't know how many times I have to school your ass. A bitch doesn't owe you shit, because she didn't make no promises or commitment to your ass. That nigga know he has an old lady, so if he creeps with the next one knowing that shit, then it's his ass," she said.

"Well, I don't feel that way, because if a bitch claim to be my friend and is smiling in my face while fucking my man, it's her ass," I sassed.

"Watch your damn mouth," she said, giving me that look to say she would still beat my ass.

I forgot that I was talking to my mother, so I apologized before taking my ass in the room before I got her started. Once I was done eating, I took a shower and took my ass to bed so that I could get up on time.

I woke up the next morning with a cramp in my damn neck because I had woken up in the middle of the night talking shit on Instagram. After showering, I got dressed, and before I headed out the front door, I went into my mother's room to tell her ass to stay out of trouble. If she decided to get her ass in some shit that day, I wasn't leaving school, so she would be on her own.

As soon as I parked in the school parking lot, I saw my ex, Byron, getting out of his car, looking good as always. He was with his new girlfriend, Shayla, causing me to cut my eyes at him. It pissed me off that the reason we broke up was because I accused him of cheating on me with her, which he denied, but here he was now in a relationship with her, wanting me to believe that he started dating her after we broke up. I didn't care if he wasn't messing with her before we broke up, because dating her a few weeks after the breakup still made his ass look guilty. I felt like making a scene, but I wasn't going to give that bird bitch the satisfaction. It still bothered me to see them together, but I was that bitch, so in public, no one would ever know that I was bothered.

I had no idea what he saw in this trick, who was always dressed as if she were about to walk the ho stroll. It boggled my mind as to why the college never sent her ass home when clearly, they could see her attire, which consisted of a whorish lace tank that showed her hot pink bra. She had on jeans so tight that they looked as if they were painted on with six-inch heels, looking stupid.

Chapter Two

Reign

I was convinced that she had to have a relative that worked in the dean's office because her attire was against the dress-code policy. This was my second year at LaGuardia Community College, so I had witnessed females being asked to leave for wearing things that didn't come close to what she was wearing.

"What's up, Reign?" Byron fixed his face to say to me.

No, I didn't have no words for him, but I was going to speak to him just to piss her ass off. I knew she was already pissed that he had spoken to me from the look on her face, which he ignored.

"How are you?" I smiled, causing her to roll her eyes at me.

"Byron, you do see me standing here, right?" she spat.

"I'm good. Are you still fucking with that nigga Dame?" he asked me.

He was being mad disrespectful to his shorty right now, but I was loving it because she hadn't cared when she was disrespecting me by calling and texting his phone when she knew that he had a girlfriend. I had spoken to her woman-to-woman to let her know that his ass was spoken for because I knew how men be lying. She sat on the phone, stating that she didn't know that he had a girl and how she wasn't going to call or text him anymore—all lies. So, the last time she called his ass, I beat the brakes off her ass and sent his ass to be as single as a fucking dollar. I refused to allow any man to keep disrespecting me when I knew my worth, so his time was up.

"I don't know where you're getting your information from because I was never fucking with Dame," I told his ass.

"Yeah, a'ight." He smirked.

That was my cue to walk off, because all I had wanted to do was show her ass that if I wanted him back, I could get him back. I was still chuckling when I walked inside of the school because he was a damn joke. These bitches swore that they were winning when they got the man, not realizing that they had got that nigga by default.

Thirty minutes later, inside of my macroeconomics class, his ass was messaging me. That was probably how long it took him to calm her ass down, but I left his ass on seen.

After my classes were done for the day, I called Jamila to see why her ass hadn't shown up for classes that day, but she didn't answer. I decided to do a drive-by to make sure that her ass was good. If she wasn't going to make it to classes, she would have called me, so I was worried that some shit done went down.

Pulling up to her house, I saw her blue Charger parked out front. Her brother had gotten it for her birthday last month. I knocked on the door. It took her so long that I was about to walk away, until I heard the locks being turned. She opened the door wearing nothing but a damn nightshirt that was turned inside out, letting me know what was up.

"I came over here to find out why you didn't bring your ass to classes today, but I think I know why," I said.

"I'm sorry. I should have called you, but Anthony came by last night, so you already know." She smiled.

Anthony was her on-and-off-again boyfriend for about three years now, so she was right. I already knew. Whenever he found time for her, she would drop every damn thing for his undeserving ass, but who was I to judge?

"Call me later so that I can tell you about Byron's ass," I told her.

As soon as I pulled up to my block, I heard a commotion, already knowing that it had something to do with my mother without even seeing her. Getting out of my car, I could now see Mr. Jimmy manhandling my mother. I was ready to whoop his old ass until I saw he was trying to stop her from beating the shit out of Ms. Trina. My mom had one hand wrapped around Ms. Trina's hair, and she was punching her with the other hand.

I told Mr. Jimmy to grab her other hand while I pried her hand from Ms. Trina's hair. This shit was so embarrassing because they were too damn old to be out there fighting like this.

"You came in my house pretending to be my friend, but I catch you sucking my man's dick with your ho ass!" my mother screamed as I was pulling her toward the house.

"Mom, stop it," I snapped.

I loved my mother, but she was starting to make me second-guess not moving out, because this shit was becoming too much. I didn't mind her when she was just talking shit, but lately she had been getting physically out of hand.

Mr. Jimmy was trying to come inside, but I told his ass that he had to go. I told him from the beginning not to get involved with my mother if he wasn't going to do right by her. His old ass wanted to cheat with Ms. Trina, so this was the end of him in my eyes. He was almost 55 and still cheating, giving me little hope that men could ever grow the hell up.

"Why did you talk to Jimmy like you grown? You don't dismiss my company unless I tell you to dismiss them." She was now shouting at me.

"Mom, this behavior has to stop because I'm getting sick of it. You just fought Ms. Trina, claiming that you caught them together, so why the hell would you want to invite him in?" I spazzed.

"I was inviting him in because all he's going to do is go to Trina's house, being his ass don't have nowhere else to go."

All I could do was shake my head because I was standing there witnessing shit from my mother that I had witnessed in high school. If she wanted to let him in after she had just said that she caught Ms. Trina sucking his dick, then that was on her. I grabbed my cell and keys and left the house because I needed a breather from the crazy lady.

Mr. Jimmy was still standing out front, probably already knowing that she was going to let his ass back inside. I didn't say two words to him as I walked to my car, getting in and driving away. I had no idea where I was going, knowing that I couldn't stay out too long because I had assignments to complete.

I ended up going to Starbucks. I could sit in there and get my work done before going back to the house. I placed my order for a vegetable panini with an iced coffee before taking a seat in the back.

When I looked up, I saw Jahiem walk in the front door with a female, causing me to roll my eyes with a twinge of jealousy. His ass always claimed to be single, so seeing him with another female made me even more happy that I didn't give him the time of day. He must have felt my eyes on him, because he turned in my direction, smiling at me like he wasn't with a female.

"Hey, you," he said with a smile on his face after walking over to my table.

"How are you, Jahiem?" I rolled my eyes playfully as if he were bothering me.

"Why are you always giving me attitude? You be acting like you not feeling a nigga when you know damn well that's not the case." He smirked at me.

"Well, it really doesn't matter how I feel about you at this point," I said, pointing over to the female who was now waiting for him.

"I see you got jokes." He laughed.

"Nah, I'm just pointing out the obvious," I said to him.

He walked over to the female and returned a few minutes later, taking a seat as if I would be impressed that he had dismissed her.

"That was rude," I spat, but he just stared at me. "What?" I asked with a roll of my eyes.

"I'm just curious why you always be in your feelings. You always fix your face to say you not feeling a nigga but always stress when you see me with a female."

"Trust me when I say I'm not stressing. It's just comical to see the look on your face when I do see you with another female, Mr. I'm Single."

"What do I have to do to convince you that I'm single?" he questioned.

"For starters, it would be nice if you stop saying you're single. 'Single' to me means not entertaining these females."

"Well, we have a different definition of what it means to be single. When I say that I'm single, that means not one of these females could put claims on me," he said, still staring at me intensely.

I knew that I was cute with my cinnamon complexion, hazel-brown eyes, and full lips, but I needed him to stop staring.

"Why you staring so damn hard? I heard if you take a picture, it lasts longer," I joked.

"I wouldn't have to take a picture if you would stop playing and be my fucking girl," he responded seriously.

I couldn't even look him in the face because he had my ass blushing, so I knew he was smirking at me right now. I'm not going to lie and say the thought of us together had never crossed my mind, but a bitch was scared to go there with him.

"Jahiem, I'm not trying to catch a case fucking with you," I said, just as serious.

"Do you think that I have been pursuing you all this time just to break your fucking heart? I'm not that nigga."

I wanted to believe him, but for as long as I'd known his ass, he had a hard time being with just one woman. In all my 20 years, I played the fool only one time for a nigga who wasn't worthy of me, and I was not trying to do that shit again. He was my first heartbreak, so I wasn't trying to ever go through that kind of hurt. That was something Jahiem needed to understand.

"Jahiem, I don't know if I'm ready to be in another relationship right now. When I do decide that I'm ready, I'm going to need a man who is going to respect me. When I love, I love hard, so I don't think that I could deal with another nigga playing with my heart," I told him.

"On some real shit, I would never disrespect you. You already know that I been feeling you for a minute, so do you think that I would fuck the shit up? Any bitch I've ever entertained will be nonexistent as soon as you say that you will be mine."

I hadn't met a street nigga yet who was able to fuck with just one bitch, but if I agreed to be his girl and he hurt me, it was his ass. I didn't know how Jamila was going to feel about me dating her brother, but I guessed I'd find out soon enough. I knew she was probably going to say that her brother was too old for me, but I begged to differ, especially when he was only four years older.

"So, are we going to do this?" he asked.

"Do what?" I responded, messing with him. "Jahiem, we're doing this, but I swear that if you hurt me—"

"I'm not going to hurt you," he cut me off.

"Okay. Now, I just hope that your sister isn't going to stop speaking to me for going out with your ass." I smiled.

"She'll be okay being she already knows how I feel about you," he assured me.

"Well, I have to get home because I have an early class tomorrow morning," I said to him.

"What time do you get out of school tomorrow?"

"My last class will be over at two. Why?"

"I want to spend some time with you tomorrow, so I'll come scoop you up about six so that we can do something together."

"Okay." I stood, and he pulled me into his arms, hugging me tight. He smelled so good that I didn't want to move out of his arms. I knew I had to let go if I was going to leave and not go with him back to his place.

When I got home, my mom was sitting on the couch with Mr. Jimmy, causing me to shake my head. There was half a bottle of Bacardi Light sitting on the table, so he most likely bribed her with liquor to let his ass stay. I was on cloud nine right about now, so I wasn't going to let my mother's twisted-ass love life ruin my good mood.

After going into my room and putting my things away, I sat on the bed to call Jamila so that I could tell her I was now dating her brother.

Chapter Three

Jahiem

I prematurely asked Reign to be my girl knowing that I was still fucking with Monica, but in my defense, I didn't think she was going to say yes. I had been trying to get with her for a long time now, and she always shot my ass down.

I had just pulled up to Monica's crib to tell her that I couldn't fuck with her anymore, and I already knew she was going to be pissed. I wasn't in love with her. She was basically something to do because she was cool as fuck.

When I walked in, I could already tell that she had an attitude. I had told her that I was coming to chill with her last night, but I had stayed at my homegirl Ginger's crib. Ginger was who Reign had seen me with at Starbucks. I could have told Reign that she was just my homegirl, but I loved that jealous side of her. I thought that seeing me with Ginger might have forced her hand to stop fighting her feelings for me. She probably thought that

Ginger was someone I was interested in, but that shit was far from the truth.

"What happened to you coming through last night?" Monica asked with attitude evident in her tone.

Just looking at Monica, you wouldn't think that someone as petite as her would be an aggressive person. Whenever she got upset, she was a force to be reckoned with, so most times, I just walked away from her ass to avoid putting hands on her.

"I didn't make no promises about coming through last night. I told you that I would come through if business was handled, which it wasn't," I lied.

"So, you couldn't pick up the phone and call to say that you wasn't going to come through? I don't know what's been going on with you lately, but the shit is starting to blow mine," she spat.

"Well, that's why I'm here now, to talk to you about this thing we been doing," I said.

"What about it?" She rolled her eyes, getting defensive.

"I think that it has run its course, so I feel it's best that we not see each other anymore," I blurted.

"So, when did you decide that we shouldn't be together anymore? Because you wasn't saying none of this shit before. You never expressed to me that you were unhappy with our arrangement, so what changed?" she asked.

"I'm not going to stand here and lie to you because that wouldn't be me. I been crushing on someone for a long time, but she refused to give me the time of day. She believes me to be a player, so to be with her, I need to prove her wrong. We both know that we have been spending time together, but we never was in a relationship where I claimed you to be my girl. I will admit that we talked about it, but that was mostly you who wanted more than I was willing to give," I said, keeping it real with her.

"Who is she?" she asked on the verge of tears.

I never understood why females always wanted to know who the person was, as if knowing was going to make them feel better.

"You don't need to know who she is because it's not going to change anything with you knowing. I'm not trying to hurt you, but if you keep it real, you know that we were just friends with benefits."

"Wow. Trust, if I thought we were only friends with benefits, I would not have been wasting my time with you. I thought I was in a relationship, so don't try to downplay the shit now because you want to be with someone else."

"I didn't come over here to argue with you. I said what I needed to say, so I'm going to get up out of here," I said.

"Why the fuck would you do this to me? You really want me to believe that we were just friends

with benefits for all these few months, Jahiem?"
She was now crying.

"We have been kicking it off and on for a few
months, so don't make it something that it wasn't,
Monica. You're acting like you didn't know I was
fucking other females. If we were in a relationship,
why would you accept that from a man who was
supposed to be your man? I don't want this shit
ending with ill feelings, so all I ask is that you
respect that I'm going to be with someone else."

"I'm sorry if it's easy for you to do, but it's not
that easy for me to just move on when I have
feelings for you. I can't promise you that I won't
have ill feelings, because I'm pissed right now at
how you chose to handle me."

"Would you rather I continued to fuck with you
and fuck with her too?" I asked.

She was hurt, and I felt bad, but I wasn't going
to continue fucking with her just to appease her
when I didn't want to be with her. She needed to
find a man who was going to feel the same way
about her that she felt about him. I wished that we
could continue to be friends, but I knew that she
would misconstrue that as my still wanting to be in
a relationship with her.

I had some business to take care of, so I needed
to leave. It was time to wrap this conversation up.

"I'm sorry," I said in a low tone.

I didn't want her to think that I enjoyed this, because I didn't. So, I was trying to avoid having an aggressive tone. I just wanted to leave without the conversation getting physical, because it wouldn't be the first time she had expressed herself with her hands.

"I'm just going to grab my things from upstairs, and then I'm going to go," I told her.

I didn't need the things that I left there, but I wanted her to know that I would not be coming back to her place. I also didn't want her to have a reason to call me once I left.

When I came back downstairs, she was sitting on the couch with tears in her eyes, but I kept it moving. I knew if I even attempted to comfort her, I was going to end up staying with her that night out of pity. Walking away and leaving her in that condition was one of the hardest things that I ever had to do, but it needed to be done. If I wanted to be in a relationship with Reign, I had to tell Monica the truth, even if it made me seem like a coldhearted nigga. Could I have handled it differently? Maybe, but I only knew how to be real and up front the way my pops had taught me.

My cell rang as soon as I was back in the car. It was my sister Jamila calling, and I had an idea why.

"What's up, big head?" I chuckled.

"What the hell do you think you're doing?" she asked with bass in her voice like she wasn't the little sister.

"What are you talking about? And take that damn bass out of your voice when speaking to your older brother."

"I don't understand how you plan on dating Reign when you already have a girlfriend."

"I already told Monica that it was over, and she wasn't my girlfriend. She was just someone I was fucking with," I let it be known.

"I'm not talking about Monica. I know that Reign hasn't been my friend for long, but it's still not right starting something with her before ending things with Samantha," she stressed.

"I have to go," I told her, ending the call before she said anything else.

Jamila of all people knew that Samantha was a sensitive subject for me, so I wasn't trying to have that same conversation with her. Samantha and I had dated in high school and had become official about a year after graduation. She stuck with me even when I was being a dog all through high school, so it was only right to make it official. I had decided to give her the same loyalty that she continued to give me even when I didn't deserve it.

About a year ago, she was invited to a party with some friends, so I offered to take her and pick her up. She insisted that she wasn't going to be drinking and decided to drive, stating that she didn't want to be waiting around for me to pick her up. She ended up having quite a few drinks and made the decision to drive home. She lost control of the car after falling asleep behind the wheel. Instead of making sure the person she hit was okay, she left the scene.

She made it home and called me, so I rushed to her place because she was hysterical. I couldn't understand anything that she was saying on the phone. I found out that she had hit someone. We had no idea if the person she hit lived or died because, at the time, my only concern was making sure she was good. I got rid of the car and told her that everything was going to be okay if she didn't say anything to anybody.

After about a week, she was still having an issue coping with the accident, so she decided she would go away for a while. We led everyone to believe that she left to go be with her grandmother who was sick and needed her. I never expected her to be gone for so long, so I started doing me.

Jamila didn't approve of me doing me, and she never had a problem voicing it. She believed Samantha was in North Carolina taking care of her sick grandmother, so in her eyes, I wasn't shit. Jamila and Samantha had a tight bond, so I did understand why she felt the way she did. I never had a conversation with Samantha about us ending the relationship, but how long did she expect me to wait?

I hadn't admitted it to anyone, but Samantha leaving and having no intention of coming back had fucked me up. Every time I spoke to her, she tried to convince me that nothing had changed and she still loved me. If she loved me, she should have proved it by bringing her ass home, but she had yet to do that. I knew I needed to have a conversation with her to let her know that I was moving on.

After handling some business, I couldn't believe that I was getting home at a reasonable hour and not breaking day. I decided to give Samantha a call to have the conversation that I had been dreading, but it needed to happen.

"Hello," she answered, sounding like I had woken her up.

"Did I wake you?"

"What happened?" she responded.

"I just wanted to talk to you about something, but I can call you tomorrow," I suggested.

"I'm up now, so just talk," she said.

"I wanted to revisit the conversation about you leaving and being gone for so long. I tried to be patient because I still love you, but I think it's time that we move on," I blurted.

"How can you say you love me and tell me you want to move on in the same sentence?" she spat, letting me know the conversation was going to end with an argument.

Chapter Four

Reign

Jahiem and I had been dating for a few weeks, and I was kicking myself for not taking him seriously sooner. This man was not the man I thought he was. He was something special, and I had never met a man like him.

As I sat in my car at a traffic light, I remembered what a good time we'd had the other night. He had come to my house, and we played cards and had drinks with my mom and Mr. Jimmy. He wasn't the least bit bothered by her drunken ways. He treated her with so much respect that I fell in love with his ass. My mom put on some music and pulled him up to dance, and the shit was so cute. He enjoyed her just as much as I enjoyed her crazy ass. He wasn't annoyed with her, and he didn't turn his nose up at her, so he was a keeper in my eyes. This was the most fun I had seen her have since my father passed away a year ago, so it warmed my heart that he was able to do that.

I didn't realize the light had changed until the car behind me started blowing the horn, causing me to stop daydreaming. I was on my way to visit my grandmother, who I hadn't seen in about a week or so. I tried to visit as much as my time permitted because she didn't have my dad anymore to make sure that she was good. My Aunt Brenda wasn't worth shit, so she really had no one checking on her. So, I took on the role of making sure she was good.

I stopped at the store to pick up a few things that she said she needed, and as soon as I walked in, I saw Anthony with some female. I had been trying to tell Jamila that his ass was no good, but she just kept taking his sorry ass back. I rolled my eyes, letting him know that I didn't approve of him playing my friend. He didn't look bothered because he knew that, no matter what he did, she was going to take his ass back. I also knew that he would deny that he was even in the store with a female, so I pulled my iPhone out and snapped a picture.

"Who the fuck is this bitch?" the girl asked him.

"Why are you violating by taking pictures, just assuming that I'm doing something wrong? This is my homegirl, so stop trying to start some shit," he said, knowing he was lying. The look on her face confirmed that he was lying.

"Oh, so now I'm your homegirl?" she spat.

I decided to just leave them to it because they were making a scene. I sent the picture to Jamila, telling her that his ass was up in Walmart shopping with a bitch who was pushing a fucking stroller. When he saw me, he tried to stand in front of the stroller as if it would become invisible. I wouldn't be surprised if the baby in the stroller belonged to his ass. I already knew that he probably was going to say that she was family and I just jumped to conclusions, and sadly, Jamila would believe him.

My phone alerted me that I had a text message, so I was now sitting in the car, smiling at the text that Jahiem had just sent. It said that he was thinking about me. He asked if he could see me later. I couldn't contain the smile that he had just put on my face as I pulled out of the parking lot on my way to my grandmother's house. I wasn't going to respond to him until I made it to her house to avoid texting and driving.

As soon as I pulled into my grandmother's yard, my phone started to ring. Looking at the phone, I saw that it was Jamila, so I answered before exiting the car.

"What's up?" I asked, already knowing that she was calling about the picture—or so I thought.

"Why did you feel the need to attack Anthony? We cool, but we are not that cool that you can be in my business," she spat.

I had to remove the phone from my ear for a second because I couldn't believe that she was coming at me like that. And when did she determine that we weren't cool to the point where I couldn't step to her man if he was stepping out on her? I was utterly confused, but if she wanted to come at me like this over his cheating ass, it was all good. I wasn't going to sit on the phone and argue with her about his sorry fucking ass, especially when I had sent her the picture.

"Well, if we're not cool to the point where I can share with you when your man is stepping out on you, I didn't get the memo. I promise you from this point on I will never get in your business when it comes to your relationship with that nigga."

"Why you got to be in your feelings? All I'm saying is that if you see my man and you believe that he's stepping out on me, send the picture. Why did you have to get in his face? I just feel that it wasn't your place. You should have let me handle it. You sent me a picture of him standing with a female, which proves nothing."

"Say no more," I spat, ending the call because I felt myself on the verge of saying some shit that I knew I wouldn't be able to take back.

She was calling back, but I sent it to voicemail because my mouth could be reckless. I needed to get out of my feelings before speaking to her again.

I had planned on spending at least an hour with my grandmother, but I was so pissed that I just dropped the groceries off and left. Jamila hurt my feelings because I honestly thought that we were good friends, but maybe I read more into the friendship than I should have. It was crazy how, in this moment, all I wanted to do was talk to Jahiem. But how could I call him to vent to him about his sister?

"What's wrong?" my mother asked as soon as I walked in the door.

"Jamila and I got into it," I said.

"Did it have anything to do with you dating her brother?" she asked me.

"No," I answered.

"Good, because I like him, but I wouldn't want you to ruin a friendship."

"I don't think I have a friendship with her. Well, not the friendship that I thought we had," I admitted.

I had been so caught up in my feelings I didn't even realize that my mother wasn't drunk, so now I was looking at her strangely.

"What?" she questioned.

"I just noticed that you're not drinking today. Please don't tell me you let Mr. Jimmy's old ass knock you up." I laughed, causing her to laugh.

"I just didn't feel like having a drink today, but I didn't know that it was a crime to not indulge."

Something was up, but I couldn't put my finger on it. However, she knew that she couldn't keep nothing from my snooping ass. I was going to leave it alone for now, but I gave her ass the side-eye before going to my room. We didn't finish the conversation about Jamila. It would have to be another time.

"Reign!" she screamed like something happened.

"Mom, why are you calling my name like it is an emergency?" I asked her.

"I need you to take me to the grocery store so that I can get my Thanksgiving dinner. You do know that Thanksgiving is next week, right?"

I did know that Thanksgiving was next week, but we had stopped celebrating, and she damn sure didn't cook no dinner.

"Mom, what is going on with you? I don't want you giving me that look like I'm saying something foreign either," I said to her. I didn't know if I should be worried or if I should be happy that she hadn't had a drink that day and now wanted to cook for Thanksgiving.

"Girl, stop trying to make something out of nothing. I need for you to call your grandmother and invite her over for dinner. I already called your aunts and uncles, so we have to get this house together."

I folded my arms across my chest, standing in the middle of the living room, looking at her as if

I were trying to solve a complicated puzzle. I knew that whatever was going on, she wasn't trying to share it with me, so I decided to let her be.

I told her that Jahiem would come and take us to get whatever it was that she needed to make Thanksgiving dinner. I knew that he wanted to spend some time with me, but at the same time, I knew he wouldn't care what we were doing if we were doing it together.

We waited for him for about thirty minutes before he let me know he was out front. I grabbed my phone before going into the living room.

"Mom, let me find out you're crushing on my boyfriend," I joked at the smile that graced her face when I told her he was outside.

He was leaning against his truck, looking like the thug you love to hate with his sexy ass smirking at me, causing me to smile.

"Reign, I'm old enough to be his damn mother," she snapped with her late comeback, still smiling.

"How are my two favorite ladies doing?" he asked, opening the door for my mother and then for me.

Looking at him, you would never think that he was the opening-doors kind of man. He was indeed rough around the edges but sweet as chocolate on the inside, and I loved how he catered to my mother.

"I'm good, Jahiem, and I'll be better once I get all the things I need from the supermarket. I'm cooking for Thanksgiving, so be sure to invite your family, because I would love to meet all of them," she said.

I knew family was a touchy subject for him because his mother and father were no longer in his life. He didn't speak about them, but Jamila told me that her parents were killed during a robbery. I thought he blamed himself because the killers were trying to rob him, not knowing that he didn't live there or keep a stash there.

"Thank you for the invitation," he responded, saying no more.

I grabbed his hand and squeezed it gently, causing him to look at me briefly with a smile on his face. I knew exactly how it felt to lose a loved one, so I just wanted him to know that I understood. My mother didn't know that they were deceased. Had she known, she wouldn't have even mentioned family.

After an entire cart was filled at the store, we were at the checkout, where he paid for all her groceries. It was something that I didn't expect but appreciated.

Chapter Five

Reign

What most people didn't know about my mother was that she didn't need to beg for anything. My father left us well-off with his life insurance policy. She never touched that money to support any of her habits, only using that money to take care of me and the household. She received his social security, and she got a veteran's check monthly that she did with what she wanted. That was the reason I didn't understand her being down there at the corner store showing her ass, begging like she needed something from that man. Sometimes the liquor had her bugging, depending on her choice of liquor that day. Tanqueray had her ass tripping, but she didn't drink it that much being that it was Mr. Jimmy's choice of liquor.

"You didn't have to do that. She had it covered," I said to him.

"I know I didn't have to do it. I did it because I wanted to." Jahiem smiled as he loaded the bags into the shopping cart.

After we helped my mother take the bags inside,
I told her that I would be back in about an hour.
I had classes the next day, which would be the
last day before the break, so I wasn't planning on
staying out long.

"You good? And don't say that you are, because I
can tell that something is bothering you," he asked
as soon as I got back in the truck.

"I don't know what it is, but something is off
with my mother. Did you notice that she's not
intoxicated, and now out of the blue, she wants to
cook for Thanksgiving? She even wants to invite
family over when she hasn't cooked or had family
over since my father passed away. So that's what's
bothering me. And the fact that I got into it with
your sister today. Apparently, we aren't as cool as I
thought we were, so I'm in my feelings about it," I
stressed.

"Did you sit down and have a conversation with
your mother?" he asked.

"I asked her what was going on with her," I
responded.

"Did you do it in a tone as if you were accusing
her of keeping something from you?"

"No, I just asked her what was going on with her,
and she said nothing was going on with her. I have
seen my mother drink one or two drinks and not
get drunk, but I have never seen her not drink at
all. I'm just worried."

"Maybe she's tired of doing the same shit day in and day out. You did tell me that she jumped on her neighbor, so maybe that's the wake-up call for her," he tried, but I wasn't convinced.

"I don't know." I sighed.

"So, what's going on with you and my sister?"

"I saw Anthony at the Walmart with a female pushing a stroller. I promise you I would have minded my business, but his hand was placed on her lower back, so it didn't look right to me. I approached him and took a picture and sent it to your sister. I thought I was being a friend, but she called me, saying that we weren't cool like that for me to be stepping to her man. She hurt my feelings, because I was just looking out for her, but she doesn't have to worry about me making that mistake again," I stressed.

"I don't know what it is about that nigga that has her so defensive when it comes to him. I think that she's upset that the shit keep happening, so instead of taking that anger out on him, she took it out on you. She needs to apologize to you because that shitty attitude should have been focused on his ass. I been telling her to leave that nigga alone because he's not trying to do right by her ass."

"It's all good. I'm over it," I lied.

"Well, let's go get something to eat, since food always makes you feel better." He chuckled.

We went to eat, and then after we left the restaurant, he asked me if I wanted to go chill with him at his house for a little while.

"Are you speaking of your place or your second home that you share with your sister?" I asked. I needed to know which place he was speaking of because he had his own place but spent more time at Jamila's place. If he was speaking of her place, I was going to kindly pass because I wasn't ready to see her or speak to her right now. Most likely that fuck nigga was over there selling her the fucking bridge again that she would most likely buy as always.

"My place." He smiled, taking my hand as we walked to his truck.

His touch sent a chill up my spine that traveled down between my legs, causing a tingling sensation. We hadn't been intimate yet, and it was not because I didn't want to be intimate with him. He had been a perfect gentleman, but because of his reputation, I couldn't help but think that he was still blessing another female. He insisted that he had cut off all the other women in his life the night I told him yes. I wanted to believe him. I could admit that I had trust issues, but I was willing to trust again.

He pulled into his driveway, pressing a button inside his car that opened the garage. I'd only been there one time before, but I couldn't let him know because Jamila wasn't supposed to have anyone over. That was another reason why I was pissed off. If we weren't as cool as I thought, why would she let me know where he lived?

"Why do you always seem to be in deep thought? You do know that I can help you release some of that stress," he flirted, pulling me into him.

I felt butterflies in my stomach from the nervousness of being so close to him. The Dolce & Gabbana Light Blue cologne he was wearing was intoxicating. He leaned into me and kissed my lips, causing me to close my eyes just as I felt his tongue.

This was our first kiss, so again, I was nervous. I felt moisture between my legs once his hands explored my body. I felt his dick swell up against my thigh, so now I was ready for whatever, and apparently, he was too.

He pulled me toward the stairs to his bedroom. Once he got me inside, he pushed me down on the bed. He removed my Ugg boots, followed by my jeans and Victoria's Secret panties, before devouring my pussy. My legs were shaking so badly I had to give myself a pep talk to calm the fuck down. I had never experienced this kind of pleasure.

He bit down on my pussy before French kissing it with his wet mouth, causing me to scream out his name. I was now bucking wildly as I felt myself on the verge of exploding. I grabbed his head, gyrating my hips as I rode the wave, and my juices released into his mouth.

"Turn that ass over," he demanded, slapping me on the ass.

I looked up at him with tears in my eyes, contemplating whether this was something I wanted to do now that he was standing ass naked. His dick was inviting, and I would have loved to put it in my mouth, but the reality of the situation had me on stuck.

"What's wrong?" he asked, concerned.

"I need you to promise me that after we have sex, nothing is going to change," I said to him.

I knew that niggas said shit all the time to get what they wanted, so him telling me that he wasn't going to change on me could very well be a lie. Even if he fixed his mouth to lie to me right now, I wanted him to know where I stood. I wanted him to know that the consequences of his actions would be his fault once the words left his mouth. Byron had gotten a pass because, although he had sold me a dream, he never got the chance to fuck me and leave me. I had left his sorry ass because some bitch was always on my phone telling me she was fucking him.

"Why would something change?" he asked me.

"I just need to know that nothing is going to change once I give myself to you." I knew that I was probably fucking up the mood, but I needed him to say it.

"Are you telling me that you're a virgin?"

"Yes, I'm a virgin," I admitted.

I had no idea why men acted as if all women were out there fucking. I knew that there were quite a few, but there were still some out there who hadn't had sex. I wasn't a virgin because I didn't want to have sex. It was just that I hadn't met anyone worth opening my legs for besides for some head.

"Listen, I feel honored that you want me to be your first, so I promise you that nothing will change after we have sex. I'm a grown-ass man, so if all I wanted from you was sex, I have no problem saying that shit to you," he said, so I allowed him to fuck me for hours, no longer caring that I had class in the morning. I swore on everything I loved that if I had known sex felt this damn good, I would have been out there fucking.

After we finished, he was sleeping, and I hated to wake him up, but I needed him to take me home because school started in a few hours. I had called my mother to let her know that I was going to be getting in late, but I didn't expect to be walking in the next morning. She liked Jahiem, so she knew that I was in good hands, but I still didn't like staying out all night.

It had been a few days since I got into it with Jamila, so I was wondering what was taking her so long to call and apologize. Since meeting, we had never gone without speaking to each other every day, so maybe she chose that nigga over me. I wanted to call her to see what was up, but I didn't feel that I did anything wrong, so she should have been the one reaching out to me.

Jahiem and I had still been going strong, and I couldn't wait to spend the night with him that night. I told him that I would have to leave early the next morning to help my mother prep for Thanksgiving.

I was on my way to my grandmother's house to spend about an hour with her because I hadn't been back in a while. I had not been on my job as far as checking on her since I started dating Jahiem, so I needed to do better.

She opened the door still in her nightgown, so I knew that she must not have been feeling well.

"How are you feeling?" I asked her.

"I'm not feeling my best, but I'll be okay," she responded sadly.

I knew that she was sad when the holidays rolled around, missing my father even more, so again, I needed to do better. I went into the kitchen to make her a cup of tea before sitting in the living room with her. She admitted that she was feeling down about him not being there, so I decided to change the subject.

Chapter Six

Jamila

"So, who is this bitch, and do I need to be worried?" Samantha asked me.

Samantha had called me the same day that Jahiem told her that he was moving on. She was hurt, and I felt bad for her at the time, until she told me the real reason she left. I wouldn't have told her to come here and fight for him had I known he had every reason to move on.

She did not confide in me that her grandmother was never sick until she walked her ass through my door hours ago with all her luggage. She wanted to go to Jahiem's place, but I told her that I didn't think it was a good idea to just show up at his place.

Another reason I had told her to come and fight for him was because I was upset with Reign at the time. I handled the situation out of anger at Anthony and needed to apologize, but my pride wouldn't allow me to. I already knew that if they found out I was the one who convinced Samantha to come, they would be mad at me.

"Listen, when I told you to come fight for my brother, I had no idea that you were the one prolonging coming back home. I only felt that you still deserved him because you were back home caring for your grandmother," I told her.

"What does any of that have to do with anything? I still love him, and I know that he still loves me," she spat.

"He's with one of my friends now, and I think he's feeling her," I told her.

"What the fuck you mean, he's with one of your friends? You didn't tell her that he already had a girlfriend, so he was off-limits?"

"I had nothing to do with them being together. She didn't confide in me until after she agreed to be with him. I did tell Jahiem that he shouldn't be starting a relationship when he was still in a relationship with you. He made the decision to call you and tell you that it was over."

She started pacing the floor, so I knew that I needed to calm her ass down before she did something stupid. "Samantha, just calm down. I'm sure that once you speak to him and explain why it took you so long to come back, he will understand."

I didn't believe that anything she said would help her get him back. He was feeling Reign, and I knew this because of the way he came at me about how I had treated her. He was pissed that I didn't tell Anthony that it was over, knowing

Reign was telling the truth. I was far from naive, and I knew that Anthony was cheating on me, but I just couldn't leave him alone. I also knew that I had waited too long to apologize to Reign, so she probably didn't even want my apology now. Jahiem told me that Ms. Peggy had invited us to Thanksgiving dinner on Thursday, but I was sure that Reign didn't want me there.

I heard my phone ringing, so I told Samantha that I would be back before rushing upstairs to answer the call. I missed the call, but it was the same number that had been calling me all night. No one was saying anything on the line. I called the number back, but whoever it was just listened to me say, "Hello? Hello?" and still didn't say anything. As soon as I ended the call, my phone was ringing again from the same number.

"Why are you ringing my phone? If you don't have anything to say to me, stop calling," I spat, ending the call.

When it rang again, I released a frustrated sigh before answering the call, prepared to go the fuck off. "Hello!" I screamed into the phone.

"Who is this?" a female asked me.

"Are you serious? You been calling my phone all fucking night and day, so who the fuck are you?" I barked.

"Bitch, I haven't been calling your phone," I heard before she started calling someone. "Kami, bring your ass in here and tell me who the fuck you been calling on my phone," she screamed.

"I got the number from Anthony's phone. I wanted to find out who the number belonged to," I heard her say in a timid voice.

I was confused because Anthony was 23 years old. I wanted to know how old the female was to be getting yelled at by her mother.

"Why the fuck would you need to find out who the number belonged to? I told you to stay your ass away from that grown-ass man," she continued to yell, and at this point, I thought she forgot that I was on the phone.

I heard the girl in the background say, "Mom, I'm pregnant."

"I swear on God if you're pregnant, I'm calling the fucking cops, because he had no business fucking your young ass," she yelled just before the call dropped.

I sat on my bed in utter disbelief. Anthony got some young girl pregnant. I had just found out that he had a 1-year-old daughter with the female Reign saw him with at Walmart. I tried to stop the tears that fell from my eyes as I dialed his number. The call was sent to voicemail. I couldn't believe that I had been so stupid to keep dealing with his cheating ass.

I wiped my eyes before going back downstairs to where I had left Samantha, only to see that she was gone. I prayed that she wouldn't show up at my brother's house. I called his phone to give him a heads-up, but he didn't answer. I thought about calling Reign but decided not to out of guilt for how I had treated her. I also didn't want her to know that I knew about Samantha right now, so I thought that was the real reason I decided not to call her.

I needed to talk to someone, so I called my cousin Kelsey. She was like my best friend, so she knew what I had been dealing with when it came to Anthony.

"What's up?" she answered.

"Somebody been calling my phone all night and day, not saying shit and pissing me off. So, when the same number called me again, it was some bitch asking me who I was. I told her she been calling me, and she said she hasn't been calling me. She screams out in the background, calling someone named Kami who she was having a conversation with while I was still on the phone. Listening to the conversation, it was confirmed that Anthony got this woman's underage daughter pregnant. Her mother went ballistic, talking about how she's going to have him arrested because he had no business with her daughter."

"Are you serious? Jamila, how many times did I tell you to leave this nigga alone? You fucked around and stopped speaking to Reign because you never want to hear the fucking truth. His ass had a kid on you, and now he will possibly be having another one on the way by a child. I hope her mother follows through with pressing charges because his ass out here being reckless."

"He probably didn't know she was underage, Kelsey. You know these fast-ass little girls be out here lying about their age."

"It doesn't matter because he had no business fucking with anyone when he is in a relationship with you. If he got caught up for being a cheater, that's karma for his ass, so stop defending him. Don't even call him for an explanation, Jamila. Let his ass go before he gives you something you can't get rid of," she stressed.

"He already did," I responded just above a whisper.

"Please tell me you're not pregnant," she pleaded with disappointment in her tone. I couldn't tell her that because it would be a lie.

After getting a lecture from her, I walked back upstairs to my bedroom and plopped down on the bed and cried myself to sleep.

A while later, I thought I was dreaming when I heard banging, until the noise woke me up out of my sleep. I put my feet into my slippers and rushed downstairs and opened the door to see Anthony standing there.

"Why the fuck you're not answering your phone?" he barked.

"I was 'sleep," I spat at his ass.

I knew that I shouldn't have even let him in, knowing what I did about his disrespectful ass. Why did he have to look so damn good? This was one of the reasons I kept taking his ass back. He walked in like he paid rent up in this bitch, pissing me off but not enough to call him out on it.

"Why are you here, Anthony? Shouldn't you be home with your daughter's mother? Oh, wait. Maybe you should be over at Kami's house, explaining to her mother how you managed to knock up her underage daughter."

"I didn't know that girl was only sixteen," he stressed.

"Sixteen," I repeated as the tears fell. I had expected her to be at least 17, but 16? Her mother had every right to be ready to have his ass put under the jail. "How the fuck you didn't know that she was only sixteen? Where the fuck you meet her at?" I questioned.

"She was at one of the trap parties, smoking and drinking, so I had no idea she was underage. Her body wasn't a body that belonged to a sixteen-year-old."

"I just don't understand how you say you love me but you continue to cheat on me. I stopped speaking to my friend for you when you mean me no fucking good."

I cried at how stupid I had become. I was not 16 years old, so I should have known better and recognized game.

"I was fucked up when I cheated on you. I love you, and none of those bitches meant shit to me. I promise," he said, pulling me into his arms.

What the fuck are you doing, Jamila? Kick this nigga out.

I knew what I needed to do, but my heart wouldn't cooperate with my mind and body. I allowed him to kiss me before letting him remove my tank, exposing my breasts. He sucked on them hungrily as his fingers danced around inside of my boy shorts. He sat me down on the couch, removing my shorts and putting my legs on his shoulders. His head was now between my legs, pleasuring me with his tongue, causing tears to fall from my eyes. My body betrayed me, and I was mad at myself that I had agreed with my body. I was in love with this man.

After releasing my juices, I watched as he removed his boots, followed by his pants. Lastly, he removed his hooded sweatshirt, asking me if I was ready to feel him inside of me. I nodded my head, letting him know that I was ready for all ten inches of him.

He positioned me over the couch, entering me from behind, sucking on my neck as he hit me with long, powerful strokes. I dug my nails into the sofa as he beat up my pussy, but I enjoyed his pleasurable abuse until we finally came together.

He pulled me into his arms, whispering that he was sorry for hurting me again. I thought about telling him that I was pregnant but decided against it, because I had no idea if I was going to keep it. I already knew that Jahiem was going to be disappointed that I had let Anthony knock me up knowing that he was no good. Kelsey had already stressed her disappointment, so I really had to think about whether he was worth putting up with for the next eighteen years. I knew in my heart that he wasn't going to stop cheating on me. He continued to hurt me and believe that because he said that he was sorry it was okay to keep doing the shit.

I needed to reach out to Reign and apologize for treating her the way that I should have been treating his ass. I also needed my friend to tell me what to do because I didn't think that I was strong enough to make the decision on my own. The route I was going with him, he'd probably have me knocked up every fucking year, right along with every other female.

Chapter Seven

Reign

After the first time being intimate with Jahiem, I found myself wanting to have sex every second of the day. We just went two rounds nonstop, and here I was ready to sit on his dick again. He was turning me into a sex-crazed fool who couldn't seem to get enough. We just got out of the shower together and were now lying in bed with no clothes on. My mouth watered at how his semi-hard dick rested on his thigh. Just as I was about to put his dick in my mouth, someone was knocking on the door, causing me to suck my teeth.

"I see that I created a monster," he joked while throwing on a pair of basketball shorts to answer the door.

I sat in bed playing between my legs like a horny teenager waiting for him to come back and put out this inferno between my legs. I felt myself on the verge of an orgasm when I heard screaming from a female that halted my pleasuring myself. I dressed quickly before heading toward the bedroom door, where Jahiem appeared.

"What's going on?" I asked him.

"I have a situation that I need to handle, so can you trust me and give me a few minutes to handle it?"

"What's the situation?" I wanted to know.

"My ex just showed up, so I need to handle it," he said, but I wasn't comprehending.

If she was his ex, what was there to handle? It was simple: tell her ass that his girlfriend was here and that her ass needed to go.

"I'm not understanding. If she's your ex, why is there a situation that needs to be handled?"

"Listen, I'll explain everything to you, but let me handle this," he insisted.

I felt like he wasn't honest with me about something, and that was the reason this situation showed up at his door. I was going to give him the time he needed to handle the shit, but he had a lot of explaining to do. After he left to go back downstairs, I tried my best to ear hustle or at least get a look at the female. I was wondering if it was the same female from Starbucks I saw him with a while back. I crept into the hallway and stood close to the wall as I peeked around the balcony, making sure not to be seen. A frown graced my face when I saw that she was a white girl who looked like LeAnn Rimes with a body of a black girl. She was thick, so I could understand why he would be attracted to her. Once they started arguing, I went back into the room, but from what I heard, she was upset that he ended things with her. I was confused, because if she was aware of him ending things, why would she show up with luggage?

"So, you have the bitch here?" she yelled loud enough for me to hear.

It was clear that she was making her presence known because she was now screaming at the bottom of the stairs.

"Did you tell that bitch that you're spoken for? Jahiem, I swear you better tell that bitch to leave now!"

Again, I didn't know what was going on, but I thought, *his ass better not come up these fucking stairs and tell me to leave. If she's the ex like he claims, why the fuck is he even entertaining her ass right now?*

"Jahiem, don't fucking touch me. I'm not leaving, so tell that bitch to leave before shit gets real up in here," she demanded.

She was talking that bullshit, but if she knew what was good for her, she would use that energy on his ass. I could hear my mother's voice saying, *"Why the fuck are you hiding in the room? Take your ass downstairs and beat that bitch's ass."* I was trying to let him handle her because if I went downstairs, I wasn't going down there to talk.

"Samantha, keep your hands to yourself," I heard him say, so I rushed out of the bedroom.

I wasn't about to sit here and let any female put her hands on my man. I tried to respect him, being that he asked me to let him handle it, but fuck that. As soon as I walked down the stairs, he grabbed me because he already knew how I'd give it up.

"Let that bitch go," she said to him.

"Trust me, if he lets me go, I'm going to beat the shit out of you. He asked you to leave, so why are you still here?"

"Make me leave, bitch."

"Samantha, chill the fuck out," he said.

I pushed Jahiem just enough to get around him and attack that bitch. I grabbed her by that sandy doll hair and dragged that bitch. My hand was now wrapped around her hair with him begging me to let her go.

"Put your hands on my man again, bitch, and next time, I promise you, you will be picking your teeth up off the floor," I spat, letting her hair go.

He pulled her toward the door, still being nice and asking her to leave, so once he got her outside, I grabbed her luggage and flung that shit. She was threatening me by saying it wasn't over and how I'd better watch my back. I didn't take threats lightly, so I ran down the stairs telling her to see me now, but he pushed me back toward the house.

"Reign, take your ass back inside, and, Samantha, take your ass on," he barked, reaching his breaking point.

He was calm the entire time, but he was losing his cool now, and when he gave me that look, I knew that he was serious. She didn't take heed, because she was still in his face going off, and I saw his jaw tightened, ready to hit her ass. He pushed her toward her car again telling her he was seconds from fucking her up. She didn't bring her ass back from around that car because she knew that his ass could get just as reckless if he wanted to. He, being the man I was falling in love with, helped her put her luggage in her car when I would have left that shit on the sidewalk.

Once I was back in the house, I found myself shedding tears because that was how mad I was being that I had to square off with this bitch. My leg was shaking, and I was trying to calm down because I shouldn't have allowed her to take me there. It didn't make much sense fighting with her when the man already belonged to me. That was why I made it clear that I was only beefing about her putting her hands on him. She was the one who took it somewhere else being that she was hurt behind them no longer being together. It was only right to defend my man because I was sure he would have done the same if a man were putting hands on me.

"Don't even look at me like that, because I told you to stay your ass upstairs," he said.

"No, the fuck I wasn't going to stay upstairs and allow any female to put hands on you."

"I told you that I was going to handle it."

"Well, she was handling your ass. Where in the hood did you meet that white girl?"

"She's not white." He chuckled.

"Yeah, okay. Anyway, don't you think you owe me an explanation as to who this ex is and how long the two of you were together? I've never seen you with her."

"She was my high school sweetheart, so we were together for a long time. Some shit went down, and she said that she needed time, which I gave her. She was gone for about a year, but we never said that it was over. I just told her that it was over when you finally agreed to be with me, so that was why she's in her feelings. I know that I should have ended it much sooner being that I was already doing me, so I was wrong for letting her believe that I was still all in," he admitted.

"So, what made her show up here with luggage like she was moving in?" I asked him.

"I have no idea. She was upset when I told her that I was ending it, but not one time did she say that she was coming here."

"Do you still love her?" I asked, dreading his answer.

"We were together for a long time, so I'm going to always have love for her, but I'm not in love with her anymore."

I felt that bitch named Doubt tapping me on my shoulder, but I decided to trust and believe he wasn't in love with her anymore.

My ass was supposed to have been home helping my mother prep for dinner tomorrow, so it was time for my ass to go.

"I hate to end the conversation, being that I still have questions, but I need to get home. I promised my mother that I would help her prep for Thanksgiving tomorrow. Are you still coming?" I asked him.

"Can she cook?" He laughed.

"Yes, she can cook, so I'd better see your ass tomorrow," I said, hugging him.

I felt that tingling between my legs, so I knew it was time to take my ass home before my mom ended up prepping without my help.

After he dropped me off, I went inside, and my mother was already in the kitchen, listening to Betty Wright's "Tonight Is the Night" while seasoning her ribs.

"I'm sorry that I'm just getting here, but let me go change, and I will be right back," I told her after kissing her on the cheek.

I wanted to take a quick shower and change out of the clothes that I had on yesterday before helping in the kitchen.

"What's wrong?" she asked as soon as I walked back into the kitchen.

I swear I hated that my facial expressions always gave away what I was feeling or thinking about something. I didn't want to bring up the fact that she was sober and not a damn cigarette was in sight anywhere. I knew she was going to get defensive and we would be arguing, so I decided to tell her what happened at Jahiem's house.

"I got into a fight with an ex of Jahiem who showed up to his place," I stressed.

"If she's his ex, what business did she have showing up at his place? And why the hell did you have to fight with her?"

"He asked me to let him handle it, so I stayed upstairs until she put her hands on him. She was upset that he broke up with her and at the fact that I was there."

"First off, why the hell would you stay upstairs at your man's house? Your ass was supposed to be front and center letting her ass know you marked your territory," she said, causing me to laugh.

We continued talking and jamming to old-school music while she was now making her macaroni salad when I heard my phone ringing. It was Jamila on the phone saying that she needed to talk to me. She asked if she could come by the house, but I wasn't sure if I wanted to talk to her. A real friend wouldn't have treated me the way that she treated me over a man who fucked her over every chance that he got. I would have never treated her that way even if I felt she shouldn't have been in my business. I would have handled it differently, the way a friend should have handled it. She hurt my feelings, so I didn't even know if I wanted to continue a friendship with her right now. However, I did agree to her coming over so that I could hear what she needed to say to me.

Jamila was knocking at the door about an hour later, so Mom let her in. I didn't tell Mom that Jamila and I weren't on speaking terms. She just figured Jahiem was the reason we stopped spending so much time together.

"I'm sorry." She burst into tears as soon as she walked into my room.

I knew her tears had more to do with more than her apology, so I just waited for her to continue, showing her ass no sympathy.

"You and everyone were so right about Anthony. He's never going to change, and I feel so bad that I took my frustration out on you." She sniffed.

"You didn't just take your frustration out on me. You discredited our friendship, but I'm over it," I lied.

My mother taught me to never trust a bitch who spoke their truth when mad, so I didn't know if I was going to forgive her ass.

Chapter Eight

Reign

Jamila was still babbling about how sorry she was and begging me to forgive her. I wanted to, but I just didn't trust her. This wasn't the first time that she put Anthony before me, so I believed if she stayed with Anthony, our friendship would always be up in the air.

"Reign, I know I haven't been the best friend, but please hear me when I say that I'm going to do better."

"I honestly believe that you lose yourself when it comes to Anthony. You forget about all the people who really rock with you, including me," I reminded her.

"I know, but I just said that I promise that I will never let that happen again. I can't promise that I will never deal with him again, being that I'm pregnant by him," she admitted, causing me to shake my head.

"Jamila, you're never going to get rid of him now," I responded sadly, now sympathetic to her tears and feeling her pain. I could no longer put on a front and act as if I didn't care for her and her well-being, so to hear that she was pregnant worried me.

"Don't cry, Jamila. It's going to be okay," I said, not believing that.

"Jahiem is going to kill me once he finds out that I'm pregnant. He already doesn't like Anthony, so please don't tell him, because I'm afraid he's going to kill him," she pleaded.

"I'm not going to say anything to him, but I need you to be honest with him because you know not hearing it from you is going to piss him off."

"I know, but I'm scared to tell him just like I'm scared to tell him that Anthony got a sixteen-year-old pregnant."

"Are you serious?"

"Yes, I'm serious, and her mother is threatening to press charges, so his ass might be behind bars soon. I didn't tell him that I was pregnant, because the way I'm feeling about the situation, I don't think I'm going to keep the baby."

"I'm not going to tell you what you should do, but don't make your decision because of his fucked-up choices. Just know that whatever decision you make, I will support you if you allow me to," I let it be known.

"I know you will." She sniffed.

I wanted to ask her to tell me everything that she knew about Samantha, but she already had a lot going on. I just needed answers to why she felt so comfortable to show up after being told the relationship was over. She stayed for about another twenty minutes, promising to be here tomorrow for Thanksgiving dinner. I went back into the kitchen so that I could make my chocolate cake with lemon drizzle that I couldn't wait for everyone to taste. The last time I made it was on my mother's birthday last year, but her drunk ass dropped the entire cake on the floor. It didn't go to waste because she was screaming that God made dirt and dirt don't hurt as she ate it. I'd never forget that day because I was so pissed, and she thought that it was so funny. I told her that I would never bake another cake for her, and she found that shit funny, too.

After I baked two cakes, I waited until the oven cooled off before putting the turkey in and setting my timer. I knew that Mom probably was going to oversleep, so I was going to help her out by at least getting the turkey and ham done. She already stuffed the turkey, so there was nothing for me to do but put it in the oven. I stole me some macaroni salad out of the fridge, making sure to pat it down so that she wouldn't notice. I sat on the couch watching reruns of *Mary Jane* and texting with Jahiem, who had my ass cracking up.

Jahiem: So, Jamila told me that y'all made up.

Me: Yeah, she apologized.

Jahiem: I got in that ass, so she knew that she'd better apologize to my baby.

Me: Oh, so I'm your baby?

Jahiem: Yes, you're my baby, and if she didn't apologize, I was going to pull her damn wig off.

Me: Lol. Please don't pull her wig off, because I would have to help her jump your ass. We don't play about our weaves, wigs, or nothing hair, period.

Jahiem: So, you will help her jump your man? It's not like I said I was going to snatch her ass bald. Lol.

Me: Boy, get off my phone. I need to get some rest. Just make sure your ass is here tomorrow.

Jahiem: I will be there. Later, love.

Me: Later.

It was going on three in the morning, so once the ham was in the oven, I grabbed a blanket from the linen closet. I lay down on the couch, making sure to set my alarm for two and a half hours so that I could take the ham out of the oven.

I woke up to my mother in the kitchen, realizing that either my alarm never went off or it went off and my ass ignored it.

"Mom, is the ham okay?" I panicked.

"Yes, baby, you did good." She smiled.

"I don't know why my alarm didn't go off, being that I know I set it," I stressed.

"It's okay, and I know your ass went into my macaroni salad, too. Your ass didn't wrap it back the way I had it." She laughed.

"Sorry. It was good, too. I'll be back to help with the sides after I shower," I told her.

"Chile, I'm just about done, and your grandmother and her aide will be here in about an hour."

My grandmother used a private agency when she needed to travel. I was just happy that she agreed to come, being that my mom cursed her out so many times while under the influence.

When I walked back into the kitchen, I was surprised to see my grandmother helping my mother with the sweet potato pies.

"Hey," I greeted her with a hug.

She was wearing her good wig, and she had on a nice dress with some black old lady shoes, looking like she was headed to church. It was good seeing her out of that worn pink night coat that she was always wearing when I would go to her house.

"You look good too, baby. I guess it has to do with that boyfriend of yours you never mentioned. I hope I get to meet him so that I can put my eyes on him," she said while I was giving my mom the side-eye.

"Yes, you will meet him today, and please don't interrogate him," I pleaded.

"I will not interrogate him. I promise," she lied with a straight face.

I went into the dining area to dress the table just as someone was knocking on the door, so I was wondering who arrived. I opened the door to see my aunt Brenda and my cousin Letta all smiles, being phony as fuck. She had a dish in her hand, so I already knew she made potato salad, but nobody wanted that shit. My mom embarrassed her one year because she was intoxicated, so she didn't have a problem speaking her mind. She asked her why the fuck she put diced tomatoes in the potato salad, causing everyone to laugh. It was no secret that she never liked my mother after that day but tolerated her because of my dad. She's another one who surprised me by being here today now that my father was no longer living. I didn't know what my mother said to get her ass here, but I moved to the side to let them in.

"Peggy, you have it smelling so good up in here, girl." She hugged my mother after setting her dish down on the table.

I was holding my breath, praying that my mom didn't say anything off the wall, because she had that look on her face.

"Hey, Mama," she sang, giving my grandmother a kiss on the cheek.

"Don't 'Hey, mama' me, girl. You don't come by the house to even make sure your mama is good these days," she spat.

"I'm sorry, Mom. I promise that I'm going to make the effort to visit more," she said, but I didn't believe her ass.

Once my mother's sister and her daughter got to the house, we were still waiting for Jamila and Jahiem to show up. When she came to the house, I was looking for him, but she said that he said he would be here later. I was disappointed, but I didn't let the shit show. Me and Jamila went into the kitchen to help my mother serve our undeserving family.

Everyone was now eating except me because I was trying to wait for Jahiem, but after texting him for the third time, I fixed me a plate.

"Did you speak to your brother?" I asked Jamila.

"He said that he had some business to handle, so I'm sure he will be here soon," she tried to convince me.

"Wow, business on Thanksgiving," I responded sarcastically.

"How have you been?" my uncle Tommy interrupted like he didn't see us having a conversation.

"I'm good, Uncle Tommy,"

"Your mother told me that you're dating, so I'm trying to figure out when you got old enough to be dating." He chuckled.

I swear I hated this fake shit, because the only time so-called family came around was when they were getting something for free.

"I'm twenty, about to be twenty-one, so I've been grown for some time now," I announced.

"Well, guess who isn't grown? Your cousin Kami, who got pregnant by a twenty-three-year-old man," my aunt Cherie announced.

The look that Jamila had on her face let me know that Kami was the 16-year-old she was talking about.

"How the fuck didn't he know that she was a fucking child?" Jamila asked because my cousin Kami didn't look no older than 13, causing my aunt to look at her.

Jamila was now standing in my kitchen crying because my aunt was interrogating her, so I told my aunt that she needed to fall back.

"What the fuck you mean I need to fall back? If she knows the grown-ass man who got my daughter pregnant, she needs to tell me who the fuck this man is," she spat.

"No, you need to tell your hot-in-the-ass daughter to tell you who she was fucking," I spat back.

"Reign, watch your damn mouth when speaking to your aunt. Now I need everyone to calm down. Kami, go on and tell your mother who the hell this man is who knocked your little young ass up."

"Auntie, if I tell her, she's going to have him put in jail," Kami whined.

If you could hear my cousin speak, trust that you would know she was a child. That was how I knew without a doubt that Anthony knew that her ass wasn't of age.

"He deserves to be in jail. Now tell your mother who this man is before I beat it out of your little ass," my mom threatened, trying to scare it out of her.

"His name is Anthony Hamilton, and he lives near the South Jamaica houses near the community center," Jamila spoke up with tears falling from her eyes.

"So, his ass is from the hood, but I promise you that I have something for his hood ass," my aunt shouted.

"Mom, you can try to have him arrested all you want, because if anyone asks me if I had sex with him, I'm going to say that I didn't. You can't prove a relationship or that he's the father of my baby because I'm not consenting to no test," Kami cried.

Jamila walked off to my room, so I followed her just to make sure that she was okay because I knew this shit hurt her. I just hoped that this was enough for her to finally leave his ass alone, seeing that he didn't give a fuck about her.

"Are you okay?" I asked her.

"I really wanted to believe that she lied about her age like he said, but seeing that little girl, I know he had to know she was underage. I swear I'm so sick of this nigga playing on my fucking emotions with his lying, cheating ass. I'm not keeping his baby. That much I do know, because I don't want nothing to do with him anymore. I let him come and have sex with me even after the phone conversation confirmed that he slept with that girl. I allowed him to walk all over me and treat me any way that he wanted to treat me, but I refuse to do this with him anymore."

"Are you sure you want to get rid of the baby?" I asked just to make sure.

I didn't want her making any hasty decision based on that fuck boy. If she wanted to keep the baby, I was going to be there for her, and if she wanted to get rid of it, I was going to be there for her. I knew that I said these things to her already, but I want to say them again to let her know that I meant what I said.

"Listen, I already told you that I would be with you whether you decide to keep it or not. So, I'm going to ask you again. Are you sure that you don't want to keep the baby?"

"I'm not keeping the baby, so will you go with me to get rid of it?" she asked me.

I was hoping that she wouldn't get rid of the baby, but if that was what she wanted to do, who was I to tell her not to? I just wished that she would talk to Jahiem before going to do something like this, but I knew she wouldn't, so I was just going to respect it. Oh, and pray he didn't find out.

Chapter Nine

Jahiem

"Jahiem, I swear you're a bitch-ass nigga to be doing this shit to me. Why are you here asking me what I'm doing at your sister's house? Wasn't you the one who put me out of your shit when I showed up over there?" Samantha fumed.

I just got to my sister's house to pick something up before heading to Reign's house for dinner, just to see Samantha asleep on the couch. Now she was upset because I woke her ass up to ask her why the fuck she was here.

"Samantha, when I kicked you out of my place that didn't mean come crash at my sister's house when she's friends with my girl. You don't need to be here, so I'm going to need you to take your ass back to the place you been calling home."

"Fuck your girl. Jamila said that I could stay here if I needed to stay, so I will not be leaving unless it's to move in with you."

"Listen, I don't have time for this shit. I have somewhere to be," I told her ass.

"Dinner with your girl and her family. Yeah, I heard all about it, but fuck me, right? It's Thanksgiving, and I'm here alone when I came all this way to show you that I still care and want to make shit right."

"It's too late, so you need to figure out where you're going because, like I said, you can't stay here where I pay the bills," I barked.

She had a lot of fucking nerve to come here expecting anything from me. I had been more than patient with her ass, and I never held back expressing how much I wanted and needed her to come home. My feelings meant nothing to her, and the only reason she came back was because I told her that I was moving on.

"Wow, so you're really treating me like some bitch off the street? I know you still love me because I still love you, and with history like ours you just don't fall out of love. I'm not going back to North Carolina, so I have nowhere to stay, so please don't kick me out," she pleaded with tears in her eyes.

"This should be enough for you to stay in a hotel for about a week to give you time to figure out what you're going to do," I said, handing her some money.

"So, you're really doing me like this, Jahiem? There's a reason why I couldn't come back, and the reason isn't because I didn't love you. I was scared," she cried.

"Scared of what? Nobody was fucking looking for you, being that there were no witnesses that night, so again, scared of what?" I barked, getting frustrated.

She was starting to piss me off with making excuses about why the fuck she didn't come back. If nobody knew, she knew that I would have protected her if that shit came back to her. I would have taken a charge for her or made that shit go away, so she had no reason to run to begin with.

"This female must be something special for you to be treating me like a trick right now. All the times you stressed to me how much you love me I always believed you until this very moment."

"I will always have love for you, Samantha, but I moved on. I need you to respect that I moved on, and I need you to acknowledge why I moved on, being that we both know why."

"I know why, and if I were you, I probably wouldn't have waited as long as you have, so I appreciate you, but it doesn't change the way I feel. Can you please take a ride with me?"

"I already told you that I need to be somewhere."

"I know, but I promise you that it will not take long. I swear, once we take this ride, I will leave you alone."

"I'm taking a ride with you where?" I questioned.

"Do you remember my friend Hannah?"

"I remember her, but what does she have to do with anything?"

"I will explain everything once we get to her house," she tried to convince me.

"I'll drive just in case your ass is trying to set me up," I said seriously.

"Don't say no shit like that, Jahiem, because killing you or having you killed is the same as killing myself," she said just as seriously.

The entire ride to Hannah's place she was on mute, but watching her twiddle her fingers let me know that she was nervous about something. As soon as we arrived, she hopped out of the car and ran up the stairs to the front door. I was guessing she wanted to give Hannah the heads-up that I was with her. I walked up to the door, and Hannah was standing there, staring me down with a smile on her face.

"How have you been, Jahiem?" she asked with a smirk on her face.

A few months after Samantha went away, I ran into Hannah at a club where she invited herself into my VIP area. We ended up hooking up that night, so I knew what the smirk was about and why she was asking me how I'd been. She tried reaching out to me, even becoming stalkerish, so I had to let her know that the shit didn't mean nothing to me. She was in her feelings, but she hadn't reached out to me since after I let her ass know to stop contacting me.

I watched Samantha make eye contact with Hannah before nodding her head. Hannah walked off and came back carrying a car seat that held a baby inside. Nervousness started to seep in because I just knew this bitch was going to say that I got her pregnant that night. Samantha set my ass up just like I knew, but I had no idea it was going to be this bullshit on the word of this trick Hannah.

"Listen, let me explain," I stuttered.

"Explain what?" Samantha asked with a confused look on her face.

"I don't know what this bitch told you, but that was not my fucking baby," I barked.

"Jahiem, what are you talking about? Why would you think that this is Hannah's baby and that you're not the father? Did you two sleep together?" she asked, looking between the both of us.

"I was intoxicated, and he took advantage of me. You know that I would never betray you like this if I was in a sober state of mind. I wanted to tell you, but he told me if I said anything to you, that he would kill me," that bitch lied with a straight face.

"It doesn't matter if you was intoxicated. You should have told me, Hannah. Jahiem, how could you do some shit like this to me? All those calls making me feel bad about not coming home, but you was out here doing you. Well, for your information, this isn't Hannah's child, but it is your child who, I promise you, you will never see. You can leave now," she shouted.

"What do you mean this is my child?" I said to her back because she had picked up the car seat and walked to the back of the house.

"You need to leave." Hannah winked.

I wanted so badly to put hands on that bitch, but my mind was all over the place, so I knew that I needed to just leave. *Samantha is in her feelings right now, so I'm going to give her time to calm down.* She had some explaining to do, so she was going to need to get up out of her feelings and talk to me.

When I got back in my car, I saw that I had a few missed calls from Reign and one from Jamila, so I knew Reign must be pissed. I thought about not showing up, but I couldn't do her like that, being that I promised her mother that I was coming. I stopped at the Walmart to get a couple of Patti sweet potato pies before showing up. The pies were going to be a peace offering. I hoped I wasn't going to have to argue with her after the bullshit I just went through.

As soon as she opened the door, a smile graced her face, so I pulled her ass in for a hug with my free hand.

"What took you so long?" she asked after kissing me on the lips.

"I'm sorry. I had some business to handle, but I told you I was going to be here. So, better late than never. Now go fix me a plate," I said, slapping her on her ass, forgetting that this was a family affair.

"Hey, young'un, come let me holla at you about my niece," this big, burly-ass nigga said to me.

I hoped his ass didn't think that he was intimidating me, because I could square up with the best of them. If that didn't work, I had no problem putting a hot one in his big ass standing here looking goofy as fuck.

"Uncle Tommy, you're not about to interrogate my boyfriend." Reign rolled her eyes, pulling me to the kitchen.

Her mother was telling him to sit his ass down somewhere and to let us be before he took his ass and sat on the couch. Reign fixed me a plate, but as good as the food looked and smelled, I didn't have an appetite.

"Are you okay?" she asked me once she saw that I was picking over my food.

"I'm okay. Jamila told me that she was here. Did she leave already?" I asked, quickly changing the subject.

"She's still here," she said just as her mother walked into the kitchen.

"How are you, Jahiem?" she asked me.

"Mom, can I speak to you for a second?" Reign asked, not waiting for an answer before pulling her out of the kitchen.

"Girl, what the hell has gotten into your ass?" I heard her mother saying.

I could hear Reign and her mother arguing about something. I was going to mind my business until I heard my sister's name.

"What's going on? And don't feed me no bullshit," I barked.

"You need to go into the room and speak to your sister. It's not my place to tell you what's going on," she said, pissing me off.

She walked toward her room with me following her so that I could find out what the fuck was going on. Jamila was sitting on the bed with red eyes, so my jaw tightened, because I was ready to go to war if someone fucked with my sister.

"What the fuck did that nigga Anthony do now?" I asked, already knowing.

That was the only time her ass be in her feelings, so I knew that it had something to do with his punk ass. She was the only reason that he didn't already have a fucking bullet in his fucking head, but all bets were about to be off.

"Don't start that crying bullshit. Just tell me what the fuck this nigga fucked around and did."

It hurt me seeing her hurt, but it was time for her ass to stop being so fucking stupid for this nigga who kept fucking her over. I was losing my patience and knew that I needed to calm down, but she needed to start speaking and speaking now. I saw her look at Reign, and they made eye contact, letting me know that she was giving Reign permission to tell me. I hated how she clammed up around me. I was her fucking brother, and she should have been able to tell me anything. She never had a problem speaking to me when she was all up in my business, but when it came to his ass, it was like pulling teeth to get her to tell me anything.

"No disrespect, Reign, but I need her ass to tell me what's going on," I said to her just as she was about to speak.

"No problem," she responded, putting her hands up in the air.

"Anthony got a sixteen-year-old girl pregnant. I knew because she kept calling my phone and not saying anything. I called the number back, and no one answered, so when the number called me back, it was the girl's mother. I didn't know that the mother was Reign's aunt and the little girl was her cousin until I got here," she cried.

I was at a loss for words because I'd been telling her to leave his ass alone, and now I came to find out his bitch ass liked little fucking girls. I was going to put a bullet in his fucking head and rid my sister of his ass. I already knew that she was going to be hurt behind the shit, but it wasn't going to be enough for her ass to walk away.

Chapter Ten

Reign

I didn't feel comfortable sitting in the waiting area of the abortion clinic while Jamila was in the back. I tried to get her to change her mind, but after Jahiem went off on her about Anthony, she didn't want to tell him she was pregnant. I was also feeling like I was betraying him by not saying anything. I had to remind myself that she was my friend first, so I was obligated to keep her secret. It was two hours later, and she still hadn't emerged from the back, so I asked the receptionist what was taking so long. She told me to give her a second so that she could see if she could find out what was taking so long. I went to sit back down to wait for her ass to come back and tell me something. Jahiem was calling my phone just as the nurse came out asking for family or friends for Jamila, so I sent the call to voicemail.

"I'm Jamila's best friend who came here with her today. Can you please tell me what's going on with her?"

She was looking like she didn't want to tell me what was going on. I guessed it had to do with me not being family, but I knew that at the abortion clinic you didn't have to be family.

"Listen, there isn't anyone else, and even if there were, she asked me to be here with her, so tell me what the fuck is going on with my friend," I shouted.

"Please calm down and follow me," she responded nervously.

When I walked in the back, I couldn't believe that Jamila was freaking out, confusing the shit out of me. I thought that she had died on the fucking table, so I was relieved to see that she wasn't dead, but she needed to tell me what happened.

"Jamila, what the fuck is going on? I thought your ass fucked around and died on the fucking table," I spat.

"I'm trying to leave, but this bitch isn't allowing me to leave, talking some bullshit that I'm not trying to hear," she said, rolling her eyes at the nurse.

"Ma'am, I told you that you have to stay the entire time of recovery," the nurse tried explaining, but Jamila wasn't trying to hear her.

"I told you that I don't want no fucking stale cookies or that lukewarm tea," she shouted.

"Jamila, you have to do what they are telling you to do. Do you want to leave this bitch and pass the fuck out? I need you to sit in that damn chair, eat those stale-ass cookies, and drink that lukewarm tea before I call Jahiem's ass down here," I threatened.

"My baby is gone," she cried into her hands.

I didn't know what to say because I never had an abortion, so I didn't know how she felt in this moment. I didn't know that she would feel regret as soon as she opened her eyes from getting off the operating table. I tried to reason with her before coming here because I knew that she would probably feel regret. I just didn't know that she would feel it so soon after, but it was probably because she made the decision for the wrong reason. I was babbling right now, but I knew that I needed to try to find a way to comfort her even though I didn't know how. I was looking at the nurse, because they should have had some counselor or some shit for situations like this. I walked over and helped her to the chair, telling her that everything was going to be okay as I rubbed her back in a calming manner.

After leaving the clinic, I was driving her home, but she asked to go back to my place, so I was on my way home. She said that she was cramping some, so when we got to the house, I made her some hot tea. I knew that I needed to call Jahiem back, so I went into the living room to return his call.

"Why did you send me to voicemail?" he questioned, not even saying hello before going in.

"First off, I didn't send you to voicemail. The call rolled over to voicemail because I couldn't answer the call," I spat.

"Okay, so what were you doing that you couldn't answer my call?"

"Jahiem, I called you back, so why are you interrogating me like you're my damn father? If you called me, you must have called for a reason, so let's focus on that reason."

"I told you about that damn mouth of yours. Keep playing and I'm going to put something in it."

"Yeah, okay," I responded, shaking my head.

"I'm about to come over there because I need to speak to you about something."

I knew that I couldn't invite him over here because Jamila was here, so I needed to think of something quick.

"Can you take me to get something to eat and talk to me there? Because I'm hungry," I whined.

"What happened to that slick talk? Now you want something to eat, so now you took all of that bass out of your voice." He chuckled.

"Yes or no so that I can get ready."

"Hurry up with your spoiled ass," he said, ending the call.

We were now seated at Applebee's, where I'd requested to go because I wanted some chicken wonton tacos. He was bitching about how he didn't like Applebee's, but his ass was going in on that spinach artichoke dip.

"So, are you ready to tell me what you needed to talk to me about?" I asked before stuffing my mouth.

"That next afternoon after Samantha showed up to my house, I went to Jamila's crib, and she was sleeping on the couch. I woke her up and told her that she needed to leave, but she was like she was invited to stay with Jamila. I told her that I didn't care who invited her, but she couldn't stay, so long story short, she asked if I could take a ride with her. She said that after I took the ride with her, if I still wanted her to leave, she would."

I stopped eating and was now listening to him, because I already knew that he'd agreed to take the ride, so now I was curious.

"Did you take the ride?" I asked him.

"I told her that I would take the ride with her as long as I drove, so that was what I did. We pulled up to her friend Hannah's house. I was hesitant, but I followed her inside. Hannah left the room and came back holding a baby girl, so I felt that they were trying to set me up. I told Hannah that she better not be trying to say that the baby girl was mine, and that was when Samantha asked me why I would think the baby was mine. I knew that I had fucked up at that point, so she asked me if I slept with her friend, and when I didn't say anything, she asked Hannah. Hannah told her that I came on to her, but again, long story short, the baby girl wasn't Hannah's baby. She belonged to Samantha, and she said that I'm the father, but after finding out I slept with Hannah she said that I would never see her. I know that this is a lot to take in, but I knew that I needed to tell you the truth," he finished.

"So, where is she now?" I wanted to know.

"I been trying to get in touch with her, to no avail. I believe that she left to go back home, but it's all good."

It was all good for him, but I needed to know if she was going to be an issue in the future because I wasn't with the drama.

"Wow," I responded.

"That was all you got?" he asked.

"What do you want me to say? To be honest, what can I say when we weren't together when you conceived the baby? My only issue is that I hope she isn't going to cause future problems for us."

"I don't think that we should have any issues from her because, like I said, she left, so I think she's done. I don't understand why she kept something like that from me when her leaving had nothing to do with me."

"Why did she leave?" I asked him, but he looked like he didn't want to say why she left, so I gave him that look that I wasn't going to leave it alone.

"About a week before she left, we discussed her going to a party with a few of her friends. I was

never a fan of her friends, so I told her to take a cab
to the party and that I would pick her up. She said
that she wasn't going to drink, so she would be fine,
and although I wasn't feeling her driving, I let it
go. She called me a few hours later, crying about
how she hit someone but made it home. When I
got to the crib, she was stressing about how she
was going to jail, so I was trying to calm her down.
I asked her what happened to her not drinking, so
she admitted to having a few drinks, but she said
she felt fine to drive home. She said that she didn't
call the police or stay at the scene because she was
scared. She told me that it happened a few blocks
from the hospital so she figured the person she hit
would get help."

I felt my lip trembling, being that what he just
stated sounded similar to what happened to my
father the night he was killed. My father had just
gotten off the late shift at the hospital when he
was hit and left for dead after crossing the street.
His coworker who was entering his vehicle heard
the screeching tires as the car sped off. The only
information that he had to offer the detective was
that the car was white. He had no idea if the driver
was male or female, so no one was charged in the
death of my father.

"So, you were okay with her leaving the scene?
I understand that she may have been scared, but
you just said that the hospital was up the block.

She could have at least tried to make a phone call to make sure that the person she hit got help."

"I didn't see the shit on the news, so most likely the person was okay," he responded, pissing me off.

"So fucking inconsiderate," I mumbled under my breath.

"Are you talking to me?" he questioned.

"I wasn't, but I was speaking about you. It bothers me that you were okay with her leaving the scene of the crime. Never mind. Are you ready to go?"

"Why the fuck are you acting like it was you she hit?" he barked.

I didn't even respond because he wasn't going to like what came out of my mouth.

Chapter Eleven

Reign

I was so pissed that I slammed Jahiem's car door as hard as I could, not giving a fuck if it pissed him off. He probably thought I was mad because of Samantha claiming that he was the father of her baby, but I wasn't. I couldn't care less about that shit when I was more concerned with getting information about that night. I tiptoed into my room trying not to wake Jamila as I grabbed a nightshirt before going into the bathroom. Before setting my phone down on the sink, I saw that Jahiem left a voicemail message, but I wasn't in the mood to hear shit he had to say. If I found out that this bitch Samantha had something to do with my father's death and he covered it up, he would pay.

After getting out of the shower, I grabbed a blanket and crashed on the couch so that I wouldn't interrupt Jamila's sleep by getting into bed. I couldn't help but wonder if she knew the reason that Samantha left.

The next morning, my mother was in the kitchen cooking breakfast, rocking her hips to the music that woke me up out of my sleep. I needed to have a conversation with her to discuss how I was feeling about not going back to school. I wanted to take a break to figure this shit out about what happened to my father, and to do that, I needed to be on a mission. I knew that school would be a distraction, so I was going to take a leave and hope that my mom understood. I wouldn't tell her the truth about why I was taking a leave. I needed a believable lie because, I swear, she knew me better than I knew myself sometimes.

"What are you doing sleeping on the couch?" she asked me.

"Long story, but I need to speak to you about something," I said to her.

"I need to talk to you about something too, but you go first," she responded.

"I'm thinking about taking the rest of the semester off from school, and maybe the next one too, but I haven't decided yet," I blurted.

I took a deep breath, not wanting to lie to her, but I couldn't tell her what I was thinking just in case I was wrong. She was staring at me intensely like she knew I was about to feed her some bullshit.

"I promise you that it has nothing to do with Jahiem if that was what you're thinking," I stalled.

"I'm not thinking anything. I'm just waiting for you to tell me the reason you're quitting school."

"I honestly just need a break because I'm not doing well in my economics class, so I've been stressing. Not to mention my ex and his new girlfriend have been harassing me every day, so like I said, I just need a break," I lied.

"My advice to you would be to stick it out and maybe get a tutor, but if you feel that you need a break, then take it. As far as your ex and his girlfriend, don't let them be the reason you want to leave school."

"I would never let him or her be the sole reason I leave school, but I feel myself on the verge of snapping, so I need a break," I stressed.

"Well, make sure that you speak with someone from financial aid to find out if it's going to be an issue," she insisted.

"I will. Now tell me what it is that you need to speak to me about."

"I was trying to tell you and the family at Thanksgiving dinner, but it didn't happen. I was going to wait until Christmas, but I'm not trying to deal with this family again." She chuckled.

It was a nervous chuckle, letting me know that she was nervous, so she was now making me anxious to hear what she had to say.

"Mom, please know that you can tell me anything," I said to her.

I didn't know what was going on, but she was wiping at tears that fell from her eyes, and that caused me to tear up. She was scaring the shit out of me because I just knew that she was going to tell me that she was dying. I wiped at my tears that fell before pleading with her to tell me what was going on with her.

"Does this have anything to do with why you stopped drinking and smoking?" I asked.

"Reign, what I'm about to tell you is hard, and that was why I tried to speak on it when family was here on Thanksgiving. I just wanted to give you some support, but with your aunt's drama it didn't happen."

"I'm not a little girl, so I don't need anyone here for support. Just tell me what's going on because you have me thinking the worst right now."

"Before I met your father, I was living my life recklessly with my boyfriend at the time named Raul. All I cared about was drinking and getting high, not caring what my family had to say about him being a bad influence. One night I was at Raul's place, waiting for him to get back with the drugs, when his door was kicked in. They were there looking for him, stating that he robbed one of their corner boys the night before. I was confused because he had no reason to rob anyone because I gave him the money that I had stolen from my aunt. I told them that he went to the store and should have been on his way back, but he never showed. They beat me up so badly that night and left me for dead. I have no idea how I ended up at the hospital, but your father was the man who saved my life. I was in a coma for about two weeks, and when I woke up, I was told that I was pregnant and that it was a miracle that the baby survived. I remember being stressed out about Raul not being at the hospital and ignoring my calls, so when the police came harassing me, your father stepped in. When I say that he catered to me, even staying after his shift to care for me, it was like he never went home. I was in the hospital for about a month, and that was when I found out that Raul was killed, sending me into a depressed state. When I was discharged from the hospital I went to stay with my grandmother. She told me that if I went back to school I could stay there, and she would help me with the baby. I was finally feeling like myself again and was excited about going back to school and having my baby. I was six months pregnant leaving the school when I got the call about my grandmother being rushed to the hospital. When I got to the hospital, I was told that she had a heart attack and they couldn't save her. I fell to my knees sobbing when I felt the tap on my shoulder before I heard his voice asking me if I was okay."

She paused, looking at me with sad eyes, but I asked her to continue because I'd never heard how she met my father. I was intrigued hearing their story and her talking about family I never got to meet. She always talked about my aunt Cherie and uncle Tommy, but it was always shit talking about them. I was also pissed that she never told me about her being pregnant with another child, but I didn't say anything. I didn't want her to shut down and not finish talking to me, so I kept my feelings to myself.

"Your father took me home with him that night, staying up comforting me until I fell asleep. The next morning, he called your aunt Cherie and uncle Tommy, telling them that our grandmother passed away. Both stated that they would help me with the arrangements, but they only showed up to the funeral. While I was hosting the repast, they were back at my grandmother's house taking everything of value. I was depressed and I felt alone, being that my grandmother was gone and my siblings didn't give a shit about me. I started drinking heavily again, not caring that I was pregnant, with this going on for months. I tried so hard to do right, but I just felt empty inside, and liquor was the only thing that numbed what I was feeling. Your father tried, but I was at my wits' end at this point and pushed him away to continue doing me. When I finally went into labor, my daughter was born with cocaine and alcohol in her system, so she was being taken away from me. I knew that

I needed to get some help, and I also knew that I didn't want my child to end up in the system. I called Raul's mother and explained the situation to her, admitting that I was in a bad place. She came to the hospital and spoke with the social worker who helped her get custody of the baby."

"So why didn't you tell me that you were pregnant before? You told me that you had an addiction, so why would you keep that from me? I just don't understand how you and my father decided that it was okay not to tell me."

"It was my choice to not tell you. It had nothing to do with your father."

I closed my eyes, briefly counting to ten because how I was feeling was about to be displayed, so I was trying to calm myself down.

"So, you still haven't told me why you stopped drinking all of a sudden," I spat.

"I received a call from Raul's mother telling me that I'm a grandmother, so I knew that I needed to get my life together. His mother has always been kind enough to keep me updated, but when your father passed away, I stopped taking her calls. My daughter doesn't know anything about me and why she ended up with her grandmother. I spoke with his mom and told her that I wanted to tell my daughter the truth and possibly have a relationship with her and her child. I lied to her and told her that I stopped drinking, so that was the reason

I stopped drinking. I broke up with Jimmy because I didn't need him to mess up my second chance if she decides to give me one."

I just sat in disbelief, not believing that she never told me about her having another child, and just as I was about to speak, Jamila walked out of my bedroom.

"I'm not feeling well," she cried.

I rolled my eyes at my mother before getting up to see what was going on with Jamila, who seemed to be in pain. I figured she was just cramping from the procedure, but she was burning up, so I started to panic. I didn't want to speak to my mother, but after taking Jamila's temperature, I knew that something was going on.

"Mom, we need to get her to the hospital," I said in panicked tone.

"What's going on with her?" she asked.

"She had an abortion yesterday," I admitted as Jamila bent over in pain.

"We need to get her to the hospital," my mom said just before going into her room to put some clothes on, just repeating what I'd just said out of nervousness.

"Mom, I called 911 because she's in a lot of pain and she said that she is bleeding heavy," I told her.

I went into my room to change my clothes, now crying because I knew that I should have talked her out of having this damn abortion. My mother told me to call Jahiem, but I told her that I would call him as soon as we got to the hospital. I didn't want to tell her that he didn't know that she got an abortion, and I damn sure didn't want to call him. I already knew that he probably was going to blame me, but she was going to do it with or without me. I was her friend, so I couldn't let her do it alone, so whatever consequences came behind my not telling him, so be it.

Chapter Twelve

Jahiem

As soon as I walked into the house my phone rang, with Reign telling me I needed to get up to the hospital. She didn't go into details, only telling me that she was there with Jamila, so I grabbed my keys and rushed out the door. When I got to the hospital, I ran up on her ass asking her what the fuck happened to my sister. Her ass was on mute like she didn't want to tell me what the fuck was going on.

"Reign, what happened to my sister?" I asked again, this time using a calm voice.

"She had an abortion yesterday and woke up in pain this morning," she stuttered.

"What the fuck you mean she had an abortion? Who the fuck took her to get an abortion?" I barked.

"I went with her because if I didn't, she was going to do it with or without me."

"So, it never occurred to you to call me? At the end of the day, she's my fucking sister."

"She's your sister, but she didn't want you to know, so it wasn't my place to tell you." Her voice cracked.

"Listen, back up off my fucking daughter," Ms. Peggy said, getting in my face.

I didn't even respond, being that I felt like slapping the shit out of them both behind my fucking sister. I walked over to the nurse's station to demand to see my sister so that I could find out what the fuck was going on. Walking in the back, seeing my sister lying in the hospital bed with pain etched on her face, had me fucked up. Just the thought of her feeling like she couldn't confide in me once again was a hard pill to swallow. I needed her to know that all we had was each other and she needed to trust me, but I wasn't going to stress it right now. I knew that I needed to be here for her and not get in her ass the way I wanted to for doing this dumb shit.

"Are you okay?" I asked her.

"I'm sorry," she cried.

"Listen, you don't have to worry about that right now. I just want to make sure that you're going to be okay. What is the doctor saying?"

"He said that I might be experiencing post-procedure pain, so they about to do a sonogram to make sure I have no placental tissue or clots."

I had no idea what the fuck any of that shit meant besides the doctor who did the abortion may have fucked up. When the nurse came, I went back out to talk to Reign just to see that she and her mother bounced. I knew that she was upset at how I came at her, but she already knew how I was about my baby sister. Just as I was about to walk outside to give Reign a call, I saw Samantha walking inside the hospital.

"What are you doing here?" I asked her.

"Your sister called me, and trust that if I knew you were here, I would not have come. I thought she was here alone," she spat.

"Did you know about her getting an abortion?" I barked.

"Abortion? She didn't tell me that she had an abortion. She just told me that she was in the hospital. Who the fuck took her to get a damn abortion? Let me guess—that girlfriend of yours, right?"

"I don't know what the fuck happened to my relationship with my sister that she picked up her phone to call you but not me," I stressed.

"You're probably the reason that she snuck off and got the abortion to begin with. You never talk to her. You always talk at her, so she probably was scared to tell you she was pregnant. She already knows how you feel about dude, so in her defense, I wouldn't have called your ass either because you be tripping."

"I don't talk at her, and the last conversation that I had with her I told her that she could tell me anything," I barked.

"That may be true, but if she came to you to tell you that she was pregnant by dude, what was you going to say?"

"I would have told her how fucking stupid she was for letting that nigga knock her the fuck up when she knows he's cheating on her."

"Exactly. So that was why she didn't tell you," she said, shaking her head.

"Is that the reason you didn't tell me that you were pregnant with my child?"

"I didn't tell you that I was pregnant because I knew that you was going to tell me to come back, and I wasn't ready at the time."

"Are you sure that was the only reason you kept the pregnancy from me?"

"If you're trying to insinuate that she isn't yours, you need to check yourself because you're the only one who was cheating. You fucked my friend, a friend you claimed not to like, so it has me wondering how many other bitches you fucked."

"I need you to ask yourself if you really expected me to wait a fucking year for you without having sex. I begged your ass to come back, but you kept giving me excuse after excuse, so yes, I fucked your friend."

"Why would you fuck my friend? I'm sure you could have fucked any female of your choice, so why did you have to go there?"

"I told you, the shit just happened."

"Well, I didn't have sex with anyone else, but if you want a DNA test, we could do that. Now if you don't mind, I want to go to the back to see if Jamila is okay," she said.

She was in her feelings, but I didn't care because she was the one who chose to put the relationship on hold.

"So, are you going to let me see her?" I threw out there.

"Maybe," she said, walking toward the back to go see Jamila.

I called Reign, but she sent the call straight to voicemail, pissing me off, so I left her a message telling her to call me. I knew her mother convinced her to leave the hospital, but she should have had her ass here since she took Jamila to the clinic. I wasn't putting all the blame on her, but she should have told me that my sister was pregnant and thinking about getting rid of it. I would have promised that I wouldn't tell Jamila that she told me about her being pregnant. She didn't even give me the option to tell my sister that I wasn't happy about her being pregnant, but I wouldn't have wanted her to get rid of it.

Samantha came from the back like twenty minutes later telling me that Jamila still wasn't back from getting the sonogram. I wanted to ask her what took her so long coming back out if Jamila wasn't back yet, but I didn't.

"Are you ready to finish our conversation before you so rudely walked away from me?" I asked her.

"Jahiem, now is not the time to be discussing this shit when clearly we are in the hospital making sure that your sister is good."

"I just want to know if you're going to allow me to see my daughter. She's my daughter, right?"

"She's your daughter, Jahiem, and I had no problem letting you see your daughter until I blindly found out about you fucking my friend."

"So, you're going to keep my daughter from me because I let that bitch get me off? You left me, so what the fuck did you expect me to be doing all these months?" I reminded her ass, again tired of her bullshit excuses.

"Jahiem, you act like this shit has been easy on me. I still have nightmares about that night, so imagine being away from you pregnant and scared," she cried, so I pulled her into my arms, trying to calm her down.

"How fucking cute," I heard from behind us, and I knew that voice anywhere.

"Before you start tripping, it's not what you think," I let her know.

"Oh, so you're a fucking psychic now? How the fuck do you know what I'm thinking?" she spat, forgetting that she was in the fucking hospital.

"Yo, calm your ass down. I just told you that shit was about nothing, so stop with the bullshit," I barked on her ass.

"So, what was it about, Jahiem?" she shouted.

I wasn't about to do this shit with her, being that she didn't want to talk to me like we were in the hospital.

"I thought you left," I said to her.

"So, since I left you called your ex-girlfriend? And for your information, I did leave, but it was only to take my mom home. If I knew that I wasn't needed here, I wouldn't have come back."

"I didn't call her. My sister called her, so can you please stop tripping?" I pulled her into my arms, but she pulled away, punching me in my chest.

She was acting like she didn't want me saying anything to her, so being that Samantha had walked to the back, I was going to talk to her ass.

"Come out front and let me holla at you," I said, pulling her along. "Listen, I need you to understand why I was so upset with you. It had nothing to do with you being a friend to my sister. I just feel that you should have confided in me knowing that the only reason she was doing this was to avoid telling me. I promise you that I wouldn't have my sister get rid of a baby because of how I feel about her nigga. I do understand you feeling like your loyalty lies with my sister, but we both want what's best for her, and this wasn't what was best for her."

"I tried to talk her out of it, but her mind was made up, so I knew that she would do it without me, so I felt that I should just support her decision. I could have come to you, but it made me feel as if I was betraying her, and that was why I didn't come to you. I'm sorry if you feel like I betrayed you, but I need you to know that she was my friend before you were my man."

I got what she was saying, but I'm not going to lie and say that I still didn't feel a way about her not saying shit, but I let it go. I just hoped that my sister was good physically and emotionally, because if she wasn't, I would blame myself.

"I understand where you're coming from, and I will try to respect she's your friend and I'm your man. I just need you to promise me that if any life-threatening situations concern my sister, you will come to me."

"I promise. Now what's up with you and Samantha?"

"Nothing is up between us. I just want to see my daughter, who she claims belong to me," I said, being honest.

"No, I'm talking about you two being hugged up when I walked up in this bitch," she clarified.

"She was expressing the nightmares she's still having and how she needed me while she was carrying my child. So, she got emotional, so I was just trying to comfort her," I admitted.

"I'm so confused as to why she keeps saying she was scared to come back here after it happened when no cops came knocking. Something is off about that night that she's not telling you, because shit she's saying just don't sound right."

"I wasn't there, so I can only take her word on what happened that night," I said just before Samantha walked over to us.

"Jahiem, if you're finished trying to convince your girlfriend that you no longer have feelings for me, you can go to the back now," she spat with a roll of her eyes.

Chapter Thirteen

Reign

I swear it took everything in me not to slap the taste out of this bitch's mouth. I didn't understand why she was here to begin with when she claimed to be leaving again with her lying ass. I wasn't going to say anything to her, but she was standing there with a smirk on her face pissing me off.

"Bitch, please don't flatter yourself. I trust my man. It's your ass that I don't trust," I said, even though I wasn't acting like I trusted his ass seconds ago.

"I'm sure you right being you just displayed how much you don't trust him. I would tell you that you have nothing to worry about, but I would be lying if I said such a thing." She laughed.

I knew that we were in the hospital, but I needed to let this bitch know that I wasn't the one to fuck with. I slapped that bitch so fucking hard I was sure that shit was heard around the fucking world. It took her a minute to register that I put my hands on her before she reacted, and we were going at it in the hospital. She may have looked like a white girl, but her ass didn't fight like one. She was giving it as good as she got, and I had to admit that my ass was getting winded. Security got up from sitting on his ass and was now helping Jahiem break us apart, and I was happy as shit.

"Stupid bitch," she shouted.

"I need for you all to leave before I'm forced to call the police," security threatened.

"I'm leaving, so, Jahiem, if you want to see your daughter, you better leave now," she said, playing dirty.

He looked like he was conflicted, being that we just got finished fighting, and although he knew that she was being petty, he wanted to see his daughter.

"Go see your daughter, because like I said, I trust you. If that bitch so much as tries to push up on you, you better tell me. I'll beat that bitch's ass again," I said to him.

"Bitch, you couldn't beat my ass if I stood there and allowed you to, with your weak-ass punches," she spat.

"Leave now." The security guard raised his voice.

"Nigga, calm your ass down," Jahiem barked. "I'll come to your spot after I go see my daughter," he said, kissing my lips before leaving the hospital with her.

After he walked out with her, I was so fucking pissed, but I refused to let that bitch know that I was. I thought that I was going to be able to go to the back to see Jamila, but he told me that I needed to leave too. I told his ass that he was going to have to call the police because I wasn't going no fucking where. I walked into the bathroom to clean my face, getting upset again, being that I had a cut over my left eye. It wasn't bleeding out or anything, so I was thinking that it got cut on the ring that she was wearing. When I came out of the bathroom, the security guard looked at me, but he didn't say anything as I walked to the back.

"OMG! Where the hell did you go?" Jamila asked as soon as I walked in her room.

"I had to leave to take my mother home," I sighed, not in the mood to talk. I knew she was the one who called that bitch to the hospital, so I wasn't understanding why she was worried about where the fuck I went.

"What happened to your face?"

"I got into it with Samantha because she was trying to flex on me in front of your brother," I told her.

"Are you seriously telling me that the two of you was fighting in the hospital while I'm back here fighting for my life?" She laughed.

"We wouldn't have been fighting if you didn't call her ass to be here," I said, getting upset.

"I didn't call her. She called me to find out how my appointment went, so when I told her that I was in the hospital, she came. So, don't blame me for the two of you acting like dumbasses."

"Whatever. What did the doctor say?" I asked, changing the subject.

"He said that he didn't see anything on the sonogram, but he wants to keep me overnight for observation. I don't even care as long as he give me some more of this pain medication, because I'm feeling good right about now." Her crazy ass smiled.

I didn't even notice that she wasn't in pain anymore because that was how upset I was about the fight and Jahiem's ass leaving.

"Where's my brother?"

"He left with his baby mama." I rolled my eyes.

"Samantha one, Reign zero." She laughed this stupid laugh letting me know her ass was high as shit.

"Whatever. Get some rest. I'm about to go," I said before giving her a hug.

I was in my feelings, so I just wanted to go home, praying that my mother's ass was in her room because I was still mad with her, too. The nerve of her wanting to get right for a child she basically gave up when she couldn't get right for the one she raised.

I stopped at McDonald's so that I could grab something to eat before taking my ass home. I rolled my eyes in the back of my head after seeing Byron at the register flirting with the cashier. I started to walk right back out, but I reluctantly walked to the line that he wasn't on, hoping he didn't say shit to me. I felt his gaze on me, so I looked in his direction, and he smiled, causing me to roll my eyes again. When I saw him take his bag and walk out the door, I was relieved—that was, until I left the restaurant.

"Reign, let me talk to you for a quick second."

"Byron, I'm not in the mood for your bullshit, so go holla at your girlfriend."

"Why are you acting like that toward me?" his dumb ass had the nerve to ask.

"Look, we are no longer together, so why would I waste my time talking to you when I can avoid having to fight your girl?"

"Well, it looks like you were already fighting with someone. Look, I'm not trying to upset you. I just want to be friends."

"No, we can't be friends, so please leave me the fuck alone," I said before getting in my car, pulling off and leaving him standing there looking stupid.

I didn't have the time nor energy to be playing with his ass tonight while my man was somewhere spending time with that bitch. When I got home, I sent him a text message asking him what time he was going to be coming. He didn't answer, so I was getting pissed, so I called his phone, and he sent me to voicemail.

After getting out of the shower, I saw my mother sitting on the couch, so I was second-guessing going to get a snack from the kitchen.

"Reign, come and let me speak to you," she said, causing me to suck my teeth at the fact that she saw me.

I wasn't in the mood to talk about a sibling I knew nothing about. If she wanted to have a relationship with this daughter of hers, I wasn't interested. I was good being the only child, so since she didn't feel the need to share this information, I was good. I went into the living room and plopped down on the sofa, waiting for her to say what she needed to say. I wanted to go back into my room so that I could attempt to get Jahiem's ass on the phone again.

"After you dropped me off at home, I got the call that I'd been waiting for from my daughter, who agreed to meet me. I gave her the address, so she's going to be here in about an hour, so all I ask from you is to be nice."

"Be nice? I don't understand why you're involving me in this when it was you who lied about your child. I shouldn't have to meet a sibling I knew nothing about, so I'm going to pass on this meeting," I said, getting up.

"Reign, sit your ass down. I'm not finished speaking to you," she shouted. "I know that you're upset about me keeping this from you, but I told you that I was in a different space back then. Do you ever ask yourself why I started drinking so heavily again after your father was taken from us? I blamed myself for your father's death, figuring that karma had finally caught up to me. That day at the corner store I was high on a drug that I haven't attempted in a long time. I was just trying to numb the pain and, at the same time, crying out for help from my daughter who had become immune to her mother's reckless behavior. I love you, and I don't love the child I gave up any less because she came from me. All I want to do is right my wrongs, so I need your support," she said, getting emotional.

"Mom, what if she just agreed to meet with you to tell you how much she hates you for giving her up? I don't want you getting your hopes up of having a relationship with her when you know nothing about her. I will support you, but if she comes out of her face to you, I promise you that I'm going to whoop her ass."

"That was the daughter I know. Thank you." She pulled me in for a hug.

As much as I didn't want any part of this sister of mine, I was going to do it for my mother, being that it meant so much to her.

"I'm going to need you to promise that no matter how this meeting goes, you don't let it drive you back to drinking again. I know that I was more concerned as to why you stopped drinking instead of telling you that I'm proud of you."

"I promise you that I will not pick up another liquor bottle, baby." She smiled.

I went into my bedroom to give Jahiem a call, which he picked up this time. He didn't say hello because he was tending to the crying baby I heard in the background.

"Hello," I repeated into the phone.

"Hey, what's up?" he asked.

"That was what I'm calling to find out, being that you said you were going to come here after seeing your daughter."

"Samantha had something to take care of, so she asked me if I could keep the baby until she got back. If you want to come here, I'll be here," he said.

"I have to do something with my mother, so I'll call you later," I said, ending the call.

I wasn't upset that he was with his daughter. I was upset because he didn't call to tell me that he wasn't going to make it because he had his daughter. I heard someone knocking at the door, so I had to put my attitude toward Jahiem on the back burner for now.

When I walked into the living room, I couldn't believe that I was making eye contact with Samantha's ass.

"Why the fuck are you here, Samantha? If you don't want that ass beat again, I suggest you leave right fucking now," I said, walking up on her before my mom stood between us.

"Reign, what the hell is going on?" my mother asked with a disappointed look on her face.

"This is Jahiem's ex, who is clearly stalking me by showing up here acting like I didn't just kick her ass," I shouted.

"First off, you didn't kick my ass, so stop saying that stupid shit. I was here to meet the woman who gave me up, but if you're her daughter, I want no part of this meeting," she said.

The look on my mother's face almost broke me down, so I knew that I needed to say something to get this bitch to stay. I felt sick to my stomach that I was about to beg her to just stay and hear my mother out. She was standing there with a smirk on her face because she knew she had me right where she wanted me.

"Listen, what's going on with me and you has nothing to do with why you're here, so could you please just hear her out?" I cringed.

"I didn't know anything was going on with us. Jahiem is my ex, so I have no idea why you dislike me for being his ex," she responded, causing me to roll my eyes and mumble under my breath.

Chapter Fourteen

Samantha

Reign was just popping off trying to fight me again, but now she wanted me to let her mother explain why she left me. My family on my father's side was somewhat there for me, so I was thankful for that, but I still felt a way about her walking away from me. My grandmother told me that my father was killed before I was born, so if I already lost a parent, why would she leave me too?

"I apologize to you, ma'am, because I didn't come here to argue with anyone, so I'm willing to hear you out," I said to her.

If Reign didn't like me, she wasn't going to like me when I took her mother and her boyfriend. She would not be able to compete with my daughter or a mother who was feeling guilty about leaving her newborn. I was going to milk this shit until she felt like she was being abandoned the same way I felt all these years. Reign told her mother that she was going to be in her room, so I was sure she was about to hit Jahiem up.

"First, let me say thank you for agreeing to come here to hear me out. I know that nothing I say today will justify my leaving you to be raised by your grandmother,"

"I don't think that it would, being that you were married and had another child. You didn't think to come back for me once you got your life in order?" I wanted to know.

I wasn't going to make this shit easy for her because I had felt a way my entire life, so I wasn't going to just say I understood. I didn't understand anything about a mother leaving her child never to return, leaving me to wonder, why now?

"I was in a bad place when the social worker reported me to child welfare, so that was the reason I let your grandmother take you. After your father was killed, I tried to get right, but I just couldn't. I told your grandmother that I was going to come back for you, and when I tried, she had moved. It wasn't like I went a day without thinking about you. Even on my worst days you were thought of."

"Just not enough for you to try to find me, so I'm not understanding why you want to be in my life now. My grandmother moved, that was true, but I never moved. I was always here in New York living with my aunt. Your daughter and I already have bad history, so I honestly don't know how this is going to work. My ex is her boyfriend, but he and I have a child together, so I'm sure that she's not going to want to share you with me."

"You don't have to worry about Reign. I will handle it and make you feel as comfortable as possible whenever you're in my home."

"Are you still using drugs or drinking? I don't mean no disrespect, but I need to know because I do have a child of my own. I don't want my daughter to get attached just to be disappointed the same way I been all my life."

"I stopped doing drugs years ago, and I recently gave up alcohol, so I assure you that it will not be an issue." She teared up. "I'm sorry. It's just that you look so much like your father." She wiped at her tears.

I'd seen pictures of my father, so this wasn't my first time hearing I looked like him, being that I had his same sandy brown hair. My light brown eyes and long nose were inherited from him, so I looked nothing like the woman who sat across from me. Reign walked out of the room with a smug look on her face. I had no idea what that was about, so I went into my bag and pulled out my album from when I was a baby. I handed it to her mother with a smirk on my face, knowing I was about to get under her skin. Her mother had tears running down her face as she flipped through the pages of the album.

"Everyone says my daughter looks just like me when I was a baby, but I think that she is the spitting image of her father."

Reign rolled her eyes when her mother asked if I had a picture of my daughter. Reign wasn't interested in what I looked like as a child, but she tried to break her neck to see my daughter's picture on my phone.

"She's beautiful. What's her name?" Peggy asked.

Yes, I called her Peggy because she wasn't my mother, so I'd be damned if I called her my mother when I didn't know her. My mother was and always would be my grandmother, who raised me from a newborn who this woman didn't want.

"Her name is Journey." I smiled.

"Such a pretty name. Do you think it's okay if I meet my granddaughter?" she asked.

I'd have rather she called her Journey, being that she wasn't a mother to me. It would only be right that she didn't refer to my daughter as her granddaughter. I wasn't going to say anything to her just yet, being that I had an agenda.

"I can bring her by to see you tomorrow if you would like." I smiled.

"Tomorrow will be fine." She sniffed, getting emotional again.

I let her know that I was going to have to go, being that I left her with Jahiem, telling him that I wasn't going to be long. I didn't mention to him that I was going to visit with the mother who gave me up at birth, so he had no idea. I knew that Reign called him, so he should know that her mother turned out to be the mother who left me at birth. Before getting up to leave, I called Jahiem, making sure to address him as my baby daddy just to strike a nerve with Reign.

"She's probably not even his," I heard her mumble under her breath, but I chose to ignore her.

I gave her mother a fake hug, expressing how much I looked forward to getting to know her, which was a lie. Once I destroyed the relationship between her and her daughter, she would never see me or my daughter again.

When I pulled up to Jahiem's place, I prayed that he wasn't going to be on no bullshit, being that Reign called him. He came to the door with Journey in his arms, causing me to smile, but he didn't return the smile. He was frowning at me as if I did something to his ass when, in fact, I didn't do shit.

"Why are you looking at me like that? I already know that your little girlfriend called you, so no, I didn't know that her mother was the mother who left me," I spat.

"I don't know if I believe that you had no idea that you were meeting with her mother," he barked.

"How the fuck would I know that the bitch who birthed her was the same bitch who birthed me? I don't know what the fuck she told you, but I have no reason to lie. I didn't even know anything about your girlfriend to even know who the fuck her mother was."

"I just find it strange how you tell me that you had something to do but didn't go into details. If you had no idea that her mother was the mother who left you, why didn't you tell me where you were going?" he questioned, pissing me off that he was questioning me.

"You know what? Believe what the fuck you want to believe," I shouted, taking my daughter from him.

I started to get Journey ready to go, so he was now trying to talk to me like he wasn't just accusing me of knowing. If he had thought about it before accusing me, his ass would have figured out that I had no way of knowing. Now that I knew and how I chose to deal with it should have been his concern. He was focused on whatever Reign said to his ass on the phone, but it was all good. I wasn't going to stop him from seeing his daughter because I was going to do everything in my power to get him back. It was game on, so I was going to play this game to the best of my ability, which wouldn't end well for Reign or her mother.

"Jahiem, I don't even want to talk about it anymore. I just want to get my daughter dressed and take her home."

"Home? Where is that?" he responded smugly.

"You already know where I'm staying." I rolled my eyes.

My friend's place was good enough to fuck her in but not good enough for me and his daughter to stay. He had a lot of nerve, but I wasn't doing this with him right now because I had to get my plan in motion. I already knew what was about to happen, and I promise you it wasn't part of my plan, so I was just going along with it for right now.

"I don't want my daughter staying at that ho Hannah's house," he said.

"Well, you told me that I couldn't stay with you or your sister, so where am I supposed to stay? If it makes you happy, I could go back home with my grandmother," I said, still gathering her things.

"Now why the fuck would that make me happy? Stop talking fucking stupid and go put my baby to bed," he barked.

"Are you sure? I mean, I can wait while you clear this with your girlfriend, because I don't want any issues with her," I lied.

I wanted all the smoke with her ass, so I was quite fine with him allowing us to stay with him. I don't care if it was for a night or permanently because all I cared about was her knowing that I was staying at his place. He already knew that she was going to be bitching about me staying here, but she was his problem, not mine.

He said that he would be back, so I already knew that he was probably going to her place to tell her in person. She was going to think that I planned this, but I honestly had no idea he was going to allow me to stay with him. To be honest, my plan was to let her mother know that I had nowhere to stay and have her offer me to stay with them. It would be easier to get her mother to love me and my daughter faster if I was living with her. When I took Journey to see her tomorrow, I would express how I didn't feel comfortable staying with him. I needed to make sure that Reign wasn't home when I had this conversation with her mother because she would see right through me.

After I got Journey down, I went upstairs to take a shower before getting in his bed, wearing nothing. I knew that he was going to be pissed seeing me in his bed when he got home, but I was praying that seeing me naked would change his mind. I was dozing off when I heard the front door open and close, so I kicked the cover off me. My smile faded when I saw him walk into the room with Reign following him. I knew she was full of shit when she said that she trusted his ass.

Chapter Fifteen

Reign

Jahiem came to my house to tell me that he let Samantha and his daughter stay the night with him until he could figure some shit out. He went on saying that he didn't want his daughter at her friend Hannah's house because of men coming in and out of there. I told him that it wasn't him that I didn't trust, it was that bitch, so he invited me to stay the night. I couldn't believe we walked in his bedroom to this bitch in his bed with no fucking clothes on. I was ready to beat her ass, but he went in on her ass, telling her that she had to go. This bitch didn't look like she just pushed out a baby three months ago, because her body was on point. A twinge of jealousy and doubt started playing on my emotions, making me feel that he would have hit if I didn't come home with him. You would think that her ass would be apologizing right now, but she was walking around his room like she was modeling for us. She wasn't looking for her clothes, because wherever she took them off at that was where the fuck they were. I was getting pissed at her level of disrespect, but I was also pissed that it seemed that every time I run into this bitch, I was going to have to fight her. I didn't feel like fighting for a man who already belonged to me, but some bitches just took you there.

"Why don't you go put some fucking clothes on and leave before I put hands on you?" I spat, having just about enough.

"When I leave, don't call asking for me to bring your daughter to see you, being that you have a problem with me being naked," she said to Jahiem, ignoring me.

I looked at him because I was starting to believe that maybe she was missing a few screws, being that she thought it was okay to be in his bed naked. She switched by me, rolling her eyes before going to the guestroom where her ass should have been.

"I told you that I didn't trust her ass, and had I not come back, who knows what would have happened."

"Nothing would have happened. If I wanted to be with her in that way, I wouldn't have come to your place to tell you that she was here."

I wanted to believe him, but at the end of the day, his ass was a man, so his dick was probably brick hard right now. I wasn't even going to look because we would have been up in here fighting if I saw any sign of hardness. She was now in the guestroom throwing things around, looking for a reaction from him. I could tell that he didn't want her to leave with his daughter, but that shit was disrespectful. She had no respect for him or the girlfriend she knew he had who happened to be me. I understood not liking me, but if that man said he was done, why try to push up on him? After she finished getting dressed, she was now dragging her feet, trying to see if he would stop her from leaving, but he didn't. He was now walking around in his feelings as if he was mad at me when I wasn't the one who invited her here.

I went into the bathroom to take a shower so that I could take my ass to bed because I wasn't about to sit up while he was having a hissy fit. Just as I came out of the bathroom, I heard the front door close, so now I was pissed. I grabbed my phone and called him, but he sent the call to voicemail. I was so confused as to why he was giving me this treatment, but I wasn't going to stay and try to figure it out. Fuck him.

"Why are you putting your clothes back on?" he asked, walking into his bedroom.

I didn't even hear his ass come back into the house with his bipolar ass, so I just rolled my eyes at his ass.

"Reign, you don't hear me talking to you?"

"I hear you just like you heard your phone ring but sent the call to voicemail," I spat.

"My phone is over there on the nightstand, so get out of your feelings and get the fuck up out of those clothes." He smirked.

"Samantha got your ass hot and bothered, so go get her ass to put that fire out," I said just before he grabbed me into a playful bear hug, kissing the nape of my neck. "Get off me, because I don't like how you took your frustration out on me when I didn't have shit to do with Samantha's ass."

"I'm sorry that I took it out on you, and I promise you that it's not going to happen again." He kissed my lips.

He was now staring at me with lust in his eyes before slipping his tongue into his mouth with me returning the kiss. He pulled my shirt over my head, standing back and admiring my perky titties, which stood at attention, sucking gently before his kisses traveled to my stomach, until he reached the jeans that I just put back on. Pulling them off along with my panties, he grabbed my ass, pulling me into him and putting his head between my legs. I felt my lips tremble as his tongue explored my pussy, licking before sucking and causing me to moan. Now he bit down on my clit, making sure to apply pressure. I tried hard not to run from his tongue-lashing. He must have sensed that I was going to try to get away from him because his grip became firm on my ass. I couldn't move as his tongue moved in and out of me until I released my juices into his mouth. I begged him to stop as he continued to suck on my now-sensitive pussy. He finally released me long enough for me to catch my breath and for him to remove his clothes. He pushed me down on the bed, licking me from my pussy to my ass before flipping me over and entering me from behind. I swear I could feel his dick at the pit of my stomach, but the dick felt so damn good. I grabbed one of his pillows, biting down once he started hitting me with strong, powerful back shots. I knew that I needed to fuck his ass back, so I tightened my pussy muscles and backed my ass up, now fucking him stroke for stroke. He started grunting in beast mode, killing the pussy until we exploded together with him collapsing on my back. He rolled over on his back, pulling me on top of him and causing me to laugh.

"I'm hungry," I whispered in his ear.

"I'm exhausted, but I guess I can feed your ass," he said, putting my hand on his semi-hard dick.

I had no dick-sucking skills, but knowing that Samantha's ass was lurking, I needed to keep his ass satisfied. I slid off him until my mouth was inches away from his dick, and I started getting a bit nervous. I had no idea what to do, so I moved my tongue around the tip a few times until he told me to put it in my mouth. I sucked on a lollipop and ice pop a million times, so I figured it couldn't be too hard. I did know that whatever I did, my ass needed to avoid biting him or scraping him with my teeth. I must have been doing something right the way he was moaning while pumping in and out of my mouth. I guessed I was nervous for no reason, and had I sucked his dick that first time, I wouldn't have been so nervous to begin with.

The next day Jahiem had some business that he needed to take care of, so he dropped me off at my house. Walking into my house and seeing Samantha and her daughter pissed me off, so I slammed the door hard as I could, causing her daughter to cry.

"Why the fuck would you slam the door?" Samantha barked.

"Bitch, don't say shit to me," I spat.

"Reign, why did you slam the door?" My mother emerged from her room.

"Mom, why is she here with her luggage?" I asked her.

"First off, get that tone out of your voice when speaking to me. The last time I checked this is my shit, so I don't owe no explanation for who I invite into my shit. You two may not get along, but she's your sister, so the both of you need to figure the shit out."

"She would have had a place to stay if she didn't try to fuck Jahiem knowing that he's my boyfriend. She's playing you just to get under my skin, because she has a friend who she can stay with."

"Like I said, she's your sister and that is your niece, so they have a home here with us. I turned my back on her before, so I'm not trying to do that again," she said with finality.

I walked down the hall to my room and slammed the door behind me. I couldn't even explain what I was feeling right now, but I could say that I was disappointed with my mother. She could have discussed moving her and her daughter into the home we shared. It must have been the guilt she was feeling as to why she made a hasty decision, but I didn't care. After taking another shower and changing my clothes, I left, headed to the hospital to see Jamila. I didn't say shit to my mother, being that I had no words for her ass right now. I called Jahiem, but just like always when he was handling business, his phone went to voicemail.

"Where the hell you been? I thought your ass forgot about me," Jamila scoffed as soon as I walked into her room.

"I didn't forget about you, Jamila," I snapped.

"What's wrong with you?" she questioned with a roll of her eyes.

"That bitch Samantha is what's wrong with me. Did you know that her mother gave her up when she was a baby? I just found out that my mother is the mother who gave her up when this bitch showed up at my house. My mother wants a relationship with her, but I want no part of that bitch or her daughter. Your brother didn't want her taking his daughter back to her friend's house, so he told her she could stay with him. He came to my house to tell me that he allowed her to stay until he could figure the shit out. I left to go back with him to his house because I didn't trust the bitch just to find her ass naked in his bed waiting for him. He told her that she had to leave, so she called my mom telling her she had nowhere to go, so my mom let her stay," I stressed.

"Are you serious? I didn't know that her mother gave her up because she never mentioned it to me."

"I don't think that she wants a relationship with my mother, and I also don't believe that she's just finding out about my mother."

"Reign, please don't start with the conspiracy theories, because you're going to go crazy making something out of nothing. If she says that she just found out her mother happens to be your mother, I believe her."

"I don't give a fuck who believes her because I don't believe shit that comes out of that bitch's mouth."

"That was because you only see her as Jahiem's ex who is trying to get back with him, so you will speculate," she said.

"Yeah, you're right. I'm speculating," I said, getting up and walking out of her room.

I was in my feelings because she was defending that bitch even after she heard all that I just said about her ass. If she wanted to believe her and disregard what I was saying, fuck her too, and I meant that shit.

Chapter Sixteen

Jahiem

I had moves to make, so after dropping Reign off, I was handling that business when I received a call from Jamila. I only answered the call because she was still in the hospital, but she was venting about Reign. I was about to tell her ass that I didn't have time for the shit she had going on with Reign. I was about to end the call until she said that Samantha moved in with Reign's mother. I had no idea what shit Samantha was on, but her ass was starting to do the most, and it was pissing me off. I called her phone thinking she was going to send me to voicemail, but she answered, sounding as if she was amused.

"Why the fuck would you take your ass over to my girl's house knowing she doesn't fuck with you like that?" I barked into the phone.

"I don't give a fuck that she doesn't fuck with me like that, Jahiem. We share the same mother, so when you kicked me and my daughter out like we were trash, I called my mother." She laughed.

"Samantha, the only reason you doing this shit is to fuck with Reign. I need you to get your shit and take your ass to Jamila's crib."

"Oh, now you're giving me permission to go to Jamila's house? Well, fuck you. I'm good," she spat, ending the call.

I needed to meet up with Black, but that shit was going to have to wait because this bitch had me tight right now. I pulled up to Reign's mother's crib, banging on the door like I was the fucking police. I had no intention of disrespecting her mom's crib, but Samantha's ass had me fucked up if she thought that slick talk was going to fly with me. She answered the door, and I hemmed her ass up, ready to take her fucking head off.

"What the fuck did you say to me on the fucking phone?" I asked, daring her to repeat that shit.

"Let me go, Jahiem," she cried.

"Just what the fuck I thought. Now take your ass in there and get your shit and do what the fuck I told you to do," I barked.

"What's going on?" Ms. Peggy asked after coming into the living room.

"She's leaving because she had no business coming here," I told her, trying to be respectful.

"I told her that she could stay here," she cried.

I could see the pain etched on Ms. Peggy's face, and it only pissed me off more because she was trying to right her wrongs, but Samantha was playing games. I didn't know what game she was playing and why, but I knew that she had no intention of forgiving her. We used to have conversations all the time where she would express that she could never forgive the woman who left her.

"I appreciate it, but she has somewhere to stay. She knows that Reign is uncomfortable with her being here, so it's best that she doesn't stay here."

Samantha came out of the back room with her bags, so I carried my daughter out of the house, causing Ms. Peggy to cry out. She was asking me to allow Samantha and her granddaughter to stay, but I couldn't. If Samantha's intentions were to try to have a relationship with Ms. Peggy, I would have no problem letting her stay.

"I'm not going to your sister's house, so you can give me my baby and leave me the fuck alone because you don't own me. Your girlfriend's name is Reign, so that is who you need to be checking, not me." She rolled her eyes.

I walked over to her car and put my daughter in her car seat before turning my attention back on her ass.

"Let me explain something to you, Samantha. I know you better than you know yourself, and I know that you're up to no good. You don't give a fuck about Ms. Peggy and having a relationship with her. Reign is my girlfriend, and nothing you do or don't do is going to change that, so get the fuck over it. Ms. Peggy has been through enough, so she doesn't need you coming into her life under false pretenses just to send her spiraling out of control. Now get your fucking ass in your car and go to my sister's house, and that is where the fuck you'd better be when I come through."

She stood at the back of her car, pouting like she wanted to say some slick shit out of her mouth, but she thought about it. I waited for her to pull away from the curb before getting in my truck and pulling out behind her. I felt bad for Ms. Peggy, so I called Reign to see where she was at so that she could get home to check on her mother. When she didn't answer I guessed she was still in her feelings about whatever happened between her and Jamila.

After handling my business, I went up to the hospital to see Jamila because I needed to know what the hell was going on. Jamila was on the phone but ended the call when she saw me walk into the room.

"You didn't tell me that you were coming up here. I tried to talk to you, but your ass ended the call."

"I didn't know I needed permission to come up here and check on your ass, and I didn't end the call. I told you that I was going to call you back after I found out what the hell Samantha was up to," I told her ass.

"So, what happened between you and Reign?" I asked her.

"Reign was tripping because I didn't agree with what she was saying about Samantha, so she left in her feelings."

"What was she saying about Samantha?" I asked.

"She didn't believe that Samantha wanted a relationship with her mother, and she didn't believe that she was just finding out about her mother." She shook her head.

"So why couldn't you just let her vent?"

"I was listening to her vent, but I wasn't going to agree with what she was saying if I didn't agree with her."

"You didn't have to say anything. All you had to do was listen and be there for her the same way she was there for you."

"What the hell is that supposed to mean?" she asked, now getting in her feelings.

"You told her not to tell me that you were pregnant, and she didn't tell me. She didn't agree with you getting an abortion, but she still supported your decision. So, all I'm saying is that you could have just let her vent."

"I'm in the hospital, so I'm not about to argue with you when I didn't do anything wrong but disagree with her. Her problem with Samantha is the fact that she's your ex, so she's not going to see nothing but negative when it comes to her. I tried to explain that to her, and that was the reason she got upset—because she didn't want to hear the truth."

"I don't want you to argue with me, because I'm not arguing with you. I just want you to be a friend the same way she was a friend to you. I know that you care about Samantha and don't want to see no wrong in her, but her ass is up to something."

"The only thing that she's up to is trying to get back with your ass and Reign knows it, so that is all she sees right now."

"Anyway, when are they letting you out of here? I told Samantha that she could stay at the house with you until I figure some shit out."

"The doctor said that I could go home tomorrow, and I don't know why you made her leave to begin with," she responded smartly.

"Whatever. I'll be back tomorrow to pick you up, being that I need to go find my girl and make this shit right," I told her ass before leaving.

Just as I was leaving, my phone alerted me of a text message from Samantha telling me that she needed me to bring a can of Enfamil. Then the next text was asking if I could bring her something to eat. I didn't bother to send a reply, just deciding to take the milk and her something to eat so she could leave me the fuck alone. Samantha wasn't going to be happy until she caused my breakup with Reign with her messy ass.

When I walked into the house with the food and milk, Samantha was sitting on the couch wearing nothing but a T-shirt. She had one leg propped up, showing that she wasn't wearing any panties and letting me know she was still on her bullshit.

"Why the fuck don't you have any clothes on?" I barked.

"I figured since you were handling me like I'm your girlfriend, you might as well fuck me like I'm your girlfriend," she teased.

"Why do you always have to be on some bullshit, Samantha? I should have known that your ass was just trying to get me over here to fuck with me."

I was trying like hell to stop looking at her fat pussy between her legs, but it was hard, being that she wouldn't put her leg down. She knew exactly what the fuck she was doing, and I knew exactly why she was doing it. She saw the lust in my eyes when I walked in my bedroom seeing her with no clothes on, but I played that shit off. If Reign thought for one second that I was aroused by what I was seeing, she probably would have been pissed.

"I'm out," I said, putting the food down on the table.

"Why are you leaving?" she said, pulling her shirt over her head and now standing before me with no clothes on.

She knew that I wasn't going to be able to resist her ass a second time standing in front of me with her big breasts, thick hips, and fat pussy. I tried hard to forget how her pussy always tasted like sweet strawberries, which I used to feast on every chance that I got. I tried my hardest to think about Reign in this moment and what I want to establish with her, but I was drawing a blank. She tried to kiss me, but I pushed her ass down on the couch and buried my head between her legs. I didn't want her to mistake this for nothing more than a fuck. I meant what I said when I said that nothing she did or didn't do would change my relationship with Reign. She grabbed my head, gyrating her hips and crying out my name as I sucked on her pussy. She started bucking wildly as she released her juices into my mouth, and I made sure to slurp every drop. I felt like shit, but it didn't stop me from wanting to feel my dick inside of her to see if she was as tight as I remembered. I pushed her down on the couch before arching her back and plunging into her with long strokes. Her pussy was tight just like I remembered, so I was in beast mode with her begging me to slow my strokes. I wasn't trying to make love, so I pounded into her until we both were screaming and grunting that we came. She was now trying to catch her breath but looking at me with a look to say she knew I wanted her.

"Are you leaving?" she asked, pouting once I got up off the couch.

"Yes, I'm leaving, because I was only supposed to be here dropping off the food," I told her.

"Well, are you coming back?" she spat.

"Samantha, please don't start tripping acting like you don't know what the fuck this was," I barked at her dumb ass.

"I know exactly what it was, and that is why I'm asking you if you're coming back, because I need for it to happen again."

It sounded like she was about to threaten me that she would tell Reign what happened if I didn't continue fucking her ass, so I was out. She was talking some slick talk at my back, but I kept it moving because I didn't want to hear the shit. As soon as I got in my car, Reign was returning my call and telling me that she just needed time to cool off. I told her that I was going to go by the crib and then I was going to scoop her up. She was asking me about what happened at her mom's crib, but I told her that we would talk about it when I got there. I didn't know if she was upset that her mother was upset, but I was positive I did the right thing by getting her up out of there.

When I pulled up to her house, I called to let her know that I was out front, being that her mother wasn't feeling me right now. She came out looking like she was pissed about something, so I already knew we were about to argue. She got in the car and didn't say shit, so whatever her mother said to her had her in her feelings.

Chapter Seventeen

Reign

"What's up?" he asked me when he realized that I wasn't going to say shit to him.

"You tell me," I spat.

"I don't know what's up. That was why I'm asking you. You're the one who got in the car not saying shit to me."

"I didn't say shit because I'm pissed," I shouted.

"Okay, so do you want to tell me why you're pissed?" he asked in a calm voice.

"My mother told me how you handled Samantha today when you came to the house. I'm bugging because she's not your girl, so why did you come to my house acting as if she were?"

"So, your mother didn't tell you that I was there to make her ass leave because I knew she was only there to fuck with you? I didn't do a fucking thing to suggest that she was my bitch, so I don't know why your mother would say that shit."

"You should have just let me handle it because now my mother mad at me. I knew the reason her being there wasn't about my mother, but my mother doesn't know. Your sister thinks that my not liking Samantha has to do with you, but it doesn't. I just feel like she knew about my mother way before her grandmother contacted her. It may seem like a jealousy thing, but I promise you that it's not. I just don't trust her ass, so I don't want her coming into my mother's life pretending she wants a relationship with her."

"Listen, I don't know what's going on with Samantha as far as if she wants a relationship with your mother. What I do know is that she shouldn't be living there knowing that the two of you don't get along. I just felt that she did that shit to get under your skin, and that was why I had her leave. It had nothing to do with me treating her like she was my girl, property, or no shit like that. It was about you and only you, so I'm sorry if your mother made it seem more than what it was, because it wasn't."

"I just wish that this bitch would disappear because she's no sister of mine. Even if I tried to be cordial, she's not going to try to do the same because she still loves you."

I was about to be in my feelings again because his ass didn't say that he didn't love her ass, so I was now giving him the death stare.

"What?" he asked.

"Nothing." I rolled my eyes.

"Why the fuck you always in your fucking feelings? I told you before that I didn't love her ass when you asked me, so why repeat it?"

When he pulled up to his place, I got out of the car not saying shit because yes, he said it before, but he could have repeated it. I knew that I needed to stop acting insecure when he was telling me it was me who he wanted to be with. I just knew without a doubt that this girl was going to do everything to destroy what I had with him. I believed that she knew he was going to show up to my mother's house to make her ass leave.

"Did you speak to Jamila?" I asked him.

I knew I said that I wasn't going to say shit to him, but I didn't feel like arguing anymore, being that I had to be here all night.

"I went up to the hospital, and the doctor is releasing her tomorrow." he responded.

"So, she didn't tell you that we got into it again?" I questioned, giving him the side-eye.

"She told me that the two of you got into it, but I told her that it was between you two and I wasn't getting involved."

I swear sometimes I felt like punching him in his throat because he knew when I asked about her that was what I wanted to know.

"So, you didn't even inquire why we got into it?" I wanted to know.

"No. When she tried to tell me, I told her that the two of you do this all the time, so not to involve me."

"If you don't mind me asking, where is Samantha staying now?" I asked, causing him to sigh, but I didn't give a shit.

"She's going to be staying with Jamila." he responded.

"She might as well since that was who your sister rocking with anyway," I spat.

"I know that you don't want to hear this, but at the end of the day, Samantha is your mother's child and your sister. I know that there is a lot of animosity because of the feelings that both of you have for me. If she's up to no good and just wants a relationship with your mother, I think that you should at least try. My daughter is your niece, who is going to be in my life, so you might as well allow her into your life."

I heard what he was saying, and I wouldn't mind being cordial, like I said, but it wasn't just me who had to want this. This girl was not going to welcome me with open arms when I was sleeping with the man she wanted to be with. I'd been trying to get my mother to understand that I wasn't just being mean, jealous, or defiant. I was willing to do this for my mother, but this bitch had to be willing to do it as well. I wasn't going to stop trying to find out more information about that so-called accident she had. I was going to ask Jamila what kind of car Samantha drove back then, but since she was Team Samantha right now, I didn't.

"I'm going to talk to my mother so that she can see if Samantha would want to come to the house, where we would both be cordial. I want my mother to have this second chance, but I'm not going to let her hurt my mother with her games."

"Well, just talk to your mother, like you said, and go from there," he said.

We spent the rest of the night watching movies until I got up to go take a shower. I thought he was going to join me, but he didn't, so I was confused as to why not. When I came out of the bathroom, he was grabbing his things to go in, so again he had my ass on stuck. I decided to wait until he came out to ask him why he didn't join me in the shower. After getting into my nightshirt, I called my mother to tell her that I wanted to try to make amends with Samantha. She was happy, but I told her not to get her hopes up because that didn't mean that Samantha wanted the same.

He came out of the bathroom with the towel wrapped around his waist, causing my hormones to go crazy. I wanted some dick, so when I watched him put on his underwear followed by some basketball shorts, I couldn't bite my tongue.

"Why are you fully clothed right now?" I asked him.

"How you figure? I'm just wearing some shorts."

"Exactly. You're wearing shorts—too much clothing when I'm trying to get some dick," I spat.

"I don't understand why everything has to be an argument with you when you could just say that you want some dick."

"I want some dick." I smirked.

He walked over to me, dropping his shorts before pulling my nightshirt over my head. His dick was standing at attention, inviting my awaiting mouth to bless him, so I kneeled in front of him, taking him into my mouth. He grabbed my hair as he pumped in and out of my mouth, causing me to gag just a little. He sensed that I was uncomfortable, so he put me out of my misery, pushing me down on the bed. He gently placed two fingers inside of me as he bit down on my clit while I fucked his fingers. I was screaming his name in a matter of minutes as I exploded in his mouth.

"Come ride this dick that you wanted so bad," he said, pulling me on top of him.

I was riding his dick like I had something to prove as he held on to my ass, meeting me stroke for stroke. I tightened my pussy muscles, causing him to growl that he was about to cum, so I put my hands on his chest, lifting my ass in a circular motion until we came together. I slowly climbed from on top of him, collapsing on my back and trying to catch my breath when my phone starting ringing.

"Hello," I answered, still out of breath. "Ms. Trina?" I questioned.

"Reign," she cried into the phone.

"Ms. Trina, did something happen? Is my mother okay?" I asked as the tears fell from my eyes.

If Ms. Trina was calling me crying, I knew that it had something to do with my mother, so I was an emotional mess.

"Ms. Trina, please calm down and tell me what happened to my mother," I pleaded.

"She said that she couldn't breathe and felt weak before collapsing, so I called 911 because I couldn't wake her up," she cried out.

"What hospital?" I sniffed.

After she told me what hospital they took her to, I tried to put my clothes on, but I couldn't get my hands to stop shaking. Jahiem stopped putting his clothes on to come and assist me so that we could get to the hospital.

"What hospital?" he asked, grabbing his keys.

"New York Presbyterian," I said just above a whisper.

I couldn't stop the tears from falling as I thought about my mother, praying that she was going to be okay. He held my hand the entire ride to the hospital, so I felt comforted with him being with me right now. When he pulled up to the hospital, my nerves kicked in and I was scared to get out of the car.

"I got you," he said after opening the passenger-side door.

I knew that I needed to be strong for my mother, so I took a deep breath before walking into the hospital. Once inside I nervously waited for someone to tell me what was going on with my mother. I already lost my father, so I wasn't trying to lose her too because she was all I had right now. When the doctor finally came for her family, we were escorted into a room where he informed us that she was having trouble breathing. He explained that she was having respiratory failure. It was a condition where she wasn't getting enough oxygen or wasn't able to rid carbon dioxide through normal breathing, so she had to be put on a ventilator. When he said she was in the ICU unit, I started hyperventilating, unable to catch my breath as I choked on my tears.

My mother had always been healthy so I had no idea what could have caused this to happen, so I needed answers. The doctor said that they were going to continue to run tests, but he didn't give me comfort that my mom was going to be okay. He said that someone would come out to let me know when I could go be with her.

"How can they save my mother when they don't even know what caused her to have respiratory failure?" I cried.

"Reign, the doctor said that they are going to run tests, so all you can do right now is pray for your mother. I know that she would want you to be strong right now," he said.

I just wanted to be with my mother to let her feel my presence, so when the nurse finally came out to tell me that I could see my mother, I tried to be strong. Before I walked into the room, she told me not to be alarmed by the tube in her airway because that was a part of the ventilator that delivered breath into her lungs. No one could have prepared me for the reaction that I had seeing my mother lying in that bed helpless. I collapsed on the floor begging God not to take my mother from me. I knew that I said that I was going to be strong, but I couldn't, so my emotions got the best of me. The nurse tried her best to calm me down, but it was to no avail because I was an emotional wreck.

I was still on the floor of the ICU when Jahiem walked in to help me up off the floor, pulling me into his arms.

"Reign, I understand how you're feeling right now, but you can't stay in ICU like this. Come take a walk with me to calm down, and you can come back when you're ready," he suggested.

I didn't want to leave, but he was right. I needed to get my emotions in check if I was going to be allowed in ICU. I decided to call my family to let them know that my mother needed them and that I needed them too. I knew my mom said they didn't show up for their mother, so I was praying that they showed up for her. I didn't even call my grandmother, being that she wouldn't be able to leave the house without her aide. I decided that I would give her a call tomorrow to let her know that my mom was in the hospital. Once I calmed down, I went back to the ICU and sat at her bedside holding her hand. She couldn't speak, so I let her know that I was here and wasn't going anywhere until she was better. I also said to her that she was going to be okay even though I didn't know if she would be.

Jahiem was waiting for me when visiting hours were over in ICU when I clearly told his ass to go home. He had to pick his sister up in the morning, so I didn't want him waiting around for me, being that I could have taken an Uber home. I was disappointed that they weren't allowing me to stay in the ICU unit with her. My aunt and uncle showed up. They didn't stay long but said that they would be here tomorrow. Jahiem wanted me to come back to his place, but I just wanted to go home to be alone. He offered to stay, but I let him know that I just needed to be alone with my thoughts. He wasn't happy about it, but he respected my decision, so I just got home and started crying like a baby. I heard someone knocking at the door, so I was praying that it wasn't Jahiem changing his mind. When I opened the door, I was now praying that it was Jahiem's ass because I wasn't in the mood to deal with Byron's ass right now.

"Byron, what do you want?" I asked with a roll of my eyes.

"I heard about your mother, so I was just coming through to make sure that you're okay."

"Well, I'm fine," I spat.

"Why do you always have to act like you don't need anybody?" he said, pulling me into his arms as I cried into his chest.

Chapter Eighteen

Jahiem

"Are you ready to blow this joint?" I said, walking into Jamila's hospital room.

She was sitting on the bed, fully dressed, attitude written all over her face, causing me to laugh at her ass.

"I knew I should have gotten someone else to pick me up. Your ass is always late, so I have no idea why you wear a watch," she spat.

"Let's go before your ass be walking to the crib," I told her, grabbing her bag.

I was so busy fussing with her ass, I bumped into the nurse coming in the door as I was leaving. I bent down at the same time she did to retrieve the bag that fell out of my hand, causing us to bump heads.

"Damn, shorty, you good?" I asked, rubbing my head.

"I'm okay," she stuttered, looking at me with lust in her eyes.

"Nurse Emily, look away." Jamila laughed.

"I'm sorry. I should have been paying attention," she apologized when it wasn't her fault.

"It's all good," I offered with a wink, causing her to smile.

"Jamila, I was just coming to say feel better and get home safe," she said.

Jamila gave her a knowing look that caused her to giggle, showing off some cute-ass dimples. She was a redbone with a few cute freckles on both cheeks. What stood out the most about her was her light brown eyes, but I wasn't trying to get caught up.

"It was nice bumping into you." She extended her hand with a smile.

"Likewise." I chuckled at how bold she was before shaking her hand.

"Nurse Emily, would you quit? Jahiem, let's go before you get into trouble," Jamila said, sticking out her tongue at me.

She was blocking when there was no need to because I wasn't doing shit but returning the damn gesture.

"What took you so long picking me up?" she asked once we were in my truck.

"Ms. Peggy was rushed to the hospital last night so—"

"OMG! Why didn't you say anything? That should have been the first thing out of your damn mouth," she spat, cutting me off.

"I didn't think you wanted to know with you and Reign beefing."

"Did you fall and bump your head, Jahiem? Why the hell wouldn't I want to know that my best friend's mother was rushed to the hospital?" she cried.

"My bad," I apologized.

"What happened to her?" she asked.

"The doctor said she has respiratory failure, so she was having trouble breathing. They have her on a ventilator, so she's in the ICU."

"OMG! Please take me to Reign's house."

I felt like shit for not calling her to tell her about Ms. Peggy. I was in my feelings last night when Reign pushed me away, so I took my ass to bed. I drove toward Reign's house as fast as I could, being that Jamila was a mess, same as Reign was last night.

"I'm sorry," I offered.

When I pulled up to Reign's house, Jamila jumped out of the car while I slowly exited the car stuck on who the nigga was leaving. When I got closer, I noticed that it was her ex, pissing me the fuck off.

"What the fuck is this nigga doing here?" I asked her but looking at him.

"I just stayed the night to make sure she was good," he offered with a smirk.

"Oh, is that right?" I asked before punching his ass so hard he fell down the steps.

"Jahiem, stop," Reign screamed, trying to stop me from stomping that nigga.

"Get the fuck off me. Fuck you and that bitch-ass nigga," I barked, kicking him one last time for good measure.

That nigga had me out of breath, making me mad that I didn't just put a bullet in his fucking head with his bitch ass.

"Jamila, I'm out. Call an Uber or have your ho-ass friend take you home," I told her before jumping in my truck and pulling out.

Reign was calling my phone, but I kept sending the call to voicemail. I should have felt bad, being that she was dealing with her mother being in the hospital, but fuck that. Nothing she could say would justify her letting that nigga stay the night. She was cool with pushing me away but had open arms for the nigga who cheated on her.

I pulled up to the block, seeing Black's ass doing what his ass did best. He was the only nigga I knew who didn't have a problem fucking bitches in a two-block radius from where his baby mama lived. He was hugged up with this chick named Brenda, knowing that if his baby mama came through, it would be over for his ass and Brenda's ass. I had no idea what that nigga was slinging, but he had these tricks fighting over his ass knowing he was no good.

"What's good, nigga?" he asked after slapping ol' girl on her ass, sending her on her way.

"Yo' ass not going to be happy until Nikki kill your ass." I chuckled.

"Nikki's ass ain't killing shit. What brings your ass to the block?"

"Reign's mom is in the hospital, so last night she tells me that she just wants to be alone, which I respected. I dropped Jamila off at her crib just to see her ex leaving, saying he spent the night making sure she was good. I fucked that nigga up and bounced on her ass, so now she's blowing me the fuck up."

"Damn, nigga, I thought I was the only one with drama." He laughed.

"Nah, I'm done with it, so trust me when I say I'm drama free."

"I know your ass lying, knowing you love Reign's ass."

"Yeah, I love her so much that I fucked the shit out of Samantha the other night," I admitted.

"Say word with your lying ass."

"Nigga, I don't lie on my dick, and that shit was good as hell," I told his ass.

"I guess your ass no different from me," he clowned.

"Whatever. What the hell are you getting into tonight? Because I need to get my fucking drink on," I said to him.

"We can chill at Creepers tonight," he suggested.

"That's cool. I'll see you later, and make sure those niggas working," I barked before jogging to my truck.

Walking into Creepers a few hours later, looking good and smelling good, I was ready to get fucked up. I walked over to the section where Black and a few other niggas I fucked with were to get shit popping.

"What's up," I greeted my niggas.

They were passing blunts around, but my ass needed to hit the Hennessy because my ass had been stressing all day. Reign had been on my mind, but I couldn't find it in me to call her ass, being that that nigga had no business being at her crib. Samantha's ass had been blowing me up, begging for me to come through to bless her ass again. I downed a few shots before lighting up, trying to get blazed when I felt someone watching me. I looked across the room to see the nurse from the hospital burning a hole in my ass. When I tell you that this girl was bold, she was as she walked up on me. She took my drink from my hand, putting the glass to her lips and downing my drink with a smirk on her face. She was now in my personal space as she backed her ass up on me, winding her hips to Cardi B song "Money."

"Don't start some shit you're not ready for," I whispered in her ear.

"I'm ready, willing, and waiting," she mouthed, facing me now.

I didn't know what was happening and what her eyes were doing to me because she had me tonguing her down like she was my bitch. My dick was pressed against her, begging to be released.

"Let's get out of here," I said, breaking the kiss.

"Lead the way and I'll follow." She laughed.

I knew that I should have walked my ass away from her, but her aura along with her eyes were intoxicating. As soon as we made it out of the door, tires screeching could be heard, causing me to reach for my gun until I recognized the car.

"So, you're really out here about to fuck another bitch while my mother is laid up in the fucking hospital?" Reign spat, getting in my face.

"Yo, move the fuck around the same way you did last night," I barked, pushing out my face.

"Listen, I didn't know that he was seeing someone," Emily tried.

"How the fuck you didn't know he was seeing anyone when I told you he was with my best friend when you asked about him?" Jamila said, coming out of nowhere.

"You also told me that his baby mama told you that they fucked the other night at your place, remember? So, while you was asking me for advice about whether you should tell her, I figured, why not shoot my shot when I saw him?" Emily giggled, but I wasn't impressed with those deep-ass dimples this time.

Jamila had always been so fucking gullible, trusting motherfuckers she didn't know, and that was the reason that nigga Anthony was able to do her ass dirty. I tried to instill in her ass that motherfuckers wasn't always to be trusted, but it seemed that the shit always landed in one ear and went right out the other. She had no business repeating some shit Samantha said to her the same way Samantha shouldn't have repeated it to her.

"What did you just say? Jamila, what is she talking about?" Reign questioned on the verge of tears.

I wanted to know how they knew where to find me when I hadn't spoken to either of them since leaving Reign's crib.

"Did you fuck Samantha?" she asked me while Jamila was stuck on mute.

"Can we not do this right now?" Jamila said once she found her voice again.

"Just tell her the same shit that you told me. I mean, she is your best friend, right? You didn't know me to be telling me all the business, but you did. All I wanted was some dick minus this drama that you all have going on." She switched away with my eyes following, causing Reign to slap the shit out of me.

I let her have that slap because she was running on her emotions, but when she went to hit me again, I grabbed her hands.

"Get the fuck off me, Jahiem. I'm done, so if you want to continue to fuck other bitches, be my guest," she yelled, pulling away from me.

I felt like shit, but at the same time I felt like slapping the shit out of Jamila for opening her fucking mouth to begin with.

"Why the fuck was you talking to a stranger about shit that concerns me? I swear you're so fucking gullible, and that was why that nigga was able to run all over your ass. You kept screaming how Reign is your friend, but you keep doing the same bullshit to her. If Samantha told you anything about me and her, you should have told her not to involve you. She knew exactly what she was doing when she told you knowing the shit was going to get back to Reign," I barked, not giving a shit about sparing her feelings.

"So that was how you feel about me? I'm gullible because your baby mother involved me in your mess, and I needed to talk to someone about it. Had I just gone to Reign I would have been wrong, right? I stressed to you not to get involved with my friend, but you didn't listen and have no problem hurting her just like I knew you would. So, miss me with how gullible you think I am because I don't give a fuck what you think about me," she screamed, walking off.

It was crazy how I was the bad guy when Reign allowed that fuck nigga to stay at her crib last night as if he were her man. Shouldn't that have made me single? She had no proof that I fucked Samantha, so she had no reason to be pissed at me. I wasn't going to deny that I was going to fuck the shit out of that nurse, because I was, but I considered myself to be single.

I walked back inside of Creepers and asked Black if he told Jamila I was here. He said that he didn't, so I didn't know how the fuck they knew where to find me, being that Creepers wasn't a place that I frequented.

"Shit just went left," I stressed, downing a drink.

I should have just walked the fuck off with that bitch because at least I would have gotten my dick wet behind this bullshit.

"Nigga, I never seen you stressing like this over no female, so I know you love that girl," Black said.

"I have to make this shit right," I said, giving him a brotherly hug before heading out.

Chapter Nineteen

Reign

It'd been a few weeks since that shit went down with Jahiem, but I was still in my feelings at how he jumped to conclusions. Byron said that shit just to get under his skin because his ass didn't spend the night with me. I did let him in that night, but I kicked his ass out like a few minutes later when he started talking some other shit. He tried to play on my emotions thinking that I was going to fall for his bullshit, so I asked him to leave. Byron came over the next morning to apologize for his behavior the night before, and that was it. I would have never done him dirty the way that he did me by sleeping with Samantha, and how was he about to fuck the next female over a misunderstanding? He beat the shit out Byron for no reason other than him being an asshole for saying that shit, knowing it wasn't true.

My mom was doing much better, so she was no longer on the ventilator. She pissed me off because as soon as she was able to talk, she was asking about Samantha. I was the one here every day making sure she was good. I was positive that Samantha knew that she was in the hospital, but her ass didn't show her face. I just wanted my mother to understand that this girl was playing a game, but she was still not trying to hear me. The hospital had her in a private room now, so when I walked into the room hearing her on the phone, I frowned. She was talking to Samantha, and once again it just didn't sit right to me that she let what I said go in one ear and out the other.

"How are you feeling, Mom?" I asked her.

"I'm feeling much better now that Samantha is going to visit today and bring my granddaughter with her," she sang happily.

"Why now?" I questioned.

"What do you mean?"

"I mean, her ass didn't show up when you was in the ICU when you needed the support and prayers the most. So again, why now?"

"Reign, what is it that you have against that girl? I understand that you're dating her ex, but you need to get over it. I want you to be just as happy about having a relationship with them because they are your family."

"How many times do I have to tell you that I have no problem having a relationship with her, but she doesn't feel the same way?" I stressed.

I didn't want to tell her that Samantha slept with Jahiem knowing that we were together and that told me she just didn't care. She could have Jahiem's ass because I really didn't give a shit anymore. I didn't want to be smiling in her face knowing that she was as phony as they came with her fake ass. My mother had her blinders on right now, but I just hoped that she saw what I did before it was too late.

"Well, when she gets here, we need to have a conversation because we all need to be on the same page. She told me that she wants to get to know us, but this thing with Jahiem is causing animosity between the two of you," she tried.

I knew what she was told by Samantha, but guess what? She was a fucking liar, but I wasn't going to say shit else. My phone started ringing, so I told my mother that I was stepping out of the room to take the call.

"Are you serious?" I asked my classmate Lori, who was on the other end of the phone.

She worked at the DMV, so I asked her if she could look up Samantha to see what kind of car she drove last year. She told me that a white Ford Fusion was registered to her last year, so the wheels in my head were spinning right now. I had no proof that her car was the car that hit my father, but her accident happened around the same time. I thanked Lori before ending the call, now standing in the hallway in deep thought. I was trying to figure out how to go about questioning her ass about her accident without interrogating her ass.

I walked back into the room acting as if everything was fine, watching *The Real* on the television with my mother. I made sure to come to the hospital early so that I could be here when the doctors made their rounds. All we knew so far was that she didn't need ventilator support anymore or oxygen therapy. Her condition wasn't chronic, so she wasn't going to need any long-term treatment, so we were basically waiting for the underlying cause. I just wanted to know what happened to cause this, and if there was anything, what we could do to prevent it from happening again. She was breathing much better and was no longer getting winded as much as she was when she first came off the ventilator.

I heard the room door open, thinking that it was the doctor, but it was Samantha walking in with that innocent look on her face. She always had that good-girl look whenever she was around my mother, but I knew better.

"Where's my grandbaby?" my mother asked with disappointment in her voice.

"Jahiem didn't want me to bring her to the hospital because of the germs, scared that she might get sick."

"I understand, even though I really wanted to see her."

"Don't worry, because as soon as they release you, I will be bringing her to visit you as much as you would like. How are you feeling? I'm sorry that I'm just coming to see you, but I didn't know if you wanted me here."

"That should go without question. I know your reason for not coming had more to do with Reign than me. Now that both of you are here, I think it's time for us to have a conversation," she said, causing me to frown.

I didn't mind having the conversation, but now wasn't the time. I had questions, but they had nothing to do with how we could fix our relationship. I wanted answers about her accident, so that was where my mindset was right about now. My mom gave me the look, letting me know that she would go off in this hospital if I attempted to show my ass.

"So, tell me the real reason that the two of you refuse to acknowledge that you have the same blood running through your veins."

"I just feel that if she weren't threatened by the fact that I'm Jahiem's ex and the mother of his daughter, we could acknowledge that were family."

"Threatened? Girl, please come back to earth, because clearly your ass is on another planet if you believe me to be threatened by you or any female for that matter. My problem with you is that you don't respect that Jahiem has moved on," I said.

"I don't have a problem with him moving on, but that was not what he did. He started a relationship with you knowing that we were still together."

"According to who?" I snapped.

"According to your friend, who told me when the two of you started dating. That let me know that we were still together."

"Well, I don't understand why you blaming me. I had no idea when the two of you started or when you ended. I can only go by what he told me, and he told me that he was single, so take it up with him," I told her ass.

"I'm not blaming you, but there are some things that you need to discuss with him as well. You say that he's moved on, but that was not the case. He's telling you that were not together anymore, but we are, and that was the only reason he didn't want me staying at your house. If I stayed there, he wouldn't be able to see you and continue to see me too."

"So, if the two of you are still together, how is it that you allow him to be with me?" I asked her because she knew she was lying.

"Reign, you know that I have taught you from an early age that a man is going to be a man no matter the woman."

I was on the verge of going off because my mother was believing the shit that was coming out of her mouth. I knew for a fact that if Jahiem slept with her, she seduced his ass, and no, I wasn't saying he wasn't in the wrong, because he was. It was just that she wasn't happy seeing us together, so she was doing everything to break us up. Yeah, I told him that I was done and not taking his calls, but I wanted him to know that I knew my worth. He had a decision to make, so until he did, I was good on not speaking to his ass. As far as Jamila, it just felt like we had grown apart, being that we never kept anything from each other. If Jahiem was still with this chick, Jamila should have told me, but she didn't.

"Mom, that was no excuse, so I refuse to accept it and share a man when I don't have to, so if he wants to be with her, so be it," I spat.

I was over this conversation just like I was over arguing with her about Jahiem. If Mom wanted me to play nice, that was what I was going to do and revert to my original plan.

"Listen, I'm willing to be cordial if you're willing," I said to Samantha.

"I never had a problem being cordial, but if we're going to be cordial, how do we do that when we are both in love with the same man?"

I swore this girl just couldn't shut the hell up. If she was in love with Jahiem, she didn't have to share that with me. I wanted to tell her that I didn't think that he still felt the same way, being that he was been blowing my ass up.

"I'm going to be honest with you just so there will be no misunderstanding later. You will have to ask yourself if you are willing to accept him being with someone else. I understand if you still have feelings for him, but if he doesn't share those same feelings, you have to let go. I'm not saying that he doesn't still care for you, because he does, because he admitted it. You have a beautiful baby girl with him, so have that conversation with him. If it's not what you want to hear, I still say that the two of you should continue to co-parent without all of the drama."

Since meeting her, I had never seen her show any type of emotion. She was always talking tough or smirking to get under my skin. She looked as if she was on the verge of tears, and I thought it was because she knew that he didn't feel the same way anymore. When she got up, excusing herself, my mother told me to go and make sure that she was okay. I told her to let her have her moment that she didn't want to have in front of us.

"Reign, I hope that you're serious when you say that you want to try to have a relationship with your sister," she said, pushing it, because that was not what I said.

Chapter Twenty

Reign

Samantha walked back into the room at the same time the doctor and his team walked in, making rounds.

"Hello, Ms. Peggy, how are you feeling today?" he asked her.

"I feel much better." Mom smiled.

"You're doing much better, but before we let you leave, we have to perform another diagnostic test. We just need to check your oxygen and carbon dioxide levels in your blood, so if the test comes back okay, we will talk about you going home."

"Do you know what caused her to have respiratory failure?" I asked him.

"Respiratory failure can occur as a result of many things, and according to your mother's history, none of them apply to her. She explained that she used to drink heavily but never had a drug or alcohol overdose," he responded, letting me know that they still didn't know what caused this shit to happen.

"Do you want to formally meet your niece?" Samantha asked me after the doctors left.

"Are you sure?" I asked, unsure that she was being genuine.

"I'm sure. I heard what you said, and I agree with you. If you and Jahiem are going to be together, I guess I'm going to have to respect it."

I didn't know if I believed her, being that her ass just slept with him knowing that we were together.

"Look at my girls playing nice." My mother laughed, which caused her to start coughing.

Samantha was asking her if she was okay while I was pouring her some water, but Mom was waving her hand, saying that she was okay. That shit scared me because it was one of those "I smoked all my life" coughs. She was feeling better, so I hoped this wasn't a setback. I hated that they didn't know what caused her to get sick, but most doctors don't know until you're dead. After she got her cough under control, she practically pushed us out the door before we could change our minds. I didn't know how I felt about going to Jamila's place to meet my niece, but that was where she was staying. I kissed my mom, telling her to call me if she needed me, before telling Samantha I would meet her at Jamila's place.

When I pulled up to Jamila's place, I took a deep breath, praying that we didn't get into it, being that this was still her place. I was tight with her, so to be honest I didn't even want to be coming here, but I was on a mission. I wondered if Samantha told her that I was coming over or if this was going to be a surprise. I knocked on the door, and Samantha answered with a smile on her face, inviting me in.

I walked inside, sitting on the couch that I frequented on so many occasions, waiting for Samantha to bring her daughter to me.

"Hey, can we talk?" Jamila asked, coming from the kitchen.

I was now wondering if this was a setup on Samantha's part to get me over here so that Jamila could speak to me. I didn't want to speak to her because I wasn't ready, so that was the reason I hadn't been taking her calls.

"I know that you don't want to speak to me because if I were you, I wouldn't want to speak to me either. We have been friends for a long time, and I'm not trying to end that with you because of a misunderstanding. I know you're upset that I kept this from you, but you need to understand that since you started dating my brother I have been in the middle. I told him not to date you out of fear that he was going to hurt you, and look what happened. The only thing I was trying to do was spare your feelings. I also know talking to the nurse about the situation wasn't the smart thing to do, but I was stressed the hell out. I would never do anything to hurt you the same way I wouldn't stand around and allow someone to hurt you. I know that you think that I'm Team Samantha right now, but that is not the case. Yes, we're cool, but I told her that my brother was with you and that she needs to move on. She was wrong for getting in bed with him again the same as he was, so I understand how you're feeling. I hate when we stop speaking, but again, I understand why you stopped speaking to me. I'm asking you if we can be friends again with the promise that I will never keep anything from you again. Well, I won't have anything to tell because I already told my brother and Samantha not to involve me in shit."

I looked around before speaking just to see if Samantha was around ear hustling before saying what I wanted to say.

"I don't want to speak on the situation with Jahiem, but I want you to understand that the day at the hospital you hurt my feelings. Have you ever known me to be jealous of any female or any situation with a dude concerning a female? I was trying to share something with you about what I was feeling about the Samantha situation concerning my mother. You disregarded what I was saying and automatically believed that it had something to do with your brother. I would never have any ill feelings toward your brother if he was honest with me about still wanting to be with her. So that day at the hospital, that wasn't what it was, and I just wished that you would have heard me out. Not to throw anything in your face, but you put me in a situation when I lied to your brother for you. So, all I ask is that you be here for me the same way that I have always been there for you. You don't have to agree with it, and it's okay to offer your opinion, but don't shut me out before hearing me out."

"I'm ready to hear you out." She offered a smile.

Just as I was about to talk, Samantha walked back into the room saying that her daughter was fussy, so she put her back to sleep. This was the type of shit that I was talking about with her, but nobody wanted to believe she was playing games.

"It's okay. I'll have plenty of time to meet her," I told her, trying hard not to roll my eyes at her lying ass.

"You don't have to leave. Come upstairs to my room so that we can get caught up," Jamila said.

I was glad that she said it because I really needed to talk to her about this shit, and I prayed that she listened this time.

"So, what was you trying to tell me at the hospital? I'm ready to hear you out," she said once we made it to her room.

"I think that Samantha is the one who hit and killed my father," I blurted out.

"Reign, what would make you think that she was responsible for what happened to your father that night?"

"I was talking to your brother about the reason that she left that night, and he told me it was because of an accident. When he told me about her stating that she hit someone coming home from a party it just sounded similar to what happened to my father. Now she shows up as the child my mother gave up, claiming to want a relationship with her. I just feel that she knew she was my mother's child and she hated her for abandoning her, so she set out to hurt her. I know that it sounds like I watch too much television, but I just feel it in my gut that something isn't right about her. I just found out that a white Ford Fusion was registered to her the time of the hit and run. The car that hit my father that night was white according to the witness, so again, I just feel that it was her."

"Let's just say that it was her that night. Do you think that it wasn't an accident and she set out to hit him with her car?" she asked me.

"I honestly don't know what to believe. I'm just telling you that from what Jahiem told me she sounds like the culprit. I could be wrong, but I'm not going to stop trying to find out the truth until it's proven I'm wrong. I just feel if she had an accident that night, whether it was my father or not, she knew that she hit someone. So, why leave the scene?"

"I was never told that she had an accident the day that she left. They only told me that a family member got sick and she was leaving to care for them. I want to help you find out, so what do you need me to do?" she asked.

"First, I need to find out if she's just finding out about my mother like she claims. My mom said that she received a call from Samantha's grandmother. Do you think that you could get into her phone to get her grandmother's number?" I asked her.

"I believe I have the number already. She called me a few times from where she was staying, so I think that number belongs to her grandmother," she said, going through her phone.

After about twenty minutes she found the number, so I told her that I would let her know what I found out. I needed to get home, so I told her that I would give her a call to let her know that I made it home. As soon as I was walking out the door, Jahiem and Black were walking up the walkway, causing me to suck my teeth. I had no problem ignoring his calls, but I knew that I wasn't going to be able to avoid him in the flesh. Even if I could, I already knew that he wasn't going to allow me to. He looked at me with that cocky-ass smile of his, causing me to smile back at him. My smile faded when I saw an image sneaking up behind them, but

I couldn't warn them because my voice was caught in my throat. By the time Jahiem turned around to see what spooked me, shots rang out. I watched in horror as Black's body fell to the ground, knowing that I needed to move, but my feet wouldn't allow me to. Jahiem reached for his gun, shooting who I now knew to be Byron as the streetlight revealed his face. I just knew my screams could be heard miles away as I kneeled over Jahiem's body, realizing he was hit. Jamila rushed out of the house with Samantha behind her screaming Jahiem's name.

"I'm good," he tried to convince me, but the pain was etched on his face.

The tears continued to fall once the police and EMS arrived. I just knew that they were going to place him in custody, but Jamila told them his gun was registered. I felt so bad at the sight of Black's lifeless body on the sidewalk as blood seeped from his body. Byron wasn't moving, so I didn't think that he was going to make it either. I was starting to blame myself because this could have been avoided if I never let him in my space.

Jahiem was being put on a stretcher while Black's and Byron's bodies were being covered with a sheet. My heart ached, and I swear I was trying to be strong, but I ended up breaking down to the point where my chest hurt. I couldn't even comfort Jamila right now, so Samantha was doing her best trying to calm her. The EMT asked if anyone would be riding with him to the hospital, so I told Jamila to ride and I would meet her there.

When I got inside my car, I allowed the tears to flow freely as the guilt invaded my body like the plague.

Chapter Twenty-one

Jamila

"I don't understand why we have to sneak around like you're embarrassed to be seen with me all of a sudden."

"That is exactly the reason we're sneaking around. My brother will kill us both if he knew I was seeing your ass again."

"I'm not scared of your brother, Jamila," Anthony barked.

"Well, your ass better be scared of the law because they're looking for your pedophile ass," I spat.

"I told you that little bitch lied about her age, so they can keep fucking looking because I didn't know she was sixteen."

"So that was your story and you're sticking to it?" I rolled my eyes.

"If you believe me to be a pedophile, why the fuck are you still fucking me?"

"That is the million-dollar question that I have no answer to," I responded honestly.

"It's because of this good dick that I bless your ass with." He chuckled while grabbing his dick.

"Anyway." I ignored his ass while I put my clothes on so that I could go.

"So, you're leaving?"

"Yes, I'm leaving because my brother is probably worried, being that I didn't come home last night, so I have to go," I lied.

I already spoke to Jahiem, so he was fine because my bestie was taking care of him and hadn't missed a day. I didn't tell anyone but Samantha where I really was just in case Anthony was on some bullshit. Jahiem was blaming himself for Black's death, being that he was the reason Byron came gunning for him that day. Reign was blaming herself as well, but I was trying to convince them both that it wasn't their fault. Byron was the one who came back with a gun being a punk instead of using his fucking hands the same way Jahiem did.

"Hold up, we might as well leave together so that I can take my ass home too." He got up, putting his jeans and boots on.

Just as I was about to go into the bathroom to use it before leaving, someone was knocking on the door. I knew that it wasn't room service since his ass had me in this cheap-ass hotel, so I had no idea who it was. As soon as I opened the door, police were rushing through the door with guns drawn telling Anthony to put his hands up. He was always talking tough, but now he looked like he was about to shit his pants.

"You set me the fuck up, bitch?" he yelled.

He must have bumped his head to think that I would fuck him and set his ass up at the same time with his dumb ass.

"Do you really think I would do something like that to you?" I spat.

He was being read his rights but looking at me like he didn't believe that I had nothing to do with him being locked up. He should have turned himself in because by running he made himself look guilty. I never judged him or stated that I didn't believe that she told him that she was older, so why would I call the cops? After they took him out in cuffs, I got on my phone and called Samantha because she was the only one who knew where I was.

"Hello," she answered.

"Samantha, did you let the cops know that Anthony was here at the hotel?" I asked, not beating around the bush.

"You damn right I did. I have a daughter, so his pedophile ass needs to be locked the fuck up under the jail."

"Are you serious? If you felt that way, you sure didn't express it when I told you that I was going to see him," I snapped.

"Would that have made sense to tell you? If I told you that you were being stupid for his rapist ass, you wouldn't have told me shit."

"I thought that you were my friend, but I guess not."

"I'm not your friend, Jamila. I'm your brother's ex-girlfriend, so I care for you the same way I care for him. You almost lost your life getting an abortion, so I don't understand why you'd get rid of the baby just to keep his ass. That shit doesn't even make any sense, so if you're mad at me, I'm okay with it because I know I did the right thing."

"You're such a bitch, and I should have listened to Reign. I swear I want you out of my place by the time I get home," I barked into the phone.

"Last time I checked, this home belongs to your brother, so if anybody can put me out, it's not your ass." She ended the call.

I swore I was going to knock the fucking taste out of her mouth if she was at my place when I got home. This bitch was so fake and phony when she could have expressed her feelings to my face and not do this shady shit behind my back. I grabbed my shit and headed to my spot to put this bitch and her baby to the fucking curb.

As soon as I walked inside my place, Jahiem was there with a pissed-off look on his face, letting me know she snitched.

"Jamila, what the fuck is wrong with you? Why would you still be messing with that fuck nigga when you know what the fuck he did?" he yelled while Samantha stood off to the side with a smirk on her face.

"I want her out of here, and I'm not fucking playing," I said, ignoring his question.

He wasn't my father, so he needed to stop acting as if he was because I was sick of it and sick of him.

"You better watch your fucking mouth, Jamila." He stood up on his cane, making me want to push his ass back down.

"Why is she here? You and she are no longer together, so if you want to put a roof over this bitch's head, take her where you lay your head. Keep smirking, bitch." I tried to walk up on her, but his ass stopped me.

"Jahiem, if she stays here another night, she better not go to sleep because, I promise you, her ass will not wake up," I threatened before going upstairs to my room.

I was so mad I started pacing my bedroom floor trying to calm my ass down before I caught a case. I heard them arguing, so I cracked my door to see what that trick was screaming about with her stink ass.

"So, now it's okay for me to go to Hannah's place? You know what? I'm not about to keep being tossed around. My daughter and I will take our asses back home where I didn't have to worry about where we were going to lay our heads," she yelled.

She should have thought about not having nowhere to live before she decided to get all up in my business. I swore if he fell for this act she was putting on and told her she could stay with him, I would be calling Reign. She just took his ass back, so I had no problem letting her know that his ass is still on the same bullshit. He needed to kick that bitch to the curb and let her ass be, and now that I saw her true colors, he needed to get a DNA test.

"Samantha, what did you think was going to happen after you snitched when she confided in you?" he asked her.

"So, were you okay with that piece of shit still fucking your sister and molesting little girls, too, when you have a daughter?"

"No, I wasn't okay with the shit, but you went about the shit the wrong way, so the two of you can no longer live under the same roof."

"Cool," she said, walking up the stairs, so I closed my room door.

I sat on my bed, waiting until I heard the front door open and close before I went into the bathroom to take a shower. It was time for me to get on board and help Reign find out what this girl's game was.

I pulled up to Reign's place about an hour later to tell her what the hell happened between me and Samantha's ass. She opened the door with that same pissed-off look that my brother was sporting, so I was assuming she spoke to him.

"How's Ms. Peggy doing?" I asked her.

"Don't even try it. What the hell possessed you to hook up with Anthony's ass?" she asked.

"He hit me up to meet him up at the hotel so that we could talk. I told Samantha where I was going and who I was meeting up with just in case he was on some bullshit. I had no idea that she was going to send the police to my location to arrest him. I just feel that she could have said how she was feeling about him instead of doing that sneaky shit. Then she goes and tells Jahiem who I was with, causing his ass to trip like he always does."

"I wouldn't have gone about it the same way she went about it, but I think I would have turned his ass in too. You know just like I know that he knew my cousin was only sixteen, because if you believed him, you wouldn't have had an abortion."

"I was conflicted, but like I said I was only going there to talk to him, in my mind. I even convinced myself that I was going to talk him into turning himself in. No, it didn't happen like I planned, and I ended up sleeping with him again, but that was my business."

She was looking at me like I done lost my mind, but she wouldn't understand unless she was in the situation.

"Did you get a chance to call Samantha's grandmother?" I asked, deciding to change the subject before we got into it.

"I did, but she has yet to return my call. But don't be trying to change the subject with your silly ass."

"I'm not silly. I just wanted to give him the benefit of the doubt because we both agreed that females do be lying."

"See what I mean? Silly. The benefit of the doubt was given to him until we saw who the female was and how young she looked. You saw her with your own eyes, and she looks like she's younger than sixteen, so how the hell would he believe her to be his age? Just admit that you love that nigga and you didn't want to believe that he intentionally had sex with her."

"Well, they got his ass now thanks to that backstabbing bitch," I said with a roll of my eyes.

"Jamila, if he was innocent, then his ass should have turned himself in instead of running because it made his ass look guilty."

"I agree with you. I told him the same thing, but he wasn't trying to hear me. He had to know that this shit was going to catch up with him. Anyway, I'm ready to take this bitch Samantha down so that Jahiem can send her ass packing."

"You do know that was my sister you're talking about?" she joked, knowing her ass couldn't stand her ass.

"Well, let me be the first to tell you that I no longer care for your sister and I need her ass to get ghost," I said seriously.

"I was thinking that maybe we could find something out from this Hannah friend of hers at least until her grandmother returns my call," she suggested, and I agreed.

I only met Hannah a few times, but she seemed nice enough, so it was worth giving it a try to see if Samantha confided in her. She couldn't be a loyal friend if she slept with my brother knowing that he was still kicking it with her. Samantha probably showed her true colors a few times, and Hannah wasn't feeling her ass like she thought. After leaving Reign's house I prayed that Jahiem took his ass to where he lived because I wasn't in the mood.

Chapter Twenty-two

Reign

I just finished helping my mother out of the shower and into the nightshirt that she lounged in during the day when someone knocked at the door. I opened the door to a short, chubby white woman, thinking that maybe she had the wrong door.

"Can I help you?" I asked her.

"I'm looking for Reign," she responded, confusing me, being that I didn't know this woman.

"I'm Reign, but who are you?" I asked, getting defensive.

"I'm Rosa, and you called me a few days ago," she said.

"Samantha's grandmother?" I questioned.

I did leave a message for Samantha's grandmother, but her name wasn't Rosa I was calling her Rosalind, and I never left my address.

"Yes, I'm her grandmother, and I need to speak with you and your mother," she responded.

As soon as I invited her in, I noticed a young woman exit the car and walk up the walkway, coming up to the door.

"This is my granddaughter, Persia," she informed me.

I let them both in before going to help my mom from her room to the living room. She was feeling much better, but her body still wasn't strong enough to do things alone.

"Hello, Rosa." My mom's face lit up.

"I'm sorry to just show up like this without notice, but this is important," she stressed.

"It's no problem, but why didn't you call to let me know that you were coming?" my mother asked her.

"I changed phones a few years ago, so I no longer had your number. Your daughter left me a disturbing message, so I decided to make the trip here. I never forgot where you lived, but I couldn't remember your number. Had I not been looking for Samantha, I would have just returned your daughter's phone call."

"What do you mean? I received a call from you telling me that I had a granddaughter and that my daughter was ready to meet me."

"That call must have come from Samantha, because like I said, I haven't had your number since I got my new phone. When Samantha turned sixteen, she was told about her father being killed, and her mother was not able to care for her. She has been bitter and in a dark place since that day, which made her act out. She came to me, asking me why it was that you had another child you were caring for but never came back for her. I tried to explain to her that you were still dealing with your demons, but if she wanted, I could reach out to you. She declined, so I let it be, thinking she was over it, but the acting out started to become a bit much. I've always kept you updated on her, but you stopped communicating, so once I lost your number, we lost touch. I had to send Samantha to live with her aunt because the older I got, the more I couldn't deal with her shenanigans anymore, so I moved. She showed up at my door last year, stating that she was just coming for a visit, but she ended up staying over a year. I felt that she was running from something, but she never shared what that something was. I know that she was having some relationship issues with her boyfriend, but I didn't know what those issues were. She called and told Persia that she could only babysit for her one last week because she was leaving. She never said where she was going, but when she left, she took Persia's daughter with her. The North Carolina police have already been notified that she's in New York, so they will be contacting the authorities."

I was so confused as to why she just went through all of that when she should have just started with "Samantha kidnapped a damn baby."

"So, the little girl she has with her isn't her child? She came here stating that the child belongs to her ex-boyfriend, who I'm now dating," I said to her.

"Do you know where she is staying right now?" Persia asked as tears filled her eyes.

"She was staying with her ex-boyfriend's sister, but she got kicked out of there today, so I have to ask him if he knows where she went," I said, grabbing my phone.

Jahiem's phone was going straight to voicemail, so I called Jamila to find out if she knew where she went. I told her that I needed for her to get to my house and try to get in touch with Jahiem and get him to my house too. She wasn't speaking to him right now, but we needed to locate this girl and the baby who didn't belong to her. Her grandmother called the detective from North Carolina to find out if he spoke to the NYPD.

It was about an hour later when two detectives showed up at our house asking questions that we didn't have the answers to. We knew nothing about her ass besides the fact that my mother birthed her, she was Jahiem's ex, and she was staying with Jamila. Jahiem was here after I finally was able to reach him, but he wasn't saying much. He was hurt, and I understood how he was feeling to have someone deceive him this way. When he first got here, he asked the grandmother if she was sure that the baby wasn't Samantha's, as if he didn't believe them. She informed us that Samantha had to have a hysterectomy from complications from fibroids when she was 16. He stressed that he never knew that she had a hysterectomy, but she was good at keeping things from a lot of people. It sounded like she was dealt a bad hand, but it didn't give her the right to steal a damn baby and lie about that baby being hers.

"Did you speak to Jamila?" I asked him.

She was supposed to be here, but she still hadn't arrived, and her phone was going straight to voicemail. Jahiem picked up his phone and called his friend Ginger to ask her if she could go by the house to see if Jamila was good. It wasn't like her not to answer her phone, especially if the call was coming from me. I had a bad feeling in the pit of my stomach, but I didn't say anything to him just in case it was nothing. The detectives said that they were going to be in touch with Rosa and Persia if they found anything at Hannah's place.

"Mom, are you okay?" I asked her.

"You tried to tell me that something wasn't right with her, but I wouldn't listen," she sobbed.

"Mom, even if you had listened, we still wouldn't have had any idea about what she done or what was going on in her mind. Just before you got sick, I was looking into if she was the cause of Dad dying that night," I admitted to her.

"What do you mean she may be responsible?" she asked me in a hushed tone.

"I don't know if she is responsible, but the reason she left New York was because of a hit and run coming from a party. Only facts that I have are that she was driving a white car and her accident was on the same night he was killed."

I just found out the date of her accident, so I now believed that she was responsible for hitting him knowingly. Now that I saw what she was capable of, I was even more convinced that she did this.

"Why didn't you say anything to me?" Jahiem asked.

I didn't even know that he was listening, because he was still trying to get Ginger on the phone to see if she made it there yet.

"I didn't want to say anything when I had no facts, but my friend confirmed that she was driving a white car last year. You confirmed the date that she left, so I'm just putting all the pieces together, but it looks like she killed him."

"This shit is crazy." He slammed his hand down on my mother's glass table, causing all of us to jump.

I was thankful that he didn't break it, but he put a look of fear on Rosa's and Persia's faces, so I told him he needed to calm down. I was upset too, but there was nothing we could do because her ass was off in the wind some fucking where. She picked up the phone to call the cops, getting Anthony locked up, when she needed a fucking cell right next door to his ass.

Jahiem, no longer willing to wait to get in touch with Ginger, decided he was going to go to Jamila's place. I told my mom that I was going to go with him just to make sure that everything was good with Jamila. She didn't want me to go now that it was a possibility that Samantha killed my father. I let her know that Jahiem was going to be with me, so nothing was going to happen to me. When Samantha's grandmother said to be careful, that let me know that she was worried as well. I went upstairs to grab my bag that held the Taser my mother had no idea I carried, just in case. I knew that Jahiem wouldn't let anything happen to me, but he wasn't back to being himself after being shot.

When I walked back out to the living room, Samantha's grandmother was on the phone with tears falling from her eyes. When she got off the phone, she said that the detective said that there seemed to be signs of struggle at Hannah's place, but nobody was in the home. I didn't know what the hell was going on, but how much damage could this girl do toting around a 3-month-old baby? Persia tried to calm her down when I would have been freaking out if it were my baby missing. I told Jahiem to try to reach Hannah again just to see if she would pick up the phone this time. He still was getting her voicemail, so we were on our way to Jamila's house. The entire ride I was praying that she was okay as Jahiem drove like a maniac to get there. I asked him to slow down so that we wouldn't get pulled over, prolonging us getting there. The detectives said to leave the police work to them, but by the time they found something, it would be too late.

When he pulled up to Jamila's house, her car was still parked in the driveway, and Jahiem noticed that Ginger's car was parked as well. He pulled his gun from the glove compartment, telling me to wait in the car, to which I gave him a stiff no. Walking inside, we didn't see anything out of the ordinary, so Jahiem called out Jamila's name but got no answer. I went upstairs to see if I saw her or Ginger but not before taking my Taser out.

"What the hell are you going to do with that shit?" he asked me.

"I'm going to light someone the fuck up if I need to," I let his ass know.

"Get your ass behind me," he said, walking up the stairs with his gun drawn like he was the damn police.

We went from room to room, but nobody was here, so I didn't know what the fuck was going on, causing me to start freaking out.

"How the fuck is it humanly possible for Samantha to do something to Jamila and Ginger when she has a baby with her ass?" I asked, getting frustrated.

"I know for a fact that Ginger would beat the brakes off of Samantha's ass, so if she bowed down, it must have been to save Jamila and the damn baby," he said.

This shit just didn't make any sense how far a woman would go to get a man. Snatching someone's damn baby, pawning it off as her own, and she still didn't get the damn man.

Chapter Twenty-three

Samantha

I was just on my way to Ms. Peggy's house to take my daughter to visit her when I saw my grandmother and cousin Persia. I knew for sure that she was going to expose me to them, so I needed to come up with a plan B. I had no idea how they found me when I didn't tell them where I was going. I really didn't have any plans on keeping Persia's baby. I just needed her to get Jahiem's ass back and get pregnant. This shit was almost over, but now they were going to ruin everything by being here. The only good thing was that I was kicked out of Jamila's place, because now they were going to believe me to be at Hannah's place. I did go to her place, but this bitch was talking out the side of her neck, so I beat the shit out that bitch. I owed her that ass whooping for fucking Jahiem knowing he belonged to me. She had the nerve to tell me that I couldn't stay with her because I was nothing but trouble. What fucking trouble did I bring to her fucking door? I still tried to be cordial to her lying ass knowing that she always wanted to fuck him. I decided to go by Jamila's place, praying that she didn't know what I'd done yet so that I could leave the baby with her. I figured if they got the baby back, the cops wouldn't be gunning for me as much.

When I walked into her place, I could tell by the expression on her face that she knew something, but she tried to play it off.

"Are you leaving?" I asked because she was headed toward the door.

"Why are you here, Samantha? I told you that I wanted you gone," she spat while trying to make a call on her phone.

I slapped the phone out of her hand, causing her to look up at me like I was crazy, but I didn't give a fuck.

"What the fuck is wrong with you?" she shouted before bending down to pick the phone up, but I beat her to it. "Samantha, give me my fucking phone," she said, following me outside of the house.

"I'm not giving you the phone back because you were being rude. I was trying to ask you if you could keep your niece for a few hours," I said, continuing to walk to my car.

"I'm not doing you no fucking favors, and you best believe I'm going to have my brother do an

DNA test. I don't trust your ass no more, so if I don't trust you, I damn sure don't trust nothing coming out of your mouth," she said, getting in my face.

"You know what, Jamila? Fuck you," I spat, pretending to go in my pocket to get her phone, but instead I pulled out my gun. "What were you saying?" I asked her, now pointing the gun in her face.

"Bitch, you crazy," she said with fear written all over her face.

"Get in the fucking car," I demanded.

"I'm not going anywhere with you, so if you're going to shoot me, go ahead," she challenged.

I didn't know if she noticed the silencer on the gun before she opened her big fucking mouth, so I shot her ass in the foot. She screamed out in pain, but I didn't care, telling her that she had one last chance to get into the car. I wasn't worried about anyone seeing the blood and thinking foul play because it was in the grass where she stood. She got in the car screaming all types of threats as if she were the one with the fucking gun. I took the handle of the gun and hit her ass as hard as I could, knocking her ass out cold.

"That was for waking the baby up, bitch," I spat before closing the door.

Just as I was about to get into the driver's seat, a car pulled up, but I calmed my nerves when I saw who was driving.

"What the fuck are you doing here?" I asked her ass.

"Something is up because Jahiem sent me here to check on his sister," she said.

"The jig is up, so I have to come up with a plan B, so get the fuck in the car," I spat at her ass.

"Don't you think he's going to know something happened if I don't call him back to let him know his sister is good?"

"I don't give a fuck what he thinks. Now get in the fucking car before you get me locked the fuck up," I barked.

"Why you do his sister dirty like that?" she asked once she got in the car.

"Don't question me about shit," I said just as her phone rang. "Who the fuck is that? And reach back there and put the pacifier in the baby's mouth so that she can shut the fuck up."

"It's Jahiem. He's not going to stop calling until I answer the phone," she responded.

"Ignore the call and let me think," I shouted.

I had so many skeletons in my closet that I believed that every one of them was about to bite me in the ass. I need to figure out how the fuck I was going to get out of this shit, but I couldn't think with this damn baby screaming at the top of her lungs. I didn't believe in harming children, but I was five minutes from pushing her ass out of the car. A loud noise could be heard, letting me know that Hannah's ass woke up, pissing me off. Everything was falling apart, so I didn't know how much longer I was going to be able deal with it all.

"What's that noise?" Ginger asked me.

"That bitch Hannah is in the trunk," I said, stopping the car on the side of the road.

I got out of the car, popping the trunk and hitting that bitch until she passed out again, and that was when I threw her out of the car.

"Don't look at me like that," I spat at Ginger.

"I didn't sign up for killing no damn body, Samantha," she bitched.

"Who the fuck did I kill? That bitch is still breathing," I said, pulling back onto the main road headed toward Main Street.

"I hope we are not going where I think we're going." She sucked her teeth.

"We have to go somewhere that nobody will think of looking," I told her ass.

I pulled up to Emily's house, making sure to park in her garage before calling her out to take the baby inside. She came out of the house from the door that led to the garage with a pissed-off look on her face.

"You said this shit was going to be like taking milk from a baby, but we still broke, and you still didn't get the man," she pointed out.

"This is just a minor bump in the road, but I promise you I will pull this shit off, just not the way I planned it," I assured her.

She rolled her eyes as she took the baby from the car seat, beefing at the same time about me bringing a bleeding Jamila to her place. I wasn't in the mood for her complaining, so I told her to shut the hell up so that I could think.

"Why don't you put a ransom out on this damn baby so that we can get the hell out of here before we end up in jail?" she suggested, thinking the shit was that easy.

"I say we rob the trap house tonight to get enough money to get out of town and ditch his sister and the baby," Ginger chimed in.

"Just tie that bitch up and feed the baby while I try to get my thoughts together," I said to them as I started stressing.

I had a voicemail from Persia saying that she wouldn't press charges if I just gave her baby back, but I didn't believe her ass. My grandmother left a few messages, speaking Spanish like I understood that shit. She didn't give a fuck about me, so I didn't know why she was pretending as if she did. She told my aunt that I was a bad spawn just like my father, but she didn't know that I knew she said that about me. Emily was my aunt's daughter, who was more family to me than any of my other family members. When her mother passed away, she allowed me to stay with her for as long as I needed to. She never judged me and, as you can see, never turned her back on me when I was being that bad spawn. Ginger was a different case, so she had no choice but to do what the hell I told her to do. She was the one who told me about Jahiem screwing Monica's ass and when he started dating Reign, who I heard he'd been chasing. I knew what he was up to even before he called to break things off with me.

"Help," I heard coming from the back room.

"Ginger, you didn't tie that bitch's mouth up?" I asked, shaking my head.

"You told me to tie her up, so that was what the fuck I did," she snapped.

"Well, go tape her fucking mouth so that she can shut the fuck up," Emily intervened.

She knew that when I started stressing, I could get reckless, and I was minutes from shooting Ginger's ass. I heard Ginger's phone ringing again, and it pissed me off, so I told her to give me her phone, and I got Jamila's phone and turned them both off. I sent Emily out to get us something to eat, being that no one was looking for her. I didn't want to order in because I was being paranoid, but it was better to be safe than sorry.

I turned my phone off as well because I didn't want them tracing my number, so I told Emily to pick up one of those Trac phones.

Emily's ass had been gone for far too long just to be going down a few blocks to pick up some Chinese food. I used her house phone, which she barely used, to call her cell phone to see what was taking her so long. She said that she had to drive to Walmart for the Trac phone because the discount store didn't have any. I went to check on Jamila to see if she would allow me to nurse the wound on her head. She kept shaking her head, refusing to be still, so I let her stubborn ass be. The baby was screaming at the top of her lungs again, so I let Ginger handle it because my nerves were bad. I swore I was ready to smother her ass with a pillow just to get her to shut the hell up. A lot of my agitation had to do with not being able to see Jahiem, and it was killing me inside. I just wanted to see his face, smell his cologne, or just be in his presence. I thought that Journey missed him too, and that was the reason she kept crying, not allowing anyone to comfort her. I hated the fact that, when this was all over, she would never see her daddy again all because of Grandma Rosa bringing Persia here.

"How much longer before she will be back with the food?" Ginger asked, interrupting my thoughts, bringing to my attention that it'd been another hour since I last spoke to her.

Chapter Twenty-four

Reign

It'd been a week since Samantha's grandmother showed up, and we were really started to worry that the baby, Jamila, and Ginger were dead. Hannah's body was found a day after the detective went to her house. She was found the next morning by a neighbor who jogged that route every morning. She died from blunt trauma to her head, so that was another reason we were all starting to think the worst. Jahiem had put the word out on the street, but I honestly thought that they were no longer in New York. He'd been going crazy trying to find his sister, saying that when he found Samantha, he was going to kill her ass.

My mom wasn't feeling well today, so she was in her room for most of the day, leaving me to keep Rosa and Persia company. I didn't know what to say most of the time because Persia was in a depressed state, not even talking much. I knew she was tired of me telling her that everything was going to be okay when I didn't know for sure. I just wanted them all found alive, but after hearing about Hannah, all hope was lost. The detectives even tried getting a location on either of their cell phones to no avail. I really felt as if they were starting to think of the worst-case scenario too, being that they had no leads. Rosa's husband has been calling for her and Persia to come back home, but neither of them wanted to leave. I knew they were sick of watching the news repeat the story asking for the public's help but getting no results.

I decided to go into the kitchen to make some lunch while I waited for Jahiem, being that he said that he was on his way. He wasn't himself after losing Black, and now his sister was missing, so I just tried my best to keep him uplifted. I was trying to be strong for everyone, but it was taking a toll on my body. My mom sure gave me the right name, because when it rains it fucking pours, and it'd been pouring and stressing me the hell out.

Once I set the table for Rosa and Persia, I took my mother some soup and a cup of hot tea before rushing out to answer the door. It was Jahiem, looking as if he didn't get any sleep with stress lines on his forehead. I let him in, and he went straight to my bedroom and plopped down on the bed. I knew he was getting tired of me asking him if he was okay, but I didn't know what else to say. I plopped down on the bed with him, putting my head on his chest, finding some comfort even if it was temporary. He pulled me on top of him, putting his tongue in my mouth, causing me to moan. I guessed he was in the mood to release some stress, so I was going to help him. He put his hand inside my sweats, caressing my ass as I gyrated into him, enjoying the dry hump that we had going on.

His fingers were now playing with my clit until I released my juices, now ready to feel him inside of me. I got up to lock the door just to be safe, making sure no one walked in on us. I knew that my mother wasn't feeling well, but that didn't mean she was incapable of getting up on her own. I slowly removed my clothes while he lay on the bed watching my every move with a smirk on his face. I crawled back on the bed and released his dick from the slit in his underwear and jeans, climbing on top. He grabbed my breast while I rode him, trying hard to keep my moans to a minimum. I didn't want anyone to know that we were in the room having sex, because they may not have understood. I knew for a fact that he needed this, and I guessed I needed it too, being that it took my mind to a serene place. It was a temporary fix but one I accepted with open arms and didn't feel the need to apologize for. I swore I hated my damn bed because it was starting to make that annoying squeaking noise, causing me to slow my movement.

He suggested that we get off the bed and that I let him hit it from the back, and I agreed because we were going to get caught. I bent over the bed and arched my back as he entered me from behind, pounding in and out of me. He was beating the pussy up, and I was trying to suppress my screams so much I had to grab my pillow. He announced that he was about to cum, so I tightened my pussy muscles, backing my ass up until we came together. We both collapsed on the bed just as someone was knocking at the fucking door, pissing me off.

"Go get the door," he said, slapping me on the ass.

Persia was just about to answer the door when I walked out, but I told her that I would get it, being that she didn't live here. I thought they knew what we were doing in the room with the way she was looking at me. Shit, I didn't mean no disrespect to the situation. I just needed to release some of the stress I was feeling. When I opened the door, I was taken aback seeing the bitch Jahiem was leaving with the night I drove up to Creepers.

"What the hell are you doing here?" I asked her.

"Listen, I didn't come here to fight. I came to talk to my grandmother," she said, confusing me.

"Who the fuck is your grandmother?" I said, getting defensive, figuring she was playing games.

"Emily, what are you doing here?" Persia asked, coming to the door.

I moved to the side and let her in because, clearly, she was speaking of Rosa when she said her grandmother.

"I just want to say that I didn't have anything to do with Samantha taking the baby. She just asked me to push up on her ex-boyfriend, and I did. She showed up to my house with Jamila bloody and bruised with her friend Ginger."

"Her friend Ginger?" I asked, cutting her off. "Jahiem," I called out so that he could hear what the fuck she was saying.

"Ginger is in on this shit. That was why you couldn't get in touch with her," I said as soon as he walked into the living room.

"Did she have the baby with her?" Persia asked with tears in her eyes.

"She did have the baby with her, but this was like three days ago. She sent me to get some food and a Trac phone, but I never went back to the house. I didn't want any part of what was going on with her kidnapping people, so I've been staying at a hotel. The guilt was killing me, so I knew that I needed to say something, so I came here, being that she said this is where she saw my grandmother."

"Do you know how worried we have been? And you just come here now," Rosa yelled, slapping the shit out of her.

"Grandma, no. She's here now," Persia cried.

"Please give us the address," I said to her.

"You better pray that it's not too late," Rosa threatened.

After she gave us the address, she said that we needed to call the police because she had a gun and wouldn't be scared to use it. I ran to the back to tell my mother that we had an address to where Samantha was staying. She told me to let the police handle it, but Jahiem already said he wasn't calling them until he had his sister. I told her that everything was going to be okay and that Rosa was going to stay here with her while we got Jamila and the baby. She had a worried look on her face, but I had to go, telling her one last time that I was going to be okay.

Jahiem was driving like a speed demon again, so I had to tell him to slow down before he killed us before we got there. He made Emily ride with us just in case she was lying, but I told him that he should have called the police for her ass. If her guilty conscience was eating away at her, why did it take her so long to say something? I had that damn bad feeling in the pit of my stomach again, but I tried hard to only think of positive thoughts. I could feel the vibration of Persia's leg going a mile a minute from being nervous. I didn't think that Samantha would harm a baby, being that she was caring for her as if she were her own. We all knew she was capable of murder, so I prayed that she spared Jamila and the baby. I just felt that we weren't going to find them at Emily's house, being that she never returned to the house. But again, positive thoughts.

Jahiem pulled up to the house, pulling his gun and telling me to stay behind knowing that I wasn't about to stay in the fucking car. Walking into the living room, we didn't see anyone, so he started going from room to room on the first floor. He said that he was going to check the basement and the garage to see if anyone was there. I pulled out my Taser once Persia and I said that we would check upstairs. I went to the left and Persia went to the right, and the first room that I walked in was clear, so I left. Just as I was about to go into the next room, Persia let out a gut-wrenching scream, causing me to run toward the room. Nothing could have prepared me for what I saw, causing me to let out that same gut-wrenching scream.

Chapter Twenty-five

Samantha

"It's been a few hours now. I don't think your cousin is coming back," Ginger voiced for the third time.

"Get the fuck on the landline and call that bitch again," I shouted.

"It doesn't take a rocket scientist to know that the bitch bailed," she stated smartly.

"What the fuck did you just say to me?" I snapped with the gun pointed at her temple.

"I'm . . . I'm just saying I don't think she's coming back," she stuttered.

"Did I ask you for your fucking opinion or did I tell you to call the bitch again?" My voice trembled from the anger I was feeling inside.

If I expected anyone to turn their back on me, it would have been Ginger. No one could have paid me to believe that Emily would betray me. I had no idea if she went to the police, so I needed to get out of Dodge.

"No answer," Ginger said, causing me to scream at the top of my lungs.

"Fuck! Listen, we need to get out of here, but first we need to get rid of those two," I said, speaking of Jamila and the baby.

"What do you mean?" she questioned with a frightened expression on her face.

"Just what the fuck I said, so get the baby and take her upstairs and put her ass in the same room Jamila is in," I demanded.

She hesitantly picked up the car seat the baby was sitting in and carried her upstairs. I didn't know how much longer I had, so I needed to be quick. Jamila could barely walk from being shot in the foot, so I couldn't take her with me. She and the baby would only slow me down, so I had to do what I had to do.

"Samantha, you don't have to do this. We could just leave them here and go. We still have time to hit Jahiem's spot to get enough money to get out of town," she said as soon as I entered the room.

Jamila was looking at me with wide eyes that I ignored as I raised the gun, shooting her twice in the chest. Ginger was screaming like she was fucking crazy, like there wasn't a reason that I had a silencer on the gun.

"Bitch, shut the fuck up," I barked, pointing the gun at her ass.

"Please don't shoot the baby," she cried when she should have been worried about me shooting her ass.

"Do you really think that we could get away with robbing one of the trap houses?" I asked her.

"I'm positive," she tried to convince me.

"Okay. Being that I'm not a monster, get the baby and we will leave her on a neighbor's porch," I told her.

"Thank you." She sniffed.

I waited until she bent down to pick up the car seat before shooting her in the back, causing her to go down on her knees. I shot her three more times, making sure that her ass was dead with her nagging ass. Baby Journey was awake looking at me, so I didn't have the heart to shoot her staring at me like that. I grabbed a pillow off the bed and covered her face with it, causing her to squirm. Her little hands tried to fight to remove the pillow, so I applied pressure until she was no longer moving. I closed the door on my way out, grabbing my bag, hauling ass from the house, not feeling bad about my decision to kill them. I knew no one could report gunfire because of the silencer, but they could report screams coming from the home. I also knew that it wouldn't be safe to ride around in my car for much longer, so I had to get rid of it.

Jahiem was a dumb nigga who really trusted this snake Ginger by giving her a spare key to his place. If I didn't know any better, I would have believed that he was fucking her ass on the low pretending to be friends. I parked my car a couple of blocks away before walking to his house, praying no one was around. Jahiem wasn't lying when he said he didn't shit where he laid his head, because I didn't find shit but a few hundred dollars. I grabbed the keys to his Range, figuring that would get me to my destination without being pulled over. By the time he saw that his truck was missing, I planned on being long gone. I grabbed a shirt and a bottle of his cologne before leaving his bedroom and promising myself that I would see him again.

I arrived in Middletown, New York, a few hours later, feeling exhausted and needing to take my ass to sleep, being that I hadn't slept. I ditched the truck, leaving the keys inside and praying that someone took it and drove off with that shit. I knocked on the door of the dude names Rashad who I met last year at a club in Brooklyn. He was some thirsty nigga who had been trying to get me here since the day I met him, but I gave him every excuse as to why I couldn't. I called him and told him that I had a situation and needed somewhere to stay for a few days, and he was with it. I told his ass my name was Danielle, so I hoped that I didn't slip up. I knocked on the door, and some older woman answered the door, so I started to think I had the wrong house. His ass didn't tell me he was living with anyone, so it pissed me off how these niggas were always lying. I knew that I should have walked the fuck away, but I didn't have anywhere to go, and I'd ditched the truck.

"Hello, I'm looking for Rashad," I said to her.

"Rashad," she called out.

He knew that I was coming, so I had no idea why his ass wouldn't be waiting for me, knowing that he lied about living alone. He came to the door looking as sexy as I remembered his ass, but my face expressed how I didn't appreciate his ass lying.

"Come in," he said, moving to the side and allowing me in.

"Who is that? You told me that you live alone," I said to him.

"Don't start tripping. That was my grandmother, who's visiting," he said, causing me to roll my eyes because I didn't believe his ass.

My ass stopped tripping once I saw his grandmother putting her coat on, leaving to go home, telling him she would call him later. I wanted to ask him why she was so damn rude because she didn't speak or say goodbye. I didn't know what that shit was about, but his ass didn't think to introduce me to the bitch. If Granny didn't like me already not even knowing me, that must mean that she didn't approve of me being here. If she didn't approve of me being here, that could only mean one thing. This nigga had a girlfriend who the family had a relationship with, and that was probably another reason her ass left.

"Why didn't you introduce me to your grandmother?" I asked him after she left.

"She be on that bullshit," he responded but didn't go into details, so I left the shit alone.

I didn't give a fuck if he had a girl. All I cared about was having somewhere to stay until I figured some shit out. I needed to find a computer to check out Inmate Lookup to see if Emily's ass was in custody or some shit. I didn't understand her bailing just to bail when she had always had my back, so she had to be locked up.

"So, what made you call me?" he asked me.

"I told you on the phone that I needed somewhere to stay for a few days," I reminded him.

"I know that you said you needed somewhere to stay, but you never went into details about that situation you was in. You been stringing me along for a long time now because of your situation, so what the hell happened?" he pushed.

"I got tired of that nigga putting his hands on me, so like I said, I just need a few days to figure some shit out." I sighed.

"Damn, that nigga was putting his hands on your pretty ass? It shouldn't have taken you this long to leave his ass."

"I know, but I was in love with him, so you know how that goes. But enough about his ass because

I'm done with him. I'm hungry and I need to take a shower, so do you think that you can make that happen?"

"I can make it happen. I'll get you what you need for the shower, and you can tell me what you want to eat," he said, getting up.

After he handed me a washcloth and towel, I told him that he could just get me some Chinese food or pizza. I went upstairs to his bedroom, impressed with his clean, spacious bedroom that I'd expected to have clothes lying around. I got into the shower, letting the hot water run all over my body, trying to wash away my sins of the day. I had no idea that my life was going to take this drastic turn when all I wanted was to be with my man. The mistake I made was taking my cousin's baby and telling Jahiem that she was his. I should have just gone to New York to claim my man, letting that bitch know that she had to bounce. Now I was on the run for kidnapping and murder, and I still didn't have the man. I honestly panicked when I found out that he was seeing someone else, but now I knew that I should have acted accordingly. I knew who that bitch was, so being that I was already jealous that she was the kept child, it took me over the edge knowing she was in a relationship with my man. I had resented my birth mother from the time I was told that my father passed away and she gave me up. I never understood how a parent could give up a child because of a drug issue, get clean, but never come back for the child. At what point was it okay to marry another nigga and have a kid and not try to have a relationship with the kid you gave up?

I never told no one that I approached her husband, letting him know who I was. I went to talk to him about helping me get to know my mother, but this nigga told me that he didn't think it was the right time. I had a friend I met in North Carolina who would always say to me that I was grown now, so why did I need her? I tried to explain to her that it wasn't that I needed her. I just wanted to meet her and ask her why. Why was it so easy to just forget? How could you give up a child with no intention of coming back for her? I swear, when I met her, the hate build-up was real, and her explanation just pissed me off that much more. Then she married a fuck nigga who fixed his face to basically deny me the same way she did when she didn't get clean for me. She went so far as to say that she thought about me every day and she loved me. How could she love me?

I couldn't believe that I was standing in the shower crying, and it pissed me off because she didn't deserve my tears. She just didn't know how much it hurt me feeling unwanted by the person who birthed me. The night that I told Jahiem that I was going to a party, I lied. I had already fixed in my mind that I was going to kill her husband.

After killing her husband, I was supposed to have gone to her house and killed her too, but I freaked out after hitting him. I knew that no one probably would believe that I didn't know who the daughter was, but at that time I had no idea. Jahiem never put the connection together that his sister's friend's father being killed was connected to my accident. The reason I left was because I just knew that he was going to figure it out, but he never did . . . or did he?

Chapter Twenty-six

Reign

It'd been a week since finding the bodies of Jamila, Journey, and Ginger. I had been trying to process how someone could be so evil as to take innocent lives. I knew that something was off with Samantha, even suggesting that she was responsible for killing my father, but I never expected her to do this. I hadn't had a good night sleep because every time I closed my eyes, I was being haunted by the sight in that room. I hadn't seen Jahiem since the day we walked into that house because he wasn't speaking to me. He wanted to kill Emily, but I stopped him from killing her, so in return he said some harsh words to me. I understood why he wanted to kill her, but I tried to explain to him that death would be too easy. I had no idea if he even had a funeral for Jamila because he made it clear that I wasn't invited. He even went so far as to say that if he saw me, he would kill me, even pointing his gun in my face. We were all running off emotions, but if he had killed Emily, he would have been locked up. I didn't stop him to spare her life. I stopped him to spare his, but he didn't see it that way. My heart was broken in a million pieces losing my friend and not being able to properly say goodbye. I felt like I lost two people I loved since he decided to walk away from me. He didn't even know how much I needed him right now knowing he was the closest thing to Jamila that I had left.

"Reign," I heard my mom call from the other side of the door.

I'd been holed up in my room since it happened, so she knew that I didn't want to be bothered right now. She was still in denial, believing that Samantha couldn't do something like this. She had so many scenarios fixed in her mind with none of them having to do with Samantha being responsible. I had never disrespected my mother on the level that I disrespected her that day because that was how pissed I was.

I wasn't going to apologize because she was speaking as if she raised her and knew what she was capable of. I wanted so bad to tell her that she birthed a fucking crack baby, but she was already crying, so I didn't.

"Reign," she called out again, which I ignored.

She started banging on the door, so I got up and unlocked the door before swinging it open so hard it hit the wall.

"What?" I yelled.

"Listen, I let that slick talk that came out of your mouth slide because I know that you're hurting, but guess what, little girl? You're not the only one. You got one more time to disrespect me and I'm going to lay you the fuck down. Now take your ass out there to the living room because someone is here to see you," she spat before walking off, cursing about how I done lost my mind and how she was going to help me find it.

I walked out to the living room not in the mood to see anyone but was shocked to see Jahiem and Jamila's cousin Kelsey.

"Hey, Kelsey," I said, hugging her and trying hard not to shed any tears.

She and Jamila were close but hadn't seen each other in a while, being that she was away at school, but they talked every day. She couldn't even speak, getting choked up on the words that she tried to speak.

"I'm so sorry. She didn't deserve to die like that," I cried.

"I was on the phone with her when you called, so she said that she was going to call me back. If I knew that was going to be our last conversation, I would have told her that I loved her."

"She always told me how you were her favorite cousin, so she knew that you loved her the same way she loved you."

"She would always say that I was her favorite cousin, and we would always joke that I was her only cousin. I'm going to miss her so much, and I would give anything for my phone to ring with her being on the other end. I came here to talk to you because you weren't at the ceremony, and when I asked Jahiem about it, he said he didn't want to talk about it. Does he blame you for her death? Also, I came to tell you that I'm worried about him because he has been drinking and reckless. I've been trying to keep him levelheaded, but I'm leaving tonight because I need to get back to school. I can't help but to think that I'm going to lose him too if he don't put the bottle down," she stressed.

"He doesn't blame me for her death, but he's mad because I wouldn't let him kill Samantha's cousin, who knew what was going on. I didn't care if she was killed. I just didn't want him to get into any trouble killing her. He said that he never wants to see me again because of it and that was the reason I wasn't invited to the ceremony."

"He came home the other night with his shirt bloody, so like I said, I'm worried, and I wish that I could stay. I hate to ask you this, but could you please try to talk to him before we be burying him next?" she pleaded with tears in her eyes.

I knew that she didn't have nowhere else to turn, being that her mother passed away when she was young. She was raised by her father and his side of the family, so it was just her, Jahiem, and Jamila. If they had any other family, they never spoke about them, so if it meant risking him going off on me, I was going to talk to him.

"Don't worry. I will go and see if I can get through to him," I promised her.

I went into the bathroom to take a shower—something that I didn't have the energy to do in a few days. I brushed my natural hair, which I allowed to stay matted on top of my head, not having the energy to even pick up a brush. It sounded like Jahiem needed me, so I was going to go to him because Jamila would have wanted me to. After getting dressed I was still in my feelings, so I didn't say anything to my mother before leaving. I knew that I couldn't stay mad with her forever, but right now I had nothing to say to her.

When I pulled up in front of Jahiem's house, I saw his truck, so I knew that he was home but also that he was intoxicated. His truck was parked on the grass not even close to the driveway, also letting me know that he was drinking and driving. I knocked on the door a few times before that bitch Monica opened the door wearing one of his shirts. She had an annoyed look on her face, looking me up and down like I looked bad or some shit.

"Can I help you?" she spat.

"No, but you could move the fuck out of my way," I said, pushing past her ass.

"Why the fuck are you here? Jahiem is not trying to see your ass," she said, but I ignored her.

He told me that he used to mess with this dirty ho but broke things off with her, so he had to be big mad to have gone back slumming. She had me fucked up if she thought that I was going to be the one leaving this bitch. When I walked into his room and saw the state he was in, I told that bitch that she needed to leave. His room was a mess with empty liquor bottles, swisher wrappers, and used condoms on the floor. Kelsey was right about him being reckless, but what bothered me about this bitch Monica was she wasn't a real bitch. If she was a rider knowing the caliber of this man, she would know that this wasn't him. He just lost his sister, so a blind motherfucker could see that he was hurting, but this bitch was just here to reap the benefits.

"I need for you to grab your shit and get the fuck on," I repeated.

"I was invited, so I'm not going any fucking where unless that man uninvites me."

"Well, that man is in no condition to uninvite you, so I'm telling your ass to leave. I'm trying not to fuck you up for even being here with my man, so if I were you, I would just leave," I warned.

"Girl, bye," she said, dismissing me.

I had so much anger built up inside of me that I was scared that I would hurt this bitch right now feeling no remorse. I was honestly trying to have some self-control, but I was seconds from jumping on this bitch. I just needed her to leave so that I could get this place clean and get rid of the stale smell up in this bitch. I could only imagine what her place looked like if she was okay sitting her ass up in here unbothered.

"Monica, I'm asking you as nice as I possibly can for you to leave. At the end of the day Jahiem is still my man, so respect that shit and just leave," I stressed.

"I don't believe that you're in any position to still call him your man. If he didn't want me here, I wouldn't be here. He needed someone, and if that someone were you, he would have called you, so being that he called me, I'm not leaving," she responded sternly.

"This can't be life," I stressed, causing her to roll her eyes.

I was so tired of fighting these hoes to the point that I was ready to walk out the door and say fuck it and fuck Jahiem too. I smiled because I could hear Jamila in my head, saying, *"Bitch, you better not walk out that door."* I honestly wanted to be here for him, but I also wanted to mourn my friend without all the extra bullshit. She took her dusty ass and went into the living room, sitting on the couch, going through her phone like I didn't say shit.

I walked over to her and grabbed her by his shirt and dragged her ass. She was kicking and screaming trying to get to me by grabbing at my pants, but she was having a hard time.

"Get off of me, you crazy bitch," she shouted.

"Well, you wanted to see crazy, being that you wasn't trying to hear me when I was talking nice to your ass."

I opened the front door and pulled her ass down the steps, not caring that all she was wearing was that fucking T-shirt. I should have taken that shit off that bitch, being that it didn't belong to her stink ass. It bothered me that she wasn't wearing any panties, reminding me that he fucked this skank.

"I need my clothes, you stupid bitch, and I didn't drive here," she yelled from the sidewalk.

"Call an Uber, bitch," I said, closing the door.

I went back inside and grabbed her shit before opening the door and throwing her shit out to her and closing the door again. It took me about an hour to get his place back to how it was supposed to look. His ass was still sprawled out on the bed snoring loud as shit, irritating my soul so bad that I wanted to slap him. I was tired and disgusted by the time I took the trash out back and came back inside. I called my mother to let her know that I was at Jahiem's place just so she wouldn't worry. I was still mad at her, but being that Samantha's crazy ass was still out here somewhere, I wanted to let her know that I was good. As soon as I ended the call, his ass came walking into the living room, looking a mess. He was only wearing his boxer briefs, sporting a hard-on, causing that tingling he always gave me between my legs. He hadn't had a shave or haircut, but his ass was still sexy to me, but I wasn't fucking his ass.

I crossed my legs, trying to calm the sensation, rolling my eyes and pretending as if I weren't hot and bothered. He sat across from me, now eyeing me with an expression that I couldn't read, and I wasn't even going to try to read his ass right now.

Chapter Twenty-seven

Reign

"Why are you here?" he asked rudely.

"I'm here because you need me," I spat, matching his tone.

"How the fuck you figure I need your ass? All I needed was some pussy and I got that shit handled," he barked.

"Well, I kicked that ho to the curb because that was not what you need right now," I told him, trying hard to stay calm.

I knew that he was trying to hurt my feelings, being that he was still in his, not realizing that I was only trying to protect his ass.

"Don't be kicking nobody out of my crib, because you lost that privilege when I told you that I was done with you."

"I'm not sweating that you're done. If you want a bitch who was not going to look out for you, then by all means you can have that. I'm only here to make sure your dumb ass don't kill yourself being fucking reckless. Trust that I'm only here because your sister would have wanted me to make sure that you were good."

"I'm good, so you can bounce," he shouted, causing me to shake my head at him.

"You're so good that your place looked and smelled like shit and that nasty ho you chose to lie up with wasn't even bothered. You should be thankful that I came here to make sure that you were good after shutting me out. You didn't even allow me to say goodbye to my best friend, so please believe that I don't give a shit about you. I don't have a problem bouncing knowing that I came here to do what I said I was going to do. I made sure that you're good, so I have no problem leaving your fucking house," I spat.

He had me so mad, coming at me like I was some jump-off when I was here checking up on his ass. I told myself that I wasn't going to even speak to him for the way he treated me and how he didn't allow me to be a part of Jamila's arrangements. I could no longer hold back the tears once I got inside my car because he hurt me. He turned his back on me when I needed him, so I was done just like he said he was done with me. He made this shit about him, not even thinking about how I was feeling after losing my best friend. We could have been here for each other, but he wanted to act like he was the only one hurting. He had me thinking about taking the money that my father left me and just moving away to start over. I felt myself on the verge of a breakdown because the hurt and pain I was feeling was becoming unbearable. I missed her so much and just wished that all that happened was just a bad dream. I didn't feel like going home because I wasn't in the mood to get into it with my mother, so I decided to go to my grandmother's house.

As soon as I pulled up to my grandmother's house and stepped out of the car, I saw Dame leaving his mother's house. I was hoping that he didn't look in my direction because I didn't want him to see me looking like this. I already knew that my eyes were probably red from crying over Jahiem's dumb ass.

"Fuck," I cursed under my breath when he looked in my direction.

I hadn't seen him in a long time and didn't mind seeing him again, but now just wasn't the time for a reunion. Dame and I were good friends until he started dating the neighborhood slut who lived across the street from my grandmother. His mother moved to my grandmother's block when we were young, and we just clicked.

I only visited on the weekends, so we didn't get to spend much time together. Once Deja put claims on him, he stopped hanging out with me on weekends because she wouldn't allow him to be anywhere around me.

"Hey, I was hoping to run into you. I heard about what happened to your friend, so I just wanted to make sure you were good. Do you need anything?" he asked before giving me a hug.

"I'm just trying to process that I'm never going to see her again." I teared up.

"How long do you plan on being at your grandmother's house? You look like you need a friend right now. I have to run a few errands for my mother, but I'll be back in about an hour if you want to link up."

"I'll be here," I said to him.

I had already made up my mind that I was going to stay with my grandmother tonight, so I didn't mind hanging out with him.

It was exactly an hour by the time I finished cooking for my grandmother when I heard the knock at the door. She looked at me with a smile on her face, already knowing who was on the other side of the door.

"What?" I asked her with a sly smile on my face.

"I saw you out there talking to Bernadette's son. I swear you used to visit me just to see that boy every weekend. I just knew that you and he were going to be together when the two of you got older, but nope. You let that fast-tailed little girl from across the street steal him from right under your nose. He was crushing on you just as much as you were crushing on him, and he would be sad whenever you would miss a weekend visit."

"Grandma, stop. We were just friends," I said, leaving the kitchen to go answer the door.

"Hey, are you ready?" he asked me as soon as I answered the door.

"I'm ready. Let me go tell my grandmother that I'm leaving," I said, leaving him at the door.

"Take the keys to let yourself back in," she said, already knowing.

"I'll see you later." I laughed at her.

She didn't question my decision about going out with another man. She already knew how Jahiem dismissed me and didn't allow me to say bye to Jamila. She said that the vibe that she got from him wasn't the one that he was displaying now. I tried to defend him, stating that he was hurting, but she wasn't trying to hear me.

I didn't know why I was nervous getting into Dame's truck like this was my first time meeting his ass. It could have been that I was feeling like I was doing something wrong by being with him.

"So how have you been?" I asked, making small talk to calm my nerves.

"I just been working hard, trying to stay out of trouble," he responded.

"Are you still dating Deja?" I asked him.

"We still kicking it, and she's pregnant with my seed." He sighed.

"Congrats even though you don't sound too excited about it."

"Deja has my ass stressed the fuck out." He chuckled.

"Well, you should be used to it, being that the two of you have been together for like forever." I rolled my eyes.

I couldn't believe that he was still with her after all these years. She was known to cheat on him every chance that she got when we were teenagers.

"Nah, this girl be bugging more than usual since she got pregnant, and I'm so ready to call this shit quits," he stressed.

"She never liked me because she always thought that I had a thing for you back then," I said.

"You did." He chuckled, causing me to laugh.

"No, I didn't," I lied.

"Yeah, okay, keep telling that lie with a straight face. I knew just like everyone else knew," he admitted.

"So if you knew, why did you start dating her instead of me?" I wanted to know.

"Do you want the truth?" he asked, looking at me.

"I wouldn't have asked if I didn't."

"At that time, all I had on my mind was a pretty smile and big butt and the female who had no problem putting out. I knew that you didn't rock like that and the fact that you only came around on the weekends, so that was two strikes against you," he said.

He was right about that because I was nothing like the fast-ass girls who lived on my grandmother's block. I appreciated him being honest, but it still made me feel a way that he chose her over me for some ass.

"All I can say is that you got what you bargained for, and even if you end things with her, you still have to deal with her," I told him.

"Do you have any kids?" he asked me.

"Hell to the no," I answered with the quickness.

"Damn, why you say it like that?" He laughed.

"I don't have time to be pushing out a baby for a selfish-ass nigga. I'm good," I said, thinking about Jahiem.

I noticed that we'd been driving for a while now, and I wondered where the hell we were going, being that he never said.

"Where are you taking me?" I questioned, giving him the side-eye.

"Shorty, I got this, so just sit back and relax," he said, turning on the radio.

I decided to do just that as I sang along to the song "Every Kind of Way" by Her. I couldn't help but think about my relationship with Jahiem, which I missed. I gave him all of me, so I was feeling the words as my eyes started to tear up. Dame reached over and turned the radio off, looking at me as the tears fell.

"I'm sorry, shorty. I'm supposed to be cheering you up, not making you cry," he apologized.

"It's not your fault," I told him, wiping at my tears.

He pulled up to Brooklyn Bridge Park, causing me to look at him with a smile on my face because he remembered. This was one of my favorite places to go growing up, and I used to always express that to him. My Mom and Dad had crazy work hours, so the neighbor who used to babysit me after school would always take her daughter and me there.

"You remembered," I said to him.

"Yes, I remembered, so being that you loved to come here, I figured it would put a smile on your face."

"I haven't been here in so long," I admitted.

"I've been here a few times since they had the new roller rink put in, so that was another reason I decided to bring you here. Can you still skate?" he asked.

Another memory from my childhood visits at my grandmother's house that he remembered. I used to skate up and down the block for hours until my grandmother would call me inside to eat dinner. Dame couldn't skate back then and would always try to keep up with me, but he always ended up busting his ass.

"Yes, I can still skate. Did you learn how to skate?" I joked.

"What do you mean, learn how to skate, girl? I been skating since my elementary days." He laughed knowing his ass was lying.

"Yeah, okay. I'm not picking your ass up off the floor."

We walked inside to get skates. This place was beautiful, and the view was so amazing that I wanted to admire the view.

"What size skates are you?" he asked me.

"Get me a size six please," I responded before sitting down to remove my sneakers.

As soon as my ass put the skates on and stood up, my ass stumbled, almost hitting the damn floor if I didn't get my balance.

"Let me find out the skating queen done lost her damn crown." He laughed as he busted a move on the floor.

I wasn't about to let his ass show me up, so I let go of the rail and skated away slowly, still being cautious. Once I got my balance under control, I was doing my thing moving my hips to the music. He was keeping up with me, showing me that his ass learned how to skate and showing off at the same time. When he came back around, he grabbed my hand, and we were now skating together. I was enjoying myself, and it felt good to smile again even if it was temporary, knowing that once I was alone again, I was going to be sad. We were now skating as if we were a couple, but I had to remind myself that he was taken. We skated for about forty minutes before we both were winded, forgetting that we weren't young Reign and Dame anymore.

"Are you hungry?" he asked as he kneeled to remove my skates.

"I'm hungry and thirsty," I responded.

"Cool, I'll take you to get something to eat before dropping you back to your grandmother's spot."

He pulled up to Red Lobster, and I couldn't contain the smile on my face, knowing my ass was about to go to town on some lobster and those banging-ass biscuits. We were seated right away, so I was looking over the menu with my mouth watering. I looked up for a second and saw him texting on his phone, but I wasn't about to trip. He was in a relationship, so I had to respect him communicating with her. We were only friends, so I needed to remind myself that I didn't have any claims on this man.

"I apologize," he said, putting his phone down.

"No need. Trust when I say that I understand you have to check in with the wife." I laughed.

"I see you got jokes. Anyway, are you working or going to school?" he said, changing the subject.

"I was going to school, but I recently took a semester off, and I'm still not ready to go back. A lot has changed in my life, so I honestly don't know if I'm coming or going these days. I do know that

I been thinking about moving away and starting over," I admitted.

"Nah, don't do that when I just got you back," he said, making me smile.

"You could have linked up with me at any time, being that your mother lives on the same block as my grandmother."

"I was trying to respect your situation."

"I only had a situation for about a year, so you could have gotten my number at any time if you really wanted to catch up. You didn't reach out because you know just like I know that Deja would have fucked you up if she found out."

Just as he was about to respond, the food arrived, so I dug in not caring about eating in front of him. I had my eye on the vanilla bean cheesecake, but I was going to take it to-go so that I could eat it with ice cream. I was going to be disappointed if I got back to my grandmother's house and she didn't have any.

"What you over there thinking about?" he asked.

"The vanilla bean cheesecake that you're going to buy for me to take home so I can devour it with some ice cream," I told him.

"Who said dessert was included in my offering to feed you?" he joked.

"If you don't want to see me act up in this restaurant, I advise you to get my cheesecake."

Once we finished eating and he ordered my cheesecake to-go, he took me back to my grandmother's house.

Chapter Twenty-eight

Dame

Reign thought that I was talking to Deja when I was responding to a text message, but it was my mother. She told me that Deja showed up to her house looking for me, so I was asking my mother to see if she could get her to leave. She knew that she shouldn't be on her feet chasing behind me when her ass was due any day now. I knew that she wasn't going to leave until I showed up, but I never expected her ass to be sitting on the porch swing.

"Is that Deja?" Reign asked.

Deja was wobbling down the stairs of my mom's house once she spotted my car, and I swear I wanted to pull off.

"That's her." I sighed.

"How cute." She sucked her teeth once Reign and I exited the car.

"Deja, don't start," I warned.

"What do you mean, don't start? I been telling you all day that I didn't feel well, but you told me you had some errands to run for your mother. All you do is fucking lie," she said before wobbling away.

"I'll talk to you later." Reign smirked.

I had no idea why Deja stormed off knowing her ass couldn't walk fast with her over-dramatic ass.

"Why do you always have to show out? You shouldn't even be out here driving knowing that you could go into labor," I barked.

"I didn't drive, and how you figure I'm showing out when my man is caught riding around with his ex? And don't think I missed the Red Lobster bag that she had in her hand. Did you take her on a date?" she cried.

I swore since her ass had gotten pregnant it seemed like she cried at the drop of a hat, and that shit pissed me off. All I wanted to do was go home and not be out here arguing with her ass when she wouldn't be mad if she just kept her ass home.

"I'm not about to stand out here and argue with you, so if you want a ride back to the crib, you better bring your ass on," I told her, walking back to my truck.

"You know that I'm not supposed to be dealing with stress. So, I don't understand why you always doing stupid shit to stress me out," she shouted as soon as she got inside the truck.

"So, how about you try not stressing yourself out? Reign just lost her best friend, so I took her out to cheer her up, nothing more, nothing less.

I told her that we are together and that you were pregnant with my baby. But none of that matters because you still will always find a way to trip over nothing."

"If you would have called me and told me you was going out with your ex and the reason why you were going out with her, I wouldn't be tripping," she lied.

"Stop calling her my ex when you know that we were only friends," I stressed, just wanting her to leave it the fuck alone.

"Whatever," she spat, now facing the window and calling herself ignoring me.

"Do you want to get something to eat before we get to the house?" I asked her, which she ignored.

I wasn't about to feed into her attitude, so we drove the rest of the way home in silence as I thought about Reign. I couldn't help but wonder what it would have been like if I hadn't been chasing ass and had told her how I felt about her. Just before Deja got pregnant, I had made up my mind that I was breaking up with her. I thought that I was in love with her all these years, but I thought it had more to do with settling when it came to her. I had always had strong feelings for Reign and thought about her often but respected the fact that she was seeing someone. My mother was the one who always kept me updated on Reign's life through her grandmother. When I heard about what happened to her best friend and how she was excluded from the funeral, I needed to see her.

"Are you okay?" I asked Deja, who was moaning, but she didn't answer me. "Deja, are you having contractions?" I tried again.

"Don't act like you care now when you didn't care earlier when I told you that I wasn't feeling well."

"Why the fuck you always want to fucking argue? Are you having fucking contractions or not?" I yelled at her.

I could see the pain etched on her face, but she was so fucking stubborn that she would sit there and be in pain. I swore after she had this fucking baby I would be done, because she would never grow the fuck up. I would be there for my child, but I was done with this shit and how she shut down over bullshit.

"I'm having contractions," she hastily responded.

She probably was in labor from the time she got to my mother's house but didn't say shit just to wait for me. I busted a U-turn, cursing under my breath because this chick here was exhausting and ruined my fucking night. No, I don't mean the part about her being in labor but the part about stressing me the fuck out for no reason. Yes, I could have told her that I was hanging out with Reign, but why the fuck would she sit in labor waiting for a nigga?

By the time I pulled up to the hospital, her ass was crying because the contractions were stronger and she was feeling them. I helped her out of the car, rushing her inside of the hospital and letting them know she was in labor. She was escorted upstairs in the wheelchair while grabbing my hand as the nurse pushed her. I held her hand and she was squeezing the life out of my shit, letting me know I needed to call her folks. Her mother wanted to be in the room, so when they took her into the room to prep her, I called her mother. I shouldn't have, but when I ended the call with her mother, I called Reign.

"I thought you would be in the doghouse by now." She laughed.

"Nah, I'm at the hospital. She's in labor," I told her.

"You didn't tell me she was due to deliver. She carried that baby well, because she doesn't even look nine months pregnant."

"Yeah, she was due any day, and that was why she was beefing tonight and kept calling you my ex knowing we were only friends."

"I see that she's still extra just like she was when we were kids. Anyway, I appreciate you calling me, but don't you think you need to get back to the delivery room?"

"Oh, shit. I almost forgot." I chuckled, ending the call with her ass.

"Where did you go?" Deja panted.

"I went to call your mother to let her know that you're in labor."

"And you couldn't do that inside the room?" she asked in that accusatory tone that she always used, which I ignored.

After the doctor examined her, he said that she was six centimeters and that he would be back to check on her. When her mother arrived at the hospital, she was throwing shade, and I was seconds from missing the birth. I wasn't about to be there and deal with her mother, so I wanted her to tell her mother to chill. Her mother never liked me when it was her daughter who was always running game and cheating on me. *She better be grateful that I didn't ask her daughter for a fucking DNA test.* I swore I needed a blunt right about now, but I knew that if I left to go smoke in my truck, Deja was going to be beefing. My mother texted me, letting me know that she and my aunt were out in the waiting area, waiting for the arrival of my firstborn. I really didn't want a lot of my family up here just in case the baby came out looking like the next nigga.

It was almost midnight when Deja pushed out my baby girl who looked just like my ass, so a nigga was happy. I was tired as shit, but seeing my baby girl was worth waiting hours for. My mother and Deja's mother didn't get along, so they kept going at it so much that I had to threaten that I was going to kick them out. The nurse said that Deja needed to rest, so I was thankful that all of them were about to take their asses home. I was going to spend the night at the hospital, so I told Deja that I would be back after walking my mom and aunt out. It was late as shit, so I wanted to make sure that they were inside her car safely.

"All her mother do is talk shit just like her daughter," my mother complained.

"Mom, I would think you would be used to it by now." I laughed.

"No, I'm not used to it, and she got one more time before I put my hands on her ass," she spat, with my aunt concurring.

I hugged them both before going back inside the hospital to be with my daughter so that Deja could rest. When I got back into the room, I washed my hands before picking up my daughter, who was still awake. I thought Deja's mother had left, but she was coming out of the bathroom, causing me to sigh.

"Don't sit and hold her all night or you will have a spoiled baby," she said.

"I don't plan on holding her all night."

That was the reason she and my mother got into it, because she was telling me what to do with my child. I understood that this was my first child, but I wasn't stupid, so she didn't need to treat me as if I were. I tried so hard to respect her on the strength of Deja, but she was really irking my damn nerves. I should have let my mother and aunt whoop her ass to let her know to stop fucking with me. I wanted to tell my mother that she didn't have to worry much longer about Deja's mother because I was leaving her ass. The only reason I didn't say anything was because I didn't want her to accuse me that it had something to do with Reign. My mother knew how I felt about Reign all these years because I didn't keep anything from her. When Deja cheated on me the first time, my mother told me to leave her ass. I stayed because the girl I wanted was already dating someone, so again I settled.

After her mother left, I put the baby down, covering her up before getting comfortable in the chair and dozing off.

I woke up to my phone alerting me of a text message, so I stood before checking it. The chair that I fell asleep in did a number on my damn back. My shit hurt, and I had no plans on staying another night if that was where I had to sleep.

Reign: Good morning. Did she have the baby yet?

I couldn't help but to smile that she reached out to me to find out if the baby was born yet. I knew that Deja wouldn't have been happy because she would put more into it than there needed to be.

Me: Yes, she had the baby late last night. That was why I didn't reach out. It's a girl.

Reign: She had a girl. Aww, congrats.

Me: Thank you. What do you have going on today?

Reign: No plans yet. I'm leaving my grandmother's house to go home in about an hour.

Me: Do you want to hang out later?

Reign: You just had a baby girl, so shouldn't you be at the hospital?

Me: I need to go home and shower before going to check in at my trucking business. I can scoop you up for lunch before heading back to the hospital.

Reign: Okay, just text me when you're on your way.

Me: Cool. I'll see you later.

After completing the paternity papers, I told Deja that I was going home to change and stop by the company before coming back. She was beefing until I explained to her that we didn't even have her bag or the baby bag. She wanted me to quote a time that I would be back, but I ignored her as I snapped a few pictures of my daughter. I knew if I gave her a time, she would be expecting me back at that time, and that was why I ignored her. I had no idea how long it was going to take having lunch with Reign, so no way would I give her a time. I kissed my baby girl on the forehead before heading out to go to the crib to shower and change.

Chapter Twenty-nine

Samantha

"Rashad, I don't trust her ass, and I think it's time for you to ask her to leave," I heard his grandmother say to him.

"Danielle needed a place to stay, so I agreed to let her stay here until she gets her affairs in order," he responded, causing me to smile.

I knew that I shouldn't be ear hustling, but when I let her in, I knew she was going to be on some bullshit. She was starting to rub me the wrong way, and if she knew any better, she would leave me the fuck alone.

"Well, what has she done to get her affairs in order? Whenever I come over here, which is often, she's lounging around doing nothing," she continued.

"Grandma, will you just let me do me, being that you don't trust anyone?" he stressed.

"That may be true, but when has your grandma been wrong?"

"Grandma, you're wrong this time," he stated sternly.

I hoped this nigga wasn't catching feelings, because I had no plans on being with his ass, and if he was smart, he would listen to Grandma.

"Okay, Rashad, but don't say that I didn't tell you so," she said to him, stuck on not giving up.

I walked into the kitchen, rolling my eyes at her ass because I wanted her to know that I heard her talking about me. Rashad had his face in the refrigerator, so he didn't see what just transpired between us.

"Rashad, don't forget that you need to pick up Remy and RJ," she said with a smirk on her face.

I hoped she didn't think that shit she said bothered me, being that he already told me about his son and baby mother. He wasn't my man, so I couldn't care less about what he had going on with his baby mother. As soon as I got my man back, Rashad would be a distant memory of mine with no looking back. Rashad walked out of the kitchen with a Corona in his hand, leaving me in the kitchen with his old-ass grandmother.

"So, what's your game, Danielle? Is Danielle even your name?" she questioned, causing me to look at her suspiciously.

She had me wondering if her ass saw me on the news, being that all old bitches watch the news all fucking day.

"Why would I say my name is Danielle if it wasn't? I don't know what your problem is with me, but please don't accuse me of lying," I spat.

"Did you hear me accuse you of anything or did I ask you a question? I only asked the question because when I called your name you didn't answer me," she said, playing games, because this old hag didn't call my name.

"Well, if you called my name and I didn't answer, maybe I was ignoring you because I know that you don't like me."

"I don't like that my grandson opened up his home to a female he doesn't know. It has nothing to do with you as a person, because like you said, I don't know you. I don't trust you because if you had any respect for my grandson and appreciated him letting you stay here, you wouldn't be disrespecting his grandmother."

"You're old enough to know that you have to give respect to get respect," I spat.

"My grandson will realize that he let the devil into his home. I just hope that it will be sooner rather than later," she said before walking out of the kitchen.

I walked out of the kitchen with murder on my mind with different ways to take her ass to her demise. I needed to find out a way to get him to stop her ass from coming over here and throwing shade every chance that she got. I didn't want him to ask me to leave before I figured out what my next move was. I was able to find out that Emily was being held on Rikers Island with her stupid fucking ass.

"Dani, I'm going to go handle this business, so I'll see you when I get back," he said, calling me by the nickname that he gave me.

"I hope your grandmother is leaving too," I whispered, or so I thought.

"Now why the hell would I stay behind if my grandson is leaving?" She rolled her eyes.

"Anyway, I'll see you when you get back, Rashad," I said walking away.

"Rashad, I want her out of here. She's disrespectful and I don't like her ass," I heard her say to him, causing me to shake my head.

After they closed the door, I went back out into the living room and propped my feet up, happy that they were gone. I had the burner phone in my hand, contemplating if I should call the crackhead mother who birthed me. I knew that she wouldn't throw me to the wolves once I spun my believable story, giving her no choice but to believe me. I wasn't going to get into it over the phone with her, so I was going to ask if she could meet me. I took a deep breath before calling her number, praying that Reign wasn't home.

"Hello," she answered. "Hello," she repeated, but I still didn't say anything. "Samantha?" she cried.

"Mom, it's me." I faked sniffed into the phone.

"I've been so worried about you, baby. Where are you?" she asked.

"Mom, I can't tell you where I'm at, but I'm calling to ask you if you would be willing to meet up with me. I want to explain everything to you, but I need you to trust me by keeping this call between us. Also, if you agree to meet up with me, I'm going to need you to come alone and not call the police." I cried, even squealing into the phone, giving my best performance.

"Don't cry, baby. Just tell me where you want me to meet you and I will be there, and I promise I will come alone."

Once I told her where I wanted to meet, I ended the call and sent Rashad a text message from my iPhone. I wanted to know if he could let me use the car that he had sitting in his driveway to run a few errands tomorrow. I felt better about being in a car than trying to travel on public transportation, risking my freedom. I made a promise to myself that Jahiem was going to be mine, and I would not lose him to anyone again.

Rashad got back about an hour later, walking in with his son, who was the spitting image of him. He couldn't deny him if he wanted to. He said that he had to pick him up, but he never said that he was bringing him back with him.

"I know you're wondering why they are here, but his mother insisted," he said.

"They?" I questioned just to be sure.

"Yes, she's here because she claims if I'm going to have my son, she needs to meet the female he's going to be around."

"Well, did you tell her that we are not a couple and my staying here is temporary?" I asked him.

I understood her position, but it wasn't necessary because I wasn't trying to have any interactions with her son. She walked into the house with a walk that said she had something to prove, but she was sadly mistaken.

"Dani, this is Remy and, Remy, this is Dani. Now that you met her you can leave," he said to her.

"Rashad, don't try to play me in front of your girlfriend. When I start dating, I'm sure you're going to want to meet the man who is going to be around your son."

"I wish you would have another nigga around my son," he barked.

They started arguing like a married couple while his son and I looked on amused, but he was also looking like he was used to the shenanigans. Rashad said that he was 4, but he looked more like 6 with his chubby ass. He had his dad's handsome face, but it looked like his mother let him eat whatever the hell he wanted to eat.

"Are you two done? I don't think you should be arguing in front of your son. I mean, isn't that the reason you wanted to meet me? How do you expect me to be respectful when it comes to your son when you aren't?" I instigated.

"Exactly, I be telling her that shit all the time," he barked as if his ass were any better.

"Don't tell me how to act in front of my son when you don't know me," she spat.

"I'm not about to argue with you because that would defeat the purpose of the point I was trying to make," I said, shaking my head.

"Your grandmother was right about this bitch having your nose wide the fuck open. You let her disrespect your grandmother and now you're allowing her to disrespect me. RJ, let's go because I never thought I would see the day that your father let pussy control him," she yelled, grabbing her chubby son's hand before going out the front door.

So, the only reason she showed up here was because his old hag of a grandmother was talking about me to this bitch. I swore his grandmother was going to fuck around and catch these hands continuing to fuck with me.

"I don't know what problem your grandmother has with me when she doesn't know shit about me. I could see if I was playing you or some shit, but I haven't left this house since you let me stay here. I'm not after your money, because I haven't asked you for shit since I've been here, and anything that you have done for me, you have done on your own."

"Listen, I'm sorry about all of this, and I promise you that I will be speaking to my grandmother about this shit."

"You never answered me when I asked to use the car to go visit my mother tomorrow, unless it's going to be an issue with your grandmother."

"I don't have an issue with you driving the car, but I wanted to tell you that the car used to belong to Remy. If you don't have a problem with it, then use it to go see your mother," he said.

I didn't give a shit who the car belonged to as long as it got me to where I needed to be tomorrow morning.

"I don't care that it used to be her car when I'm trying to go see my mother and not ride on the stuffy bus to get there. Just don't forget to talk to your grandmother about talking about me when I didn't do shit to her."

"I got that covered," he said, grabbing me from behind.

He smelled so damn good, and I had been trying hard not to fall victim to his sexy ass, being that I was already in a relationship. I let him eat my pussy, but that was the extent of the intimacy with him because I was trying to be faithful and not fuck anyone.

"Do you want to go see a movie?" he asked me.

I wasn't trying to be seen out in public out of fear that someone would recognize me from the news report. I got lucky that Rashad and his peoples were clueless, so I wasn't risking my freedom to catch a damn movie.

"Why can't we just order in and watch a movie? I don't like going out much," I lied.

"That is cool. What do you want to eat?" he asked me.

"Well, after you eat this pussy, we can focus on ordering food and watching a movie," I told his ass.

I swear the way his ass ate my pussy and tongue fucked me in the ass, I was ready to hop on his dick, but I would not. I'd just continue to count the days until I'd be in Jahiem's arms again, hoping it was going to be soon. I needed to make sure that the bitch who birthed me believed everything I told her tomorrow so that I could get back to New York.

Chapter Thirty

Ms. Peggy

Reign had been staying with her grandmother these last few days, so I didn't have to explain where I was going this early. I knew that she wouldn't approve of me meeting up with Samantha, so that was the reason I didn't tell her. I knew that all the evidence proved she was guilty of this horrendous act, but I didn't believe she did it. I took an Uber to the Port Authority to get the bus to Middletown, New York. Samantha wanted to meet in Brooklyn, but she quickly changed her mind, which I didn't mind. If she came here and got spotted by Jahiem or anyone who knew him, her life wouldn't be spared. He cared about her, but he cared about his sister more, so it was best for her to just stay away.

I got off the bus about an hour later after taking the express. I now looked around for her, being that she said she was going to be here waiting. My phone rang and it was her, so I guessed she wanted to make sure that I was alone.

"Hello," I answered.

"Mom, walk toward the corner and cross the street. I will be parked in front of the corner store in a black car," she said, ending the call.

I hung up the phone, looking down the block and seeing the car she was speaking of, praying she wasn't setting me up. Yes, I had just a little doubt in the back of my head from all the things I remembered Reign saying about her. I walked up to the car, and she reached over to open the passenger door, allowing me inside.

"Hi, Mom," she said, hugging me, and I returned the gesture.

"How are you?" I asked as I wiped at my tears.

"I'm okay, but I would be better if I didn't have to be away from my family for something that I didn't do. Do you mind if we go to the room at the hotel that I'm staying at so that I can tell you everything? Also, I just want to say that I really appreciate you coming alone like you promised me."

"I told you that I would come alone, and I meant it, so let's go to the room so that you can talk to me," I told her.

Once we got to the room she was staying in, she seemed a bit nervous when asking me if I wanted something to drink. I knew she was probably worried if I was going to believe her, but she didn't have to worry about that.

"I'm fine. You don't have to get me anything to drink. I just want to hear about what happened that day."

"I'm going to just start from the beginning so that you can see that I'm ready to be honest about everything. The call you received that day wasn't from my grandmother. I always knew who you were because my grandmother told me. I wasn't interested in having a relationship with you because I hated you and wanted no part of you. I didn't understand what kind of mother would leave her child behind after that child already lost her father. Last year I left New York to go back to my grandmother's house and had been there for a while. It was getting reported to me whenever Jahiem was sleeping with someone. When I got the call about him dating Reign and it was getting serious, I wanted information on her. Once I found out that she and I were connected through you, that was the reason I contacted you. I wanted her to know that Jahiem was my man and I would do anything to keep it that way. When I spoke to him on the phone and he broke things off with me, I knew he had to be feeling her.

"I knew that if I was going to get him back, I had to do more than confront her to tell her that he was my man. I swear that when I came here with my cousin's baby, I had no plans on keeping her as long as I did. The plan was to just pass her off as Jahiem's daughter until he agreed we could be a family. As soon as he would have agreed to us being together, I planned on getting pregnant."

"Pregnant? Your grandmother said that you had to have a hysterectomy done," I interrupted her.

"That was what my aunt and I agreed to tell her when she found out I was in the hospital. Instead of telling her the truth, we lied. I was having some painful cramps one morning so bad I couldn't even stand up. My aunt took me to the hospital, and we found out that I had PID: a pelvic inflammatory disease. I didn't know that I had contracted chlamydia. Being that it wasn't treated, that was the reason for the complication. If she knew that I was having sex, she would have never forgiven my aunt, so that was the reason we lied. I'm not going to lie and say that I didn't have ill feelings toward you and your daughter, because at that time I did. But once I heard you say that there wasn't a day that went by that you didn't think of me, I no longer hated you."

"So, if you no longer hate me or have any ill feelings toward me, I need you to tell me the truth about what happened that day. I don't care if you was the one who killed them. I want to know, because if you lie to me, I'm not going to be able to help you," I said to her, just wanting the truth.

"I showed up to your house that day to bring the baby to see you, but I didn't get out of the car because I saw my grandmother. She was on your porch talking to Reign, and when I saw her let my grandmother and my cousin in, I left. I knew that she was going to tell you about the baby not belonging to me, so I pulled off. I went to my friend Hannah's house to ask her if she would keep the baby, but she said no. She started getting in my face, saying the baby couldn't stay because I always came to her house with drama. I had no idea what she was speaking of, so yes, I got mad, and yes, I attacked her, but I didn't kill her. I promise you she was breathing when I left, so I'm thinking that maybe she was killed by a female. She was known for sleeping with men belonging to other women and not caring, so that might be the reason she was killed."

I was getting a headache because I wanted to believe that she was innocent, but it seemed as if she was spinning a story. None of what she was saying was making sense when all she had to do was return the baby. I needed to know how all these people ended up dead while she was walking around alive claiming to not have anything to do with it. I knew that Reign thought I was naive when it came to Samantha. It wasn't that I was naive. It was just hard accepting that a child I birthed was capable of murder.

"So, what happened next?" I asked her.

"Jamila wasn't speaking to me at the time because I got her boyfriend locked up, but I took my chances going there. I just needed someone to talk to because, at this point, I was in panic mode and trying not to go to jail. When I got there, she looked like she was on her way out, so I asked her if I could talk to her. She was still upset with me, which I understood, but I needed her, and she wasn't trying to hear me. We started arguing, but I was trying to explain to her why I felt that I wasn't wrong getting him locked up. Someone knocked at the door, and it was my cousin Emily, who I called to meet me at Jamila's place. I had Emily meet me there because if Jamila wasn't going to keep the baby, I was going to have Emily take her. Jamila was still popping off at the mouth, so Emily attacked her before I could stop it. Jamila fell and she wasn't responding, so I started to panic, knowing that Jahiem could have walked through the door. Emily suggested that we get her in the car, which we did, but as soon as we were about to leave Ginger showed up.

"I know her as Jahiem's friend, so I tried to act normal, but as I was talking to her, Emily hit her from behind. I had no idea why Emily was doing this, but she was acting crazy, saying how she was tired of these bitches fucking with me. I'm looking at her trying to figure out what really had her acting this way, and that was when she told me to meet her at her house. When I got to her house with the baby, I saw that she had Ginger and Jamila tied up in one of the rooms upstairs. Don't ask me how she was able to get them both tied up in a room because I have no idea. All I know is that I needed to get up out of there because I wanted no part of it. When I tried to leave, she started acting crazy toward me, so we started fighting. I still had no idea what triggered all this that she had going on. When I was able to break free, I left, and now I regret that I had to leave the baby behind with her," she finished and was now crying.

"So, you didn't think to call the police once you got out of the house knowing that you left the baby behind?" I asked her.

"I didn't think to call the cops because I still took my cousin's baby without her permission. I just figured that she would let them go and Jamila would get the baby. If I knew that she was capable of killing them, I promise you that I wouldn't have left." She sobbed.

"Your cousin showed up to my house and she told us that you kidnapped Jamila and Ginger, not the other way around."

"That was why I didn't come forward after she blamed it on me, because it's just my word against hers. I don't want to be in jail for something that I didn't do because it wouldn't be fair to me to do time. I know that I was wrong for taking the baby, but that was all that I'm guilty of, so I need your help, Mom."

Her calling me Mom tugged at my heartstrings, but I have no idea what she wanted me to do to clear her name. If she hadn't kidnapped the baby and called her cousin to assist her, none of this would have happened. I wanted to believe her, but it was hard to believe everything that she just said.

"What do you need me to do?" I asked, knowing that Reign would kill me if I even attempted to try to help her.

"I just need you to help me prove that the only thing that I did was take my cousin's baby without her permission. I'm willing to face those consequences, but I'm not trying to spend the rest of my life in jail for murder."

"You do know that admitting to taking the baby without permission is a crime. Had you not taken that baby, the baby would still be here. I don't think that a judge is going to just want to charge you with just taking the baby without permission," I said, being real with her.

"I understand that, but I didn't mean for any of this to happen. All I want is to be with my man, nothing more, nothing less. I want to have a relationship with you, too, but I know Reign is not going to let that happen once I'm back with Jahiem," she spat.

I was starting to think that maybe she had some mental issues because she was getting angry and speaking as if she had a chance with Jahiem. I honestly didn't know how to help her besides turning her in to get the help that she needed. I wasn't afraid of her at this point, but I knew that I needed to say the right thing to get out of here. I also knew that I didn't dare pick up my phone because earlier she was already acting paranoid.

"My husband left us well-off with money that we haven't been spending, so I can use some of it to get you a lawyer. I can tell you right now that he is going to tell you that you have to turn yourself in," I said, hoping she believed me.

"OMG! You would do that for me?" She ran into my arms, thanking me.

"Yes, I would do that for you, baby," I told her, thanking God that she believed me.

Chapter Thirty-one

Reign

My mom just admitted to me that she got a call from Samantha and she went to meet up with her, so I was trying to calm myself before speaking. She looked at me, asking for me to say something, but I'm telling you my temperament was scaring the shit out of me.

"I have no fucking words right now," I said to her as my voice cracked from being that upset.

"Reign, please just let me explain," she begged.

"Do you have any idea what that girl took from us? She murdered three innocent people, and you meet up with her and not inform the police. I just don't understand what the hell is wrong with you and this fantasy that you have with being a mother to her. That girl don't give a fuck about you, and I wish that you would understand that and move the hell on," I shouted.

I was so mad that I wanted to slap the shit out of my mother for being so fucking stupid trusting that bitch. She was lucky that her ass didn't end up dead for being stupid for this girl once again. Now she was telling me that she told her that she was going to get her a lawyer just to get out of the hotel room. I tried to explain to her if that she didn't keep her word, that crazy bitch was going to come for her with everything she had. She could have ended this if she had just confided in me so that we could involve the police. She had to pay for what she did, so why she felt the need to entertain anything that came out of Samantha's mouth was puzzling to me.

"Reign, it's not too late because she trusts that I'm not going to tell anyone, being that I showed up alone to hear her out. She knows that I'm getting her a lawyer, so I can tell her that the lawyer wants to meet with her. This time we can call the authorities and have them pick her up at the location," she said.

My tears were flowing, and I was breathing in and out of my mouth, trying to calm myself down to the point where I was shaking. She didn't even understand what she did wrong right now, and the shit was pissing me off. I couldn't even tell Jahiem that my mother was in contact with Samantha because he would lose it on her. I needed to try to see if her thinking she was meeting up with the lawyer would work. I told my mother not to contact a real lawyer because I was going to get Dame to pretend like he was the lawyer. I told her not to contact Samantha or take her calls until I got the shit figured out. My mother said that she was staying at the Sleep Inn on Route 6 in Middletown, New York, but I knew her ass was long gone. My mom was sitting on the couch with her crocodile tears, but I didn't give a fuck. *She'd better hope Jahiem doesn't find out about the stupid shit she did when he been looking all over for Samantha.* I went into my room to call Dame to see if he wanted to do this for me without asking a bunch of questions.

"Hey, you," he answered.

"Hey, are you busy?" I asked him.

"Never too busy for you. What's up?"

"I need a favor, but I can't go into details over the phone, so do you think we could meet up and talk?"

Deja had been tripping since we started hanging out as friends, so I knew that he was on a tight leash, but I hoped he said okay. I really didn't have anyone else who would agree to do this for me, so if he said no, I had no idea how we were going to catch her ass.

"Do you want me to scoop you up?" he asked me.

I couldn't help but smile but had to remind myself for the umpteenth time that his ass was taken by Deja, who had that ass on lock. He said that after she had the baby, he was going to leave her, but it seemed to me that the baby changed his mind. I wasn't waiting in line to be his girl, but I'm not going to lie and say it didn't cross my mind.

"Reign," my mother yelled from the living room.

"What, Mom?" I spat, still annoyed with her ass.

"She's calling," she said, holding up her phone.

"Well, ignore her call, and I mean it, Mom. I will be back in a few, and that is when I will let you know if you can take the call," I told her.

Dame texted me to tell me that he was out front, so I told my mother that I would be back in an hour and reminded her not to answer the phone. I left, praying that she would listen to me this time and not take the damn call.

"Thanks for coming," I said, getting into his truck.

"You owe me big time because I had to take a book to the back of my head just to get out of the house. Deja's ass is getting more physical with her crazy ass when I'm not doing a damn thing in these streets."

"I told you that I don't want to hear you complaining, because you like it, so I love it." I rolled my eyes at him.

"I don't like that shit, and trust that if it weren't for my daughter, I would have left her ass already."

"Whatever."

He had a million excuses why he was still putting up with her ass when he knew the real reason was because he loved her ass.

"If you stop playing games, we can write that love story that should have been written all those years ago." He laughed.

"I'm not trying to go there with you." I laughed, mushing him in the side of his head. "Nigga, you done lost your mind," I said when I saw him pulling up in the hotel parking garage.

"Girl, pump your brakes because we are only here to have dinner." He cracked up.

"Whatever, and since you find it so funny, dinner is on your ass," I said, getting out of the car.

"Always." He smiled, grabbing my hand, which I pulled away from him.

"Who do you know up in here?" I asked him.

We were dining at a restaurant on top of a hotel and the shit was impressive, so I wanted to know how the hell he pulled this off. I also wanted to know why we were here like we were on a date when all I wanted to do was talk to his ass.

"I'm sorry to disappoint you that I'm not lame Dame anymore as you used to call me back in the day." He chuckled.

"I only called you lame Dame when you use to ditch me to go play hide and seek with Deja and the others in her house."

She used to invite everyone over her house to play stupid games but never invited me, so I used to get mad when he would go. I didn't have many friends on the block, being that I was only a weekend visitor, so they were mostly her friends. He knew that, so that was why I called his ass lame Dame—for leaving me to sit on the porch alone with no one to play with.

"This place is amazing, and it has me feeling like a tourist, being that I've never been any damn where and I lived in New York all my life," I said, admiring the view.

"Keep hanging out with me and I will have you experiencing things you never experienced before," he said, sending a chill up my spine even though I knew he didn't mean his comment to be sexual. "Do you need a wet wipe?" he joked.

"Nah, I'm good." I shook my head at his ass.

Once we were seated, I took a deep breath to calm my hormones so that I could get to the reason I was out with him. He was so damn handsome that I could barely focus on the matter at hand, but I knew I needed to get it together. He already knew everything that happened because I filled in the parts his mother didn't learn from my grand-mother.

"So, talk to me," he said.

"Samantha reached out to my mother, and my mother took her ass all the way to Middletown to meet up with her."

"Are you serious? Well, did she call the authori-ties to arrest her ass?" he asked.

"My mother has been Team Samantha since the day that girl called her on the phone, so hell no, she didn't call the authorities. Samantha told my mother that she didn't kill anyone and that her cousin is the one who killed them."

"Bullshit. Your mother could have been killed. What the hell was she thinking?" he said, getting pissed the same as I was an hour ago.

"She wasn't thinking, and she never thinks when it comes to Samantha, but she finally saw what I been trying to tell her about that girl. She told her that she was going to pay for a lawyer to fight the case for her, and I think that was the only way she was going to leave with her life. So, the reason I asked you to come out is because I wanted to ask you if you would be that lawyer. I just want her to think that she is meeting with the lawyer and have the authorities pick her ass up."

"How do you think your ex is going to feel finding out that your mother met up with her and now you're doing the same? You told me that he's been looking for her and even drinking his life away, stressing about it."

I thought about Jahiem, but being that I still loved him, I would never hand her over to him so that he could kill her. I didn't want him spending the rest of his life behind bars even though I knew that he would for his sister.

"I wouldn't be able to live with myself if he killed her and ended up going to jail for the rest of his life."

"I don't think that Jahiem is the type of person to get caught." He chuckled.

"That may be true, but I still don't want him taking that risk, so I'm sure you can understand that."

"Yes, I can understand that you're still in love with him and only want the best for him," he responded with a hint of sarcasm in his voice.

"So, do you think that you could put a suit on and pretend to be a lawyer so that we can take her ass down?"

"What's the plan?"

"I will contact the detective who was on the case and let him know that she reached out to my mom and bring him up to speed. I don't know how it's going to play out as far as them getting involved. I just need to know if you would do it so that I can let the detective know what my plan is when I get there."

"I'll do anything for you, so I don't even know why you're acting like I would tell you no," he said seriously.

"Thank you." I smiled.

Chapter Thirty-two

Reign

After we enjoyed dinner, we were sitting outside in his truck, talking, and I didn't even realize that we been talking for hours. It was almost midnight, so I told him that I needed to get some sleep so I could be up to go to the police station tomorrow. I didn't know what was happening between us, but I was starting to feel something that I shouldn't. After I watched him smoke a blunt, his eyes got low and his words slurred, making him sound so sexy to me. I wasn't tired or worried about getting up in the morning. The truth was that I needed to get up out of his truck. I was seconds from trying to hop on his dick right there in the truck and not caring that he had a girl.

My mother was still up when I walked into the house, so now I wished that I had stayed in the truck.

"Mom, what are you still doing up?" I asked her.

"Jahiem just left," she said, causing my heart to skip a beat.

I started to panic, wondering if he saw me sitting in the truck with Dame or getting out of the truck with Dame. I didn't see him or his truck, but it could be that I was busy watching Dame's ass like a fan.

"Did he say what he wanted? And please tell me you didn't say anything about Samantha."

"He just said that he was here to talk to you, and no, I didn't tell him anything about Samantha, Reign. I would not say anything to him knowing that he would kill my daughter if he knew where to look for her," she said, but I just walked away from her.

I called his phone, but he kept sending me to voicemail, so I was almost positive that he saw me, but I didn't see him. I didn't know why I felt the need to explain myself to him when he was the one who kicked my ass to the curb.

"Mom, was he drunk?" I asked after walking back into the living room.

"No, he was looking good and smelling good." She cackled.

"Have you been drinking?" I asked her.

"No, I haven't been drinking," she spat.

I went back into the room and decided to text him to see if he would respond because he clearly didn't want to talk to me.

Me: Mom said you stopped by and asked for me. What's up?

I waited for about ten minutes, and when he still hadn't replied, I went to take a shower to call it a night. I didn't know what he wanted, but I wasn't going to sweat it since he didn't want to tell me why he was here. When I got out of the shower, my message indicator was blinking, so I grabbed my phone. It was him finally responding.

Jahiem: I came by and it was late. So where were you?

Jahiem: So, now you don't want to talk to me?

Me: I'm sorry, I was in the shower. I just wanted to know the reason you stopped by.

Jahiem: So, you're not going to tell me where you was at?

Me: I was out with a friend.

Jahiem: I didn't know you had any other friends besides my sister, so who were you out with?

I didn't want to do this with him because I didn't know if he saw me, so if I lied, he would know I was lying. At the same time, I didn't have to explain myself when he said he didn't want to be with me anymore.

Me: It's a friend from my grandmother's neighborhood.

Jahiem: Dame?

OMG! How the fuck did he know about Dame? I didn't remember mentioning Dame to him, so now I was wondering if my mother said anything.

"Mom, did you tell Jahiem about Dame?" I asked her.

"Dame? Is that who you been spending time with?" she asked.

I went back to my room and slammed the door, frustrated that I didn't know how he knew about Dame.

Me: How do you know Dame?

Jahiem: Answer the question.

Me: Yes, I was out with Dame, but we were out as friends.

Jahiem: So you sit out in a truck with a nigga who is just your friend. If the two of you were only hanging out, why didn't he just drop you back off? You was in his truck for over an hour, so I'm just curious as to what do friends talk about for hours.

My mom said that he just left, so if he knew how long I stayed in his truck, there was no way he just left, with her silly ass. I should have smelled her breath to make sure her ass wasn't drinking, being that her fucking timing was off.

Me: We were just talking. If you saw me sitting in his truck, why didn't you call me to tell me you were waiting for me?

Jahiem: It wasn't important. You have a good one.

Me: Are you serious?

I waited for him to respond, but he never did, so I said fuck it. I was pissed that he was pissed at me.

He had a lot of nerve when he only saw me sitting in a truck talking but he was fucking that bitch Monica. "Fuck him," I said, putting the pillow over my head and screaming to release my frustration.

The next morning, I was still in my feelings, but it didn't stop me from getting it together to go down to the station. My phone rang, and it was Dame calling me, so I answered the phone wondering what he wanted.

"Hey, what's up?" I asked him.

"I was thinking that if you mention to the detective that your mother is in contact with Samantha and even met up with her, it might backfire."

"What do you mean?" I asked.

"It's kind of like harboring a fugitive. She knew that there is a warrant out for her arrest, and she failed to report that she was in contact with her. I just don't want them being petty by arresting her, because you already know how these motherfuckers could be," he said.

"I didn't even think about that. So what should I tell them when I go down there?"

"Just tell them that your mother received a phone call from her, and she asked your mother to get a lawyer for her. Make sure you let your mother know not to tell them that she met up with her."

"Okay, so my mother did speak with her this morning, and she said that she would call back to tell her where she was willing to meet the lawyer. I just hope that her ass says that she is going to meet someone here and not in Middletown."

"Well, I'm headed to work, so let me know how it goes and when you're going to need me to suit up."

"I will," I said before ending the call.

I pulled up to the police station, sitting in my car and having second thoughts about going inside because Dame had me shook. I didn't want to go in here and get interrogated like I did something wrong. The NYPD was good for making you feel like you did something wrong with their line of questioning. I was now thinking if I should just give Jahiem a call or shoot him a text to tell him that she reached out to my mom. I swear this was one of those times that I needed my best friend to help me decide what the fuck to do. My phone alerted me of a text message, so I grabbed my phone, which I'd just set in the cup holder.

Jahiem: Leave the police station and meet me at my crib.

I looked around, wondering how he knew I was at the police station, but I didn't see his ass, and that was when I let the tears fall. This is going to sound stupid, but my best friend heard me, and she sent his ass. No, I didn't care if it was just him being on some stalkerish shit. I knew my bestie heard me just now, and she'd been hearing me.

I wasn't sure if I wanted to meet him at his house, being that I didn't want to tell him the truth about why I was there to begin with. When I pulled up to his house, I saw his truck parked out front, so now I was stalling by sitting in my car. I just needed to calm my nerves and figure out what I was going to say to him. I saw the front door open with him standing there waiting for me to exit the car. *I swear his ass better not be on no bullshit because I'm not in the mood when I have to figure out how to take this bitch down.* I got out of the car and walked up to the home that I thought for sure I would never visit again. He stepped to the side and let me walk inside as he stood wearing an expression I couldn't read. I could tell that he was still upset about me being out with another man.

"What were you doing at the police station?" he asked, but I didn't say anything because I didn't know how to answer his question. "Look, don't bullshit me, because I already know that it has something to do with that bitch Samantha. Your mother told me that the bitch called her, but when I started questioning her, she shut down. I knew that she shut down because you probably told her not to tell anyone that she spoke to the bitch. That was the reason I waited for you last night, and that was how I knew you were in the truck with that nigga."

I swore my mother got on my fucking nerves, because not one time did she mention that she slipped up and told him. Now he was going to expect me to tell him what the fuck was going on and blow up at me for not telling him.

"First, let me just say that who I was with in the truck was just a friend, as I said to you in the text message. You left me, not the other way around, so I don't understand why seeing me in the truck is even an issue. Now as far as Samantha reaching out to my mom, I had no idea until she told me the other night. I was just going to go to the police to let them know that Samantha contacted my mother," I told him, leaving out the part of my mother meeting up with her.

"So, why did she feel the need to reach out to your mother?"

"She told my mother that she didn't do this, and it was her cousin Emily, so she asked my mother if she could get her a lawyer. She wants to turn herself in so that she can prove that she's innocent," I stuttered.

"What's going on? I feel like you're not telling me the truth, and I need you to be honest with me, Reign. I already know that the bitch is upstate somewhere because she stole my car and they found it abandoned in Middletown. I been up there looking for that bitch, but I haven't had any luck finding her ass. I have a homegirl who stays in Middletown, so she got her people looking out for her."

"Samantha called my mother and asked her if she could meet up with her, making her promise to come alone. My mother agreed, so she met up with her at a hotel that Samantha said she was staying at in Middletown. My mother didn't tell anyone that she was meeting up with her because she really wanted to help her. She is still stuck on that was her daughter, so she didn't believe she did this until she met up with her. She said that the story she told about what happened didn't make sense. When she started saying that she wanted to clear her name so she could get you back, my mother knew something was off. I was going to have my mother tell her that she got her a lawyer so that she could show up. When she showed up this time my plan was to have the police waiting for her to arrest her. I know that you're about to be in your feelings, but like I said, you are the one who gave up on me," I said to him, causing him to just stare at me with cold eyes.

Chapter Thirty-three

Reign

I watched as his jaw tightened before he reached over, grabbing a rolled-up blunt off the table to light it up. He was mad, but he had no one to blame but himself for me not trusting him enough to come to him.

"After I smoke this blunt, I'm going to meet you at your crib so that I can speak to your mother so we can set this shit up," he barked, walking away as if he was dismissing me.

I wasn't about to argue with his ass, so I just got up to leave so I could take my ass home to let my mother know he would be on his way. When I walked in the house, she was watching *The Price Is Right* while drinking a cup of coffee.

"Mom, why did you tell me that Jahiem had just left last night but fail to mention that you told him you spoke to Samantha?" I asked her.

"I didn't tell you because I knew that you was going to be mad at me thinking that I just offered the information. I didn't mean to tell him. It just slipped out, but I didn't tell him anything else, so he left."

"He didn't leave. He was sitting somewhere in the neighborhood, because he saw when I pulled up with Dame. You could have called my phone to give me the heads-up, but I guess that would have been asking for too much. I just don't understand how you can keep a secret for a murderer but don't even have your real daughter's back," I spat.

"Reign, I'm not going to keep doing this with you. No matter how grown you think you are, I'm the fucking parent and you're the child. I'm not going to keep apologizing for not telling you that she reached out to me."

"I just want you to understand that you didn't raise that girl, so you have no idea who she is, and I need you to stop thinking that you do. I also know that you're guilt tripping, but you don't need to do that shit anymore. You apologized to her, and you even told her that you wanted to right your wrongs, but she was just using you. She said it out of her own mouth, and that bullshit about she no longer hates you is a fucking lie. All she wants you to do is help her with a lawyer when she knows she's guilty."

I was tired of explaining the same shit to her as if she were a child who couldn't comprehend what I was saying to her.

"What's the plan?" she asked me, not responding to anything I said.

I was starting to think that if it came down to who she would choose between me and Samantha, it would be Samantha. She came back from Middletown saying how she believed that Samantha wasn't dealing with a full deck. She even admitted that she now believed that Samantha killed them. Sitting here talking to her made me think that she was Team Samantha again. She didn't have to say it, but the look on her face said it all, pissing me off. When I heard the knock at the door, I got nervous hoping his ass didn't go off on my mother.

"How are you doing, Ms. Peggy?" he asked her.

So, I guessed he was only mad at me because he was smiling all up in my mother's face like he didn't just kick her daughter out of his place.

"Hello to you too," I spat.

"Why are you acting like you didn't just leave my place?" he said.

"Anyway, let's get down to the reason you're here, because I'm going out," I lied, fucking with him.

"So, you're dating that nigga now?" he barked.

"Did you hear me say that I'm going out with a dude, or did you hear me say that I'm going out?"

"I don't know why the fuck you're standing in my face lying knowing that you're going out with that nigga."

"Language," my mother said to him.

"Why you mad? You shouldn't even be questioning me about who the hell I'm going out with like you care."

"I do care," he said, throwing me off.

I didn't expect him to say that he still cared for me, so now he had me stuck on stupid with no comeback. My mom was looking at me to say something, but I couldn't find the words to say because him saying he still cared meant what? I had so much that I wanted to say to him if he ever gave me the chance, and now that the door was open, I had nothing.

"If you still cared for her, what the hell was you doing laid up with the next bitch?" my mother spat.

"I messed up, but I'm trying to make it right," he said.

I couldn't help but wonder if his change of mind had to do with seeing me out with another man last night.

"How are you trying to make it right?" I asked, finally finding my voice.

"I know that we need to figure this thing out with Samantha, but could you just give me a few minutes to talk to you?"

I got up, and he got up to follow me to my room so that we could have some privacy without my mother adding her two cents.

"Listen, I already know what you're thinking, so let me just say that I didn't say that I still care because I saw you with that nigga. I never stopped caring and I know that I was wrong for the way that I handled you. I know that nothing I say is going to give you back what I took from you by not allowing you to attend the memorial. I hope that this token gives you some comfort the same way that it has given me comfort," he said, handing me a box.

My hands shook as I held the box in my hand even though I knew it wasn't an engagement ring. The box was larger than a ring box and shaped different, so I tried to calm my nerves. When I opened the box to see a cremation urn necklace my tears fell, and I only knew that it was an urn necklace because my mother wore one on her neck. This one was shaped as a teardrop with tiny teardrops that were custom-made with a pic of me and Jamila. I couldn't stop the tears from falling as my body shook with the proof in my hand that my friend was gone. Jamila always said that if she died, she wanted to be cremated, so he honored her wish because she probably would have come back to haunt his ass. She had a fear of any kind of bug, so she always stressed that she didn't want to be put into the ground.

"I know that you probably will never forgive me, but I just want you to know how sorry I am, and I mean that shit. I couldn't see at the time that you were only looking out for me, but I understand now. The only thing I could think about that day was making someone pay for my sister's death. I didn't think that it was fair that she got to go to jail still breathing when my sister was dead. I understand that you care about me and you don't want to see me in jail, but I promise you that I got this. If I catch up with Samantha, she's going to go missing without a trace, and that is on my sister."

I reached up and wiped the tears that fell from his eyes, letting him know that I had his back this time. He pulled me into his arms, holding me tight as I cried in his chest wishing that Jamila was still here with us. His touch felt right, and it was a touch that I missed so much that I didn't want him to ever let me go. He took the necklace from my hand and put it around my neck, and that was when I noticed that he was wearing one too. I touched it to examine it, and it was the same as mine, but his teardrop was blue and mine was green. His was custom-made and his teardrop held a picture of him and Jamila.

"Let's go out here and talk to your mother so that she can call that bitch," he said, pulling me up.

When we came out of the room, my mom was in the kitchen making another cup of coffee to get her caffeine fix for the day. She drank at least three cups of coffee a day, and I didn't know how she did it.

"Mom, can you call Samantha and tell her that you hired a lawyer so she can tell you where she wants to meet with him?" I said to her.

"Reign, I only agreed to do this if the police are involved. I'm not going to stand by and watch my daughter be killed."

"Are you serious? She killed my sister, my friend, and a fucking baby, so that crazy bitch doesn't need to be breathing," Jahiem barked.

"Mom I'm starting to think that you say stupid shit just to get under my skin, but I don't care anymore. Can you just call her so that we can get her location so that the police can pick her ass up?" I was at the point where I thought that maybe her being dead and out of my mother's life for good would be best. No, I wasn't jealous, but I was tired of seeing my mother be so fucking naive when it came to this fucking girl.

Jahiem looked at me because I mentioned the cops, but I had no plans on involving the cops. I was going to show him that I had his back, even though I wasn't too keen on taking a life for a life.

She came out of the kitchen, taking her sweet time before grabbing her phone to make the call. I hated that we couldn't hear what Samantha was saying on the other end of the phone. I knew if my mother put the phone on speaker, she would know that someone was listening in on their conversation. When she ended the call, telling Samantha that she loved her, she hurt my feelings. I didn't remember the last time she told me that she loved me, so I was in my feelings. I knew she was going to say that she was just saying what needed to be said, but I believed that she really loved that girl.

"What did she say?" I asked, voice cracking. I hated that I wore my damn heart on my sleeve sometimes, because I didn't want her to know that it bothered me.

"She said that she could meet with the lawyer tomorrow but she's not turning herself in to say what happened until he gets her no jail time."

"Where did she say she's willing to meet the lawyer?" Jahiem asked.

"She wants him to meet her in Middletown at the Galleria Mall. She wants a public place in the opening to make sure she doesn't see any cops," she said, causing me to roll my eyes.

"So, she's wanted for murder, and she wants to meet in a public place? She's good for playing games, so I hope the bitch is going to show up," Jahiem said.

"Well, that was what she said, so who are you going to get to be the lawyer? She wants to meet at noon tomorrow," my mother said.

I didn't want to tell him that I already recruited Dame to be the lawyer, not knowing how he was going to respond.

"I asked Dame to put on a suit and pretend that he's the lawyer my mother hired, but this was because we weren't speaking," I said to him.

"That was cool," he said, surprising the shit out of me. "Why you looking at me like that? You said that nigga is only a friend, right?" he asked.

"He's just a friend," I responded.

"Well, call that nigga and tell him to suit up and be here to pick your mother up at ten tomorrow, and I'll figure the rest out," he said.

He said that he had some shit to handle and asked if he could come back tonight so that we could all leave together tomorrow. I told him that I didn't have a problem with him coming back, but I honestly wanted to know if we were back together. I was starting to have feelings for another man who belonged to someone else, so I needed to figure the shit out. After he left, I went to the kitchen to fix me a sandwich before sitting at the kitchen table. I chickened out and decided to send Dame a text instead of calling him. I didn't know how he was going to feel when I told him that I forgave Jahiem after how he treated me.

Chapter Thirty-four

Reign

Me: Hey, you. Do you think that you can put that suit on for tomorrow?

Dame: Why the fuck do you keep texting my man, bitch?

Me: Deja, I know that he's your man, so I don't need you to keep reminding me. Dame and I are only friends you ruined back in the day, but it's not going to happen again. If you can't accept that we are just friends, then that is on you.

Dame: If you was a real friend, you would respect that he has a girlfriend who has a problem with you being his friend.

Me: It's not my job to help you with your insecurities.

Dame: I'm not insecure. I just want you to stay the hell away from my man. I know you still have feelings for his ass. I swear if I find out that you're sleeping with him, I'm going to fuck your entire world up.

Me: Deja, get your ass off his phone and go feed your fucking baby with your insecure ass.

Dame: Fuck you, bitch.

Me: Fuck you too. Tell your man that I'm trying to get in touch with him.

She was still texting bullshit, but I was done responding, praying that Dame got his phone soon so I could see if he was available for tomorrow. I finished my sandwich and took my ass in my room, holding my necklace in my hand and thinking about my friend. It was an hour later when my mom came in my room to tell me that Dame was in the living room.

I started to panic because of what happened the last time I invited a man into my house. Jahiem knew that we had to discuss tomorrow, so hopefully if he did get here before Dame left, he would understand.

"Hey, you," I greeted him.

"I'm sorry for just showing up, but that crazy-ass Deja took my phone on some jealous bullshit that she's always on. She was going off about how you kept texting me and all she wanted was the truth. When I asked her to give me my phone, she just started tripping, and I wasn't trying to fight her, so I just left."

"When she responded to the text I sent you, I told her that we were just friends. She said that if I was your friend, I would respect that you have a girlfriend, which I do. She has always been insecure, and I let her intimidate me when we were younger, but fuck that. I'm not going to stop being friends with you just to appease her ass. Anyway, I sent you a message to see if you will be able to suit up and play lawyer tomorrow. The plan is for you and my mother to meet with her at the Galleria Mall in Middletown at noon."

"So will the police be on site tomorrow?" he asked.

"No, I didn't go into the police station because Jahiem followed me there and stopped me from going inside. He was here at the house last night and saw me in the truck with you, so after my mother let it slip that she spoke to Samantha, he followed me. He wants us to go with the original plan, and he said he would handle the rest."

"What does 'he will handle the rest' mean? I hope he doesn't plan on killing her, because I didn't sign up to be an accessory to a murder."

"Who said anything about murder, Dame?"

"If that nigga don't have plans on murdering that bitch, then why the fuck would he tell you not to involve the police? I need you to be smart and not fall into his web that he's leading you into, Reign. If she's found dead, we will all be just as guilty as the person who killed her ass."

"She needs to be killed," I admitted out loud.

"That may be true, but I still say we should allow the authorities to handle it as you wanted to do before he stopped you. Does this mean that you and him are back together after the way that he treated you?"

"Let's not speak on that when you're still with Deja. You make excuse after excuse as to why you can't leave her."

"Yeah. Whatever. I will be here to pick your mother up at ten," he said, getting in his feelings.

"How will I get in touch with you if you don't have a phone?" I asked him.

"I'll have my phone back as soon as I get back to the house," he said, walking out the door.

I just wanted Samantha's ass gone so that I could get back to my life. It was a life that was not going to be the same without Jamila, but I needed to at least try. I didn't know if Jahiem was going to be a part of my life, but it was time for me to start living my life. I had no idea what time Jahiem was going to return, so I went into my room to get my things so that I could shower. I was nervous about tomorrow, so a shower would help me calm my nerves a bit.

Jahiem got back to my house a little after midnight, and I tried hard not to think that he was with another female. He asked me if he could take a shower, so he really had me thinking that he was up to no good. I watched as he went into the gym bag that he had with him, removing clean under-wear. It was late, so I decided that I wasn't going to say anything to him about why he was showing up this late. After he went to get into the shower, I got back under the covers, dozing off until I felt his hands on my ass. I kept my eyes closed until I felt his lips caressing the inside of my thigh. I let out a loud moan as he allowed his tongue to tease me, knowing I didn't like to be teased. I grabbed his head aggressively as I gyrated my hips until he latched on and sucked my pussy, giving me an unexplainable feeling. I bit down on my bottom lip to suppress my moans, being that my mother was next door. I didn't need her hearing me having sex in her house right now, being that we were not really on good terms. Jahiem smirked at me before running his tongue across the crack of my ass. He pulled me on top of him, knowing that my ass rid-ing his dick was going to cause my bed to rock like fucking crazy. My mom was going to curse us both the fuck out, but he thought the shit was funny.

"Shit," I hissed.

He was killing the pussy now that he had me face-down, ass up, and it was a wrap on holding my screaming his name in. He was doing the same aggressive behavior he did when he thought that I fucked Byron. I hoped that he didn't think that I had sex with Dame, because I didn't want him to think that I was anything like his ass. He started stroking me with deep, long strokes, making me forget about what I was just thinking about. I backed my ass up, fucking him as I held on to the headboard that was hitting the wall, but at this point, I didn't care. I yelled that I was about to cum, so he was now in beast mode until we came today and collapsed on the bed.

"Yo, you didn't hear your mother banging on the wall." He laughed.

"Stop lying," I said, punching him in the chest.

I went into the bathroom to take a quick shower, and he joined me, bending my ass over like my shit wasn't already sore. As soon as we got in the bed, he was out snoring loudly, so I joined him and took my ass to sleep.

When I woke up the next morning, it was going on seven, and I had no idea why I was up so early. It could have been my nerves knowing what was going to go down today and not knowing what the outcome was going to be. I went into the kitchen to make me a cup of peppermint tea just to see my mom sitting at the table smoking a cigarette.

"I thought you quit smoking," I said, grabbing my Minnie Mouse mug off the shelf.

She ignored me as she flicked her ashes into the ashtray, so I was guessing she was still upset with me, but it was whatever. She was nervous about today and so was I, but it was now or never if we wanted to get this bitch.

"Mom, what's wrong?" I asked her because she was now sitting at the table with tears in her eyes, making me feel bad.

"He's going to kill her, isn't he? I don't know if I can be a part of helping him set my daughter up to be killed," she said, taking a pull from the cigarette.

"Mom, he's not going to kill her, and as soon as she shows her face, the police are going to be there to arrest her," I lied.

"Do you promise?" She sniffed.

"Mom, I promise," I said, pouring my tea before sitting down to join her at the table.

This shit was stressing me the fuck out, and I didn't know how much more I could take without speaking my real feelings.

"Mom, I don't want you to start drinking again, so please try not to stress yourself or blame yourself for the way she turned out."

"I'm not going to go back to drinking, Reign. It's just that my nerves are bad, and I didn't know how to calm them. That was the only reason I left this house to go get a pack of cigarettes, but I promise I just smoked a few."

"Mom, we are all stressed, so hopefully this entire ordeal will be over after today." I hoped.

"You must have been stressed the way you and Jahiem's ass was going at it last night, but your ass better not let it happen again. I'm not getting no dick in my house, so I'll be damned if your ass is going to be getting dick. How the fuck you go from being mad at him to riding his dick in the first place?"

"Mom! This is not a conversation that I want to be having with my mother." I scrunched up my face at her before leaving her in the kitchen.

Dame showed up a few minutes before ten, and he wasn't too happy seeing Jahiem walking out of the back room. I introduced them, and Jahiem just gave him the head nod, letting me know he wasn't feeling my introduction.

"Jahiem, let's discuss the plan before heading out so that everyone will be on the same page so there will be no fuckups," I suggested.

"The shit is simple. Just make that bitch believe that he's the lawyer who is going to get her ass off, and I will handle the rest." He huffed.

I didn't know why he had all that bass in his voice when Dame was helping us when he didn't have to do this shit. Dame didn't look too pleased on how Jahiem was acting, but he didn't say anything just looking at me. I knew that he didn't agree with me letting Jahiem handle this without the police, but hopefully this shit was about to be over.

Chapter Thirty-five

Samantha

After getting off the phone with the bitch who birthed me, I had a bad feeling she was not being honest with me. When I asked her about the lawyer, it just seemed to me like she was being coached. Usually when I got a bad vibe, nine times out of ten I was right, so if I was right, I would be dealing with it accordingly. I knew that I couldn't be in two places at one time, so I made a phone call. I told the person on the other line to be on standby just in case I needed shit to pop off. If I was right about my feelings, I was going to make the call for them to handle some business for me. I would teach that crackhead of a mother of mine that I was not to be fucked with. The reason I picked the Galleria Mall was because of the view I would have of the parking lot. I planned on being there an hour before she and the lawyer were scheduled to be there.

When I pulled up to Rashad's house, I caught an instant attitude seeing his grandmother's car parked in front of the house. She knew that I stayed here, so if she didn't like me, why the fuck was she always here? He needed to tell her to stay her old ass home and he would visit her there since she liked being up his ass all the time. When I walked inside, she was sitting in the living room watching television.

"My grandson has really lost his mind giving you a key to his house," she said smartly.

I swore on the strength of Rashad that I wanted to be respectful of his grandmother, but she just kept coming for me.

"He gave me a key so that I could come and go the same as you," I spat.

"I'm not someone he just met off the street," she shouted.

"I'm not someone he just met on the street, and even if I were, why do you care? You're not fucking me, so stop worrying about business that doesn't concern you."

"What kind of woman are you? Someone should have washed your damn mouth out with some soap. You need to get your shit and get out of my grandson's house because whatever the fuck you're running from is not his problem."

"I could have sworn I just told you to stay out of business that didn't concern you. If you don't approve of me being here and you don't like me, stop bringing your old ass over here."

"I bring my old ass over here because I will protect my grandson at all costs knowing you mean him no good. His mother had a few screws missing, so trust me, I know crazy when I see crazy. I hope that answers your question."

"Wow, so I'm crazy when I have done nothing to you or your grandson to deserve that label from you? Maybe your daughter wasn't the crazy one, because from where I'm standing, it's fair to say you're the crazy one," I said just as Rashad walked through the door.

"Hey, my two favorite ladies." He smiled, walking over to me and kissing me on my cheek before hugging his grandmother.

"We are fine, sweetie. Just getting acquainted," she lied with her old, ugly ass.

"Babe, I need to speak with you about something," I said to him before walking away toward the stairs.

I heard her suck her fake teeth as I walked away, but I had bigger fish to deal with, so I wasn't feeding into it.

"What's up?" he asked, kicking his sneakers off.

"The reason I borrowed the car today is because I had a job interview that I didn't tell you about because I didn't want to jinx it. I got the job, and I will be starting training next Monday, so I found me a place. It's available and not too far from here, but I'm going to need fifteen hundred dollars for the security, being that I only have the first month's rent," I lied.

"Why are you trying to leave when I told you that you can stay as long as you need?" he responded with disappointment in his voice.

"I know, but I'm going to be honest. I don't feel comfortable here with your grandmother coming and going whenever she wants. That was the reason why I haven't been intimate with you on the next level. You have no privacy here, so I think it's best that I get me a spot, and you can come and go as you please. Just think about me riding your dick in the comfort of my own place without having to worry about Granny walking in."

"I mean, I don't want you to leave, but since you put it that way, I have no problem giving you that small bit of change. How soon will you need it?" he asked.

"I have to be at the office tomorrow morning before ten," I lied again.

He walked over to the closet, reaching on top, pulling down a Jordan sneaker box that was filled with cash. Shit, if I knew he had a stash, I would have helped my damn self, but it was all good, being that he was giving me the money. I would just tell him that the place fell through and the landlord was taking his time to return the money.

I hoped he didn't tell his grandmother that I asked for money because she would really go in on my ass.

"I need a favor from you, too," he said, causing me to frown.

I was not about to give him no head for his measly $1,500, so I was prepared to tell him to fuck off.

"Fix your face. It's not whatever you're thinking," he said.

"So, what is it?" I asked with a roll of my eyes.

"My son RJ's birthday party is next weekend, so I need you to be there with me so that I can shut my grandmother the hell up. She thinks that you are using my spot as a hideout, but I told her that she was wrong."

"No problem," I told him but had no plans on attending.

"So, what are we about to get into?" he asked.

"What time is your grandmother leaving? Because we could watch a movie and order some dinner," I suggested.

"You done turned me into a house nigga. Why the fuck you never want to go out and chill with a nigga? I already told you if you're worried about that abusive-ass ex of yours, you don't have to because I got you," he said, reminding me of the lie I told.

"I told you the night you met me in the club that the outside scene wasn't my thing, so can we just chill? Why do we have to be in the streets to enjoy ourselves? A man should love a woman who doesn't want to hang out in the streets and only wants to be home spending time with him," I said, laying it on thick.

"Let me see how long my grandmother plans on being here," he said, walking out of the room.

I didn't know if he knew I was running game, but if he did, he didn't say anything, so that was all that mattered.

His grandmother left about an hour later, so he was now on the phone ordering us some pizza and wings. He wanted to watch *Creed 2,* so being that I made him stay his ass in, I didn't complain, even though I didn't want to watch it. I wasn't even watching the movie because I had tomorrow on my mind, praying everything went as planned. I just want all of this to be over so I could be with the love of my life again so we could get married and have some babies. I hoped Emily's ass rotted in that fucking jail cell for being so stupid trying to turn my ass in. I would swear on a stack of Bibles that she was the one who killed that baby and those bitches. I was on her boyfriend's Facebook page the other day snooping around just to see that his ass moved on already. I tried to tell her ass that he was sleeping around on her, but she didn't want to believe me. There was no way that he was in a relationship already, and he had to be with this girl before she got locked up.

After *Creed 2* was over, I had his ass watching *Acrimony* with me because I was avoiding going to the bedroom. I wasn't trying to give him no pussy, so I was praying that the Hennessy he was drinking would knock his ass out. He was a lightweight with the liquor, so I never understood why he always went above his limit. Hennessy wasn't the drink for his ass, and he would have been better off drinking some of this Moscato with me. It would have been more his speed, I thought as I watched his eyes getting low, so I suggested he take his ass to bed. As soon as he took his ass in the room, I noticed that he left his cell on the table and he didn't have a lock code. He was such a damn lame to not have a code when he knew his ass was up to no good. Now I knew why he wasn't pressing me for no pussy, because his baby mother was still giving it up. I wasn't mad, but his ass could have kept the shit real, being that he wasn't my damn man. She sent his ass nude pictures that I sent to my phone because I knew they would come in handy at some point. I also saw that he was in a lot of females' inboxes, trying to get with them with his thirsty ass. I was now in his text messages, but whoever this person was he was texting, they were speaking in code.

He wanted me to believe that he was the owner of a barbershop, but I knew he also dipped and dabbled in something illegal. I just didn't know what illegal business he was a part of, but I didn't give a shit. I knew one thing: he was too damn fine to be in females' inboxes acting all thirsty when he probably could have any female he wanted.

The next morning, I left the house earlier than I planned just in case they had the same idea to be early. I wanted to have the upper hand by arriving before they arrived just in case it was a trap. I didn't call Peggy to confirm if she was still coming. She assured me that she would be there. She knew what kind of car I was driving, so I didn't dare park anywhere near the mall. I parked about ten blocks away from the mall and took a slow walk, taking the back blocks. Once I was where I needed to be, I got to thinking about the other entrances of the mall, so I decided to enter when they opened. I told her that we could meet in the food court, so I waited on the upper level where I still had a view.

I saw Peggy and an unknown man enter the food court, with her looking around for me, but I had to make sure she wasn't setting me up. I watched closely but didn't see anyone who seemed to be with her and the lawyer. I was still nervous to approach, so I decided to wait just to be sure no one was in the cut waiting for me to approach. My cell vibrated in my pocket, and I knew it was her. I watched as she made the call on her phone. I answered the phone, and she asked me how much longer it would be before I arrived. I told her that

I was like ten minutes away before ending the call. Just as I decided to walk toward the food court, I saw her make another call, but it wasn't to my phone. It could have been that her phone rang and she was answering the call, but I wasn't sure. I prayed before walking into the food court that I wasn't going to be rushed by police as soon as I approached her.

Chapter Thirty-six

Samantha

When Peggy saw me walking into the food court, she offered me a warm smile, which calmed my nerves.

"Hey, baby, this is Attorney Parker," she introduced him.

"You look too young to be an attorney. What law firm are you with?" I frowned.

"Listen, you're in no position to sit here and interrogate me. Just be thankful that your mother found a lawyer who was willing to represent you. You're already late, so let's get started by stating your name. I also need you to tell me what your defense is pertaining to this case," he responded.

I was taken aback because he was rude and treating me as if he didn't believe that I was fucking innocent. Peggy put her hand on my leg and told me to just tell him the same thing that I told her, so that was what I did.

"So, your defense is that you were afraid for your life. Correct?"

"That is correct," I spat, getting irritated with his ass.

"So, you're telling me that you got out of the house, and it didn't occur to you to send help for the others who were in danger?" he asked.

"Like I said, I was scared, and I wasn't thinking straight at the time. If I knew that she was going to hurt them, I would have called the authorities."

"Well, I have your statement, so what I'm going to do is speak with the district attorney. But at some point, you will have to surrender. Are you willing to turn yourself in?" he asked me.

"I don't have a problem turning myself in if they are willing to set bail so that I can fight the case on the outside."

"That will be determined at your arraignment, but there is no guarantee that the judge will grant bail, due to the circumstances. Let me speak with the district attorney, as I stated, and I will be in touch with your mother."

"Do you have a card?" I asked him.

"I don't have a card with me, but your mother has my number, so if you need to speak with me, you can get it from her."

What kind of lawyer was his ass with no business card? I didn't question him about not having one, being that I didn't want to offend him when I

needed his help. I gave Peggy a hug and thanked
her for keeping her word, and she told me that she
would be in touch. I made sure not to exit through
the main entrance, so I exited from the side door,
heading back to the car. As I was walking back
to my car, I had that bad feeling in the pit of my
stomach, which caused me to become paranoid. I
started looking around, noticing the same black
car that I saw leaving the mall. I really didn't pay it
any mind because I believed Peggy and the lawyer
came alone, but now, I wasn't so sure. I was a half
a block from where the car was slowly keeping its
distance, trying to be discreet. I put a pep in my
step, trying to make it to my car, and this time
when I turned around, I saw him. I couldn't see his
face clearly because of the New York fitted he was
wearing, but I would know that walk anywhere.
He always walked with that swag that I fell in love
with, but in that moment, I knew that I was in
danger. Getting out of his car was his first mistake,
because I took off running. He was a thug-ass
nigga, so I knew that he wasn't going to chase me,
but I also knew he would shoot me.

I didn't want to believe that Peggy set my ass
up, but what other reason would Jahiem be here
in Middletown? He jogged back to the car he was
riding in, so instead of going back to the car, I
decided to hide behind one of the buildings. I saw
an older woman coming out of the building, so I

caught the door and entered the building, trying to catch my breath. My heart was beating so fast out of fear that I thought I was going to have a damn heart attack. He was still angry with me, so I needed to clear my name, but that wasn't going to happen, being that Peggy lied to me. She should have known that there would be consequences to her actions. If she didn't, she would soon enough. I went upstairs to the second floor of the building just in case he happened to come looking. He couldn't get in the building unless someone came out, and he entered the same way I did.

"Can I help you?" I heard from behind me.

It was an elderly white woman who I didn't even hear open her door or come into the hallway.

"Are you lost? If you don't know anyone in the building, that means that you're trespassing, so you need to leave, young lady," she said, meddling in my business.

"I'm not trespassing, ma'am, because my grandmother lives in this building, but she isn't home, so I was just leaving," I lied.

"Who is your grandmother, child? Is Ethel your grandmother?" she asked me.

"Yes, but she isn't home, so I'm just going to come back," I said, starting to walk down the stairs until she stopped me.

"If you want, you can wait for her inside of my apartment. I'm sure she'll be back soon," she offered.

I didn't want to go into her apartment, being that I had no idea who Ethel was and how well she knew her, but I didn't want to run into Jahiem either.

"I don't want to be a bother," I told her.

"It's no bother, and I'm sure Ethel will be back soon. She probably just went to the grocery store," she said, so I followed her inside.

Her apartment was neat and clean but smelled like mothballs, burning my damn nose, but hopefully I wouldn't be here long. She went into the kitchen after offering me a cup of tea, which I declined.

"Ethel didn't tell me that she had a granddaughter. What's your name?" she asked, wanting to talk, but I was stressing about how the hell I was going to get to my car.

"My name is Simone, and I haven't seen my grandmother in a few months, so she didn't know I would be stopping by," I lied with a straight face.

"Oh, well, I'm sure she'll be happy to see you. I met her grandson a few times, but he doesn't visit often. Are you sure that you don't want any tea? I have peppermint and black tea," she offered again.

"No, thank you. I'm going to get ready to go because I didn't plan on being out as long as I have," I told her.

"Okay, let me call Ethel to see if she got back from the store," she said, making the call before I could stop her.

When the knock came on the door, I cursed under my breath at her little old ass for being so fast making that call. I grabbed my cell, getting up to leave and prepared to explain that it was just a misunderstanding. When I got to the door and saw Rashad's grandmother standing there, I almost shit on myself.

"What the hell are you doing here at my neighbor's apartment lying about being my granddaughter?" she spat.

"I'm sorry I lied, but I just needed to speak with you," I lied, knowing damn well I had no idea her old ass lived in this building.

"How did you even know where I lived?" she asked.

"I didn't know exactly what apartment, only the building from Rashad, so that was why I pretended that you weren't home. I had no idea what door to knock on, so that was the only reason I lied to this nice lady," I continued to lie.

"So, what reason did you have to tell her that your name was Simone if you were looking for me to talk? My grandson told me that you were out paying first month's rent and security on a place, so how did you end up here?"

Damn, I forgot that I was supposed to be paying for a place I found. I could have said that was why I was in the building when the old lady approached me with her nosy ass. She was waiting for me to respond, but I didn't know what to say, and I damn sure didn't want her to call Rashad.

"Can I please just speak with you?" I pleaded, still not knowing what I was going to say if she agreed to hear me out.

"I apologize, Harriet, but I told you about letting strangers into your home, especially when she looks nothing like my family," she said, referring to the color of my skin.

I just looked at her ass and rolled my eyes, feeling the need not to explain shit to her, so I left, not caring in that moment what she told Rashad.

Chapter Thirty-seven

Reign

I told Jahiem to just stay in the damn car so we could follow her to find out where she was staying, but he didn't listen. He got out of the car, deciding to do whatever in broad daylight, and he fucked the shit up. She spotted him and took off fucking running, so now he was back in the car, shouting at me to drive faster. If he didn't want to lose her, he should have taken flight the same way that she did. He had to know if she spotted him that she was going to take off running, so what was his plan? I was so pissed because I should have gotten the authorities involved because she got away again. She was going to take that shit out on my mother now that she knew my mother set her up. We circled the block a few times, and she was nowhere in sight, so now he was mad, but guess what? I was mad too. He had me park on the block where she was last seen, and we'd been sitting here for twenty minutes. He didn't want to believe that she was ghost and he fucked up, so he was hoping that she came out of hiding.

"I should have just shot that bitch in the fucking back," he barked.

"No, you should have just listened to me when I said to just follow her to see where she was staying. At least we could have waiting until night fell before approaching the bitch, but it's too late now."

"I fucked up," he admitted.

I told him to get in the driver's seat because I needed to get on the phone to let my mother know that we lost her. I wanted her to be aware of her surroundings because who knew what the hell Samantha was going to have planned? After speaking to my mother, I called Dame to ask him if he could stay with my mother until I made it back.

"Why the fuck are you asking that nigga to stay with your mother?" Jahiem asked.

"I asked him because I don't want nothing to happen to my mother now that Samantha knows that she lied. We already know what that crazy bitch is capable of, so I'm going to make sure that my mother is okay until we get back."

He turned on the radio acting like he had an attitude, but I didn't care. All I cared about right now was making sure that my mother was okay. I hoped he didn't think that the frown he was sporting bothered me, because it didn't, and he was even more attractive when he was mad. I knew he was mad at himself for getting out of the car knowing he wasn't going to chase Samantha, so he was taking it out on me. I started thinking that maybe he still had feelings for her and didn't want to hurt the bitch because he could have given chase.

"I hope that you're not in a rush to get back to the house because I have a stop to make, if that is okay with you," he said.

"Where do you have to stop when I just told you that I was worried about my mother? I don't know how long Dame is going to be able to stay at the house with her," I said to him.

"I want to stop at my homegirl's spot that I was telling you about to let her know shit didn't go according to plan," he said.

I just sat back and let him do him because if I said anything, we would have been arguing, so I sent my mother a text. She said that they didn't make it back to the house yet, so I reminded her again to be aware of her surroundings. He pulled up on Red Barn Lane to a big house, parking in the driveway. He seemed familiar with the place, making me wonder how many times he'd been here. A female was now standing in the door, looking to see who parked in the driveway, so maybe he had never been here before.

When he exited the car, she ran down the stairs, hugging him, with her body touching his as if he were her man. I was waiting for him to distance himself, but he didn't, and he welcomed the hug, pulling her in even closer to hug her back. I stepped out of the car, and that was when he distanced himself from her grip, introducing me to her. I guessed we weren't girlfriend and boyfriend, being that I was only Reign in this moment. I didn't even bother to say hello and took my ass back in the car and let them do them. I didn't care if I was being rude because he was being rude by not introducing me as his girlfriend. He was worried about Dame when his ass didn't even acknowledge me to this bitch who was all up on his ass. I couldn't hear what they were talking about because the windows were up. I decided to be petty and blow the horn, letting him know to bring his fucking ass on so that I could get home.

"Why do you have to be so fucking rude?" he barked once he was back in the car.

"Rude would be you all hugged up with that bitch in front of me. Rude would be you introducing me as Reign. So being that I'm not your girlfriend Reign, stop sweating my comings and goings with Dame."

"Are you seriously going to sit there and make a big deal out of nothing? I didn't say that you were my girlfriend because we never said if we were back together. You could have corrected me if you consider me your man. That girl has a man she's happily married to with a four-year-old daughter, so trust I'm not checking for her. They been together since high school, and he knows that we are only friends."

"So, how come I never met this friend of yours? I asked him.

"Maybe because that friend of mine lives in Middletown with her man and child. I never heard about that nigga Dame, but he's back in your life as your best friend who I never met."

"You're so full of shit, but it's all good," I said just as my phone rang.

It was my mother, telling me that she just got home and that she told Dame that he could leave. She promised me that she locked the door and had no plans on going back out until I got back to the house. I didn't know why Dame's ass didn't listen and stay with my mother, but I knew that it was she who didn't allow him to stay. I wanted to call him and ask if he could just sit out front of the house, but I didn't want to argue with Jahiem's ass. After I got off the phone, he didn't say anything, so I didn't say anything either because we were both in our feelings.

About an hour later, he pulled up in front of my house, turning the car off before turning to face me. I swore I didn't have the energy to have a conversation with him right now, but I was going to hear him out.

"I'm going to need you to stop acting all crazy when you know that I wouldn't take you to no female's house who I'm smashing. I didn't introduce you as my girlfriend because I didn't know if you forgave me. I know that we had sex, but that doesn't mean that we are back together unless we discussed it, which we didn't. I love you and I never stopped loving you, and I told you that shit, but you didn't say that you forgave me. If you forgive me and want to be with me, I'm going to need to hear you say the shit."

"Jahiem, if I didn't forgive you, I wouldn't have slept with you," I responded.

"I just said that you need to say the shit, Reign."

"Jahiem, I forgive you and I want to be with you, but if you let a bitch get that close and personal again, it's going to be a problem," I said.

"Well, give me some love with your sexy ass," he said, pulling me in for a kiss. "I have some business to handle, so are you coming to the crib to spend the night with me tonight?" he asked me.

"It depends on what time you get home and if my mom feels okay staying home alone, so just call me when you get to the house," I said before getting out of the car.

Walking into the house, seeing my mother smoking a cigarette and looking upset, I knew she was about to go off on me. It wasn't my fault that Jahiem dropped the ball trying to run up on her and letting her get away.

"Mom, before you say anything, it wasn't my fault that she got away," I said to her.

"I'm not blaming anyone for her getting away, but I'm upset that we let Jahiem talk us out of involving the authorities. I love my daughter, but she needs help, and the longer she's out there, others may get hurt. She trusted me, so being that I broke that trust, she isn't going to believe anything else I try to say to her. I already tried calling the number back, and it has already been disconnected. Even if we go to the police now and tell them that she's somewhere in Middletown, it may be too late."

"I'm worried that the somewhere else is going to be her coming back here, trying to do something to you. Jahiem wants me to come spend the night with him, but I'm not trying to leave you here alone."

"Well, if you plan on having sex with him again, that is where you better take your ass. If you sex up in here again, I'm going to hose both of you down. The two of you were in there acting like two damn dogs in heat with your fast tail."

"We wasn't acting like dogs in heat. We just missed each other." I laughed.

"Take your ass over to his house and show him how much you miss his ass, and I mean that shit, Reign," she said seriously.

"Okay," I stressed, going to my bedroom.

I called Dame to thank him again for doing that for me, and he was asking to hang out, but again I didn't want to leave my mother. He had the nerves to say that he liked my mother and told me to invite her out with us. I didn't mind hanging out with him, but if Jahiem and I were going to be together, I didn't want to cause problems. I felt like I owed him, so I ended up telling him that I would go out with him but I couldn't stay out long. My mother made a fuss about how she didn't want to go out, so I told her not to open the door. She was convinced that Samantha wasn't going to come for her, but I was sure her crazy ass was.

Dame picked me up, and when he pulled up on my grandmother's block, I looked at him for an explanation.

"Mom invited you and your grandmother over for dinner." He beamed.

"Your mother got my grandmother to agree to leave the house and come over to her house for dinner?" I asked in disbelief.

"Nah, your grandmother declined, but I told my mother that you and I would join her for dinner tonight." He chuckled.

My grandmother was funny like that when it came to her going to someone's house and eating food she didn't see them prepare. She didn't care about knowing his mother for years because she was stuck in her ways. I was kind of curious as to why his mother wanted us over for dinner to begin with. I didn't mind, but it just felt as if she had an ulterior motive when she knew her son was spoken for by his crazy girlfriend. He came around and opened my door, taking my hand and helping me out of his truck. Walking inside his mother's house smelled good, causing my stomach to growl. All I had this morning was a cup of tea, so I was hungry, and unlike my grandmother, I was going to eat. His mother always kept a clean house, so I trusted her enough to eat her food.

"Hello, Reign, it's good to see you. How are you doing?" she asked me.

"I'm good, just taking it one day at a time. I'm ready to start living my life again," I told her.

"What are your plans?" she asked.

"I don't know if I'm going to go back to school or if I want to get a job right now, but I know I have to make a decision soon."

"Did Dame tell you that he's looking for someone to handle the books at his trucking company, being that I can't do it anymore? How good are you with numbers?" she asked.

"I got an A in my accounting class, but I don't think it will be a good idea for us to work together, Ms. Latoya." I laughed.

"And why the hell not?"

"His girlfriend doesn't like me, and she already thinks that I want to be with him, no matter how many times I tell her we are just friends," I told her, being honest.

"Deja doesn't like anyone who encounters my son regardless of who they are, and that was the reason he could never keep any female employees. Just think about it and try not to think about Deja and her jealous ways," she said taking her mac and cheese from the oven with him just shaking his head at her.

Chapter Thirty-eight

Samantha

I already knew that this old bitch called Rashad, so I was ready for any questions that he was going to have. I wasn't ready to leave his house, so if I had to fuck him to get him to forget whatever it was that she told him, I would. My boo was acting as if he wanted to cause me harm today, so why continue to be faithful to his ass? I walked inside, and Rashad was sitting on the couch smoking a blunt while watching ESPN.

"Hey," I said, trying to feel him out.

"How did it go? Did you get the place?" he asked.

"I already know that your grandmother called you, but I bet money that she didn't tell the truth about what happened."

"She said that you lied to her neighbor about being her granddaughter and even lied about your name."

"First off, your grandmother is a liar, and she lied because she doesn't like me, and she doesn't want you with me. I had no idea that your grand-mother lives in that building when I spoke with management. I went back there today with first month's rent and security when I was approached by an older lady. She said to me that if I didn't live in the building or wasn't visiting someone, I was trespassing. I told her that I was waiting for someone to return to the office so that I could speak with the manager. She offered for me to stay at her apartment because she said that most likely he was showing an apartment. As I was leaving her place, because she was nice enough to call the office to make sure he returned, that was when I saw your grandmother. She started accusing me of all types of shit that didn't even make sense when I had no idea she lived there. I tried to explain to her why I was in the building and why I was at her neighbor's house, but she didn't want to hear me out. I don't know what she has against me, but I'm telling you that I don't know how much more I can take. If she wants you with your baby mother that bad, maybe you should consider being with her," I said, wiping at my fake tears.

"I'm not trying to be with my baby mother, and I don't know what beef my grandmother has with you. But she can't dictate who I'm going to be with. I hope that you know that you don't have to find you another place, and you can just stay here. I don't want you and my grandmother living in the same building trying to kill each other." He laughed.

"I just don't understand why she doesn't like me when I have yet to do anything to her. Why is she so overprotective of you?" I asked him.

"My mom came back into my life last year saying she wanted to be a part of my life, but that was far from the truth. She was doing everything right for about a month, and I even invited her to stay with me. I came home from a business trip, and when I walked up in here, everything was gone. The part that fucked me up was that I left her with the keys to my crib and enough money to do as she pleased, and she still fucked me over. All I ever wanted was a relationship with my mother, so the shit felt good having her in my life again. The shit fucked me up so bad that my grandmother made a promise to never let that shit happen again. My grandmother really means no harm, and she's only going hard to protect me."

"Listen, I have no intention of doing you dirty. That is a promise, and I do understand going hard for family, but sheesh. She can let up on me because I'm not that female, so you need to talk to her, or this isn't going to work."

"I'm going to talk to her, but does this mean that you will stay with me instead of looking for a place?"

"Rashad, the only way I will commit to moving in with you indefinitely is if you set boundaries for your grandmother. She can't just walk up in here whenever she feels like it if I'm going to be living here. I know you love your grandmother, but I just feel that she's trying to control your life. You're a grown-ass man, and if you make mistakes, she should let you because how will you learn from those mistakes? She even has your baby mother not liking me as if I'm in here manipulating you when that is not the case."

"Trust me when I say that Remy was going to trip whether my grandmother had something to say about you or not, but I get where you're coming from."

"Well, you need to let them know that I will be moving in here with you, and make sure Granny understands boundaries. I'm marking my territory, and I'm the head bitch up in here now, so they better act like they know." I smiled but was dead-ass serious.

It'd been a few days and his grandmother hadn't been over here, so he did what the hell I told him to do. He was leaving tonight on a business trip as he told it, but I couldn't care less where the hell he was going. I was going to have the house to myself, and he left me with some cash, so I was good with him leaving. He gave me the keys to his truck and told me not to wreck his shit because it was his baby. After he left, I went upstairs to take a shower because I had plans on driving to Harlem. As soon as I got out of the shower, someone was knocking at the door, so I put on a tank and shorts to answer it. When I saw that it was his grandmother, I couldn't help but laugh because he took her key.

"Why didn't you just let yourself in?" I laughed in her face.

"I bet you're not going to find it funny when the cops arrest your crazy-ass, Samantha," she said, knocking all the laughter out of me.

"You know that is not my name, so if you're not going to address me by my name, don't address me at all," I stuttered, still taken aback as to how she knew my name.

"I thought something was familiar about you, but I couldn't put my finger on it, but thanks to Harriet babbling about you the other day, I finally did. She said that when she first saw you in the hallway, you reminded her of the girl she saw on the news. Harriet usually babbles a lot, so most times I just pretend to listen to her until that day. She said you looked like the female she saw on the news who murdered a baby and two females. So, I went looking for the story, and what do you know? It was you. What kind of person could kill a fucking baby and two females? How the fuck can you live

with yourself knowing that you're a murderer?"
she cursed.

"If I were a murderer, I promise you that I would
have killed you the first time you got on my fucking
nerves. Now I don't know what you think you
know about me, but you're wrong, so if you want to
go to the police, do you. I promise you that you're
going to feel like a fucking fool, so again, do what
you feel you need to do."

"I knew something was off about you the first
time I laid eyes on you. You have twenty-four
hours to leave my grandson's house or else," she
said, leaving with a smirk on her face.

I was so mad at myself for not bashing in her
fucking head that I was throwing shit around like
it was my house. She threatened me, so I knew if I
didn't leave her grandson's house, she was going to
make good on that threat. I couldn't afford to take
a chance that she was bluffing, so I had to do what
I had to do. She was right about her neighbor's
babbling, because she mentioned that she left her
spare key under her welcome mat. I didn't know
how true her babbling was, but I was going to find
out.

I waited until it was dark outside before leaving
the house to go take care of this bitch before she
opened her mouth. I was dressed in all black,
praying that someone left the building so that I
could get inside. I thought about pressing all the

buttons until someone let me in, but I didn't want to draw attention to myself. After I waited for about ten minutes, a man exited the building, so I smiled at him as he held the door until I was inside. My hands were shaking as I felt around for the key under the welcome mat, praying Harriet didn't open her door. It was late, but her ass seemed like a busy-body who sat up all night. Once I had the key in my hand, I was praying again that her ass was in her room, sleeping. Her apartment was dark, so I tried not to bump into anything while looking for her bedroom. Once I found her bedroom, I sat in the chair that she had near her bed, just watching her sleep. I just wanted to see if she was a heavy sleeper, and it seemed that way, because she hadn't stirred one time. I grabbed her cell off the nightstand, powering it off before going into my pocket, removing the syringe. The syringe was filled with enough drugs to stop her heart to make it look like she had a heart attack. I covered her face with the pillow and held her down until I emptied the syringe into her arm. The gloves made it kind of hard, but I got it done in record time, hoping she didn't see me when I removed the pillow. I needed the scene to look as normal as possible with no sign of struggle to rule out a homicide.

I pulled down Rashad's fitted, covering my face as I exited the building, making sure to walk as normally as possible to my car. I hoped that this bitch wasn't so evil that she refused to die, I thought as I made it to Rashad's truck. I didn't breathe normally again until I pulled into Rashad's driveway, thankful that I made it back to his house.

I opened the door and almost shitted myself seeing him standing in the foyer and hanging up his jacket, now looking at me suspiciously.

"What are you doing here?" I asked him with a shaky voice.

"Did you forget that I live here?" He chuckled.

"You know what I mean," I said to him.

"I had to postpone my business trip because Remy called to tell me that RJ isn't feeling well, so I'm about to head over there. Do you want to come with me?" he asked, knowing damn well I was not going to that girl's place.

He didn't know how much I needed his ass to stay gone because I had plans on using his truck to pay Peggy's ass a visit.

"I'll pass," I said with a roll of my eyes.

"Why you dressed like a ninja? Where are you coming from?" he asked me.

"I'm not dressed like a ninja. I'm wearing all black because that is the mood I'm in right now, if that is all right with you," I snapped.

"Why are you getting defensive when I just asked you a question?" he barked.

"Don't you have to go see about your son?" I spat, walking away from his ass.

My nerves were bad because I wasn't expecting his ass back for at least a week so I could move in silence. After he left, I went upstairs to shower so that I could take my ass to bed because I just wanted to sleep.

I don't know how long I was asleep before being jolted out of my sleep. Rashad was downstairs slamming shit around and cursing, so I rushed downstairs to make sure that he was good. He was being comforted by his baby mother as he now sobbed in her arms, mumbling incoherently.

"Rashad, what's wrong?" I asked, feigning concern.

"His grandmother passed from a heart attack," she cried.

Chapter Thirty-nine

Samantha

"OMG! Rashad, I'm so sorry," I said, pushing her out of the way.

"Why the fuck did you push me?" she shouted.

"He's my man, and if he needs comforting, that is what I'm here for," I shouted back.

"Wow. Rashad, I'm going to go, but if you need me, please don't hesitate to call me," she said, ignoring me.

"I promise you that he will not be needing you because he has me, so do me a favor and let yourself out," I told her.

"What the hell is wrong with you?" he asked, shaking his head.

"Nothing is wrong with me. I'm just letting her know that you don't need her because you have me."

"So, what you're trying to tell me is that you don't have no chill. I just found out that my grandmother is dead, and this the shit you on. Do you know how I feel right now when the last thing I said to my grandmother was that she needed to distance herself? I did that shit for you, and all you can think about in my time of need is to be selfish and make the shit about you."

"I wasn't making the shit about me. I just wanted to comfort you in your time of need, so don't fix your face to say I'm being selfish."

"Just don't make the shit out to be a competition by disrespecting her when that female was down for me for years. She wouldn't use my grandmother losing her life to try to get back with me or be on no petty shit like that. She loved my grandmother, so she's feeling the same pain I'm feeling, so that shit you just did wasn't cool."

"Excuse me for giving a fuck, and I didn't know that I was making the shit out to be a competition, but okay," I said, walking away before I hurt his fucking feelings.

I understood that he was hurting, but he wasn't going to speak to me any fucking way he wanted to, so it was best to give him space. If he didn't want me to be here for him in his time of need, I was just going to let him be.

Over the next few days, I just felt like an outsider as his family was at the house planning for the service. Remy was front and center as if she were the girlfriend and I were just someone he was fucking with. She was enjoying the fact that he was basically ignoring me, but it was all good because I would get the last fucking laugh. I didn't have a problem being behind the scenes because of my current situation, but the shit was pissing me off. He was mad at me because he wasn't man enough to choose his grandmother over me. I wished a motherfucker would tell me to tell my grandmother not to visit my home if I loved her like that. Well, I couldn't even say if I loved her like that, because if it were my grandmother, I would have been like hell no. Anyway, that was his beef with me, but I was going to let him have that if it made him feel better.

"I don't understand how this happened when my mother was healthy with no health problems or any issues with her health. I just spoke to her the other night, and she was fine besides being upset with you. She told me how you told her that she needed to distance herself, so what was that shit about?" Rashad's uncle asked him.

"She didn't like my girlfriend, so I told her that it would be best if she didn't come to the house as much, and I regret that shit. I didn't mean her no harm, and it was a situation where I let my third leg cloud my judgment," Rashad responded.

I wonder if they even took into consideration that I could hear them from where I was sitting, but I guessed they didn't care. I could see now that I may have overstayed my welcome, so it might be time for me to move the fuck on. Especially if they found out what contributed to her having a heart attack. The only person in his house who acknowledged my presence was his son RJ, who I wished would stay out of my face. I heard the doorbell ring, and when I saw that they ordered food, I got pissed off again. No one asked me if I wanted anything to eat, but again, it was all good as I switched my ass to the table and helped myself. His aunt rolled her eyes, but she didn't say anything, because if she did, the way I was feeling, I would have gone off on her ass.

I went to sit next to Rashad, but he was still acting funny style, so I said fuck it. I wasn't about to kiss his ass.

"I'm going to stay at my uncle's crib tonight so that we can go down to the funeral home early, so I'll probably be back late tomorrow," he let me know.

"No problem. If you need me, I will be here," I lied.

After everyone left, I went into his closet and emptied out his stash from the shoebox that he let me know was there. I grabbed the shit I came there with and the keys to the car he let me drive, being that he took the truck. I left on my way to Harlem to stay in a hotel until I figured out what

I was going to do next. I knew that I needed to get another phone, but I would take care of that tomorrow once I got settled.

I had something up my sleeve that no one was going to see coming so that I could get my life back. This being on the run shit was for the birds, and I was sick of it, so it was time to do something about it. I had a guy who worked at the hotel who I met on social media, or so I thought until I got to the hotel just now. He lied about being the manager, and they had no one by that name who even worked at the hotel. Now I was standing outside trying to figure out what the hell I was going to do now that I drove all this way. I couldn't use my identification, so I decided to go sit in the car until I figured something out. I even thought about calling Peggy but decided not to since her ass lied to me. I should have just taken my ass back to Rashad and put the money back before he realized I took it. Instead of listening to my better judgment, I ended up driving to Jahiem's house, parking a few houses away. I missed him so much and wanted so badly to be back in his arms, but there seemed to be too many obstacles in the way.

My phone alerted me of a text message, and it was Rashad asking me where I'd gone, being that he was back at the house. He didn't say anything about the money missing, so I assumed he thought that I just stepped out. He was nice enough to buy me this phone, and I hated that I needed to get rid of it just like the other phones. I just wished that shit could go back to the way it was before my grandmother and cousin showed up. I wondered if I showed up to Jahiem's door to explain my lie, would he shoot me on sight or hear me out? When I saw his truck pull up, my heart started pounding in my chest seeing him so close but not able to touch him. This was torture, so I had to do something to get him back by any means necessary.

There was only one other person I could reach out to, but I didn't know if she would accept me with open arms. I didn't know if her number was the same, but I was going to find out because I needed her right now.

"Hello," she answered with that stink attitude in her voice that she always had.

"Hey, this is Samantha. Are you busy?" I asked her.

"Samantha, why are you calling me? I saw your picture all over the news, so I don't want no part of whatever you got going on," she said.

"I promise you that I didn't do any of what they are saying besides taking my cousin's baby without her permission."

"That may be true, but I have a fiancé now and a child, so I can't get caught up in no bullshit with you."

"Listen, I swear I'm not trying to get you caught up in anything, I just need you to return the favor that you owe me," I said, trying to guilt trip her.

"Wow. I didn't know that I owed you when you called yourself being there for me, but it's all good. What do you need?"

"All I need right now is for you to book a room for me, and I will give you the money, so it will cost you nothing."

"My fiancé isn't home, so I will have to bring the baby with me, so as soon as I do this for you, I have to leave."

"Thank you," I said, not meaning the shit.

After I gave her the address to the hotel, I left from Jahiem's place so that I could be there. I had no idea if I could trust her, but I had to pray she was nothing like my other stupid-ass cousin. I wasn't asking for much, so that was the least she could do for me after all the shit I'd done for her.

I had no idea that she had a fiancé or baby, being that I hadn't spoken to her in years. I always knew that she had a boyfriend, but I never met him because her ass was always with different men. I couldn't help but wonder what man she snagged who was willing to marry her ho ass. I saw when she got out of the car, so I got out to meet her, but I wasn't going to go to the front desk with her.

"I can't believe that you're a mother now." I beamed, looking at the baby she held in the car seat.

"I don't believe it myself sometimes. How many days do you want me to book the room for?"

"Just book for a week, but I need you to put it on a card, and I will give you the money," I told her.

"Samantha, I swear nothing better come back to me or I'm going to be a snitch bitch and not care how you feel about it."

"Deja, I told you that nothing is going to come back to you, so stop acting like I asked you to commit a crime."

"Um, you're a fugitive, so this is a crime." She rolled her eyes and sucked her teeth.

"I already promised you that I'm not going to get you caught up in anything, so please just go book the room," I stressed because she was getting on my damn nerves, making me hate that I had to ask her for help.

"I have to use my fiancé's business card, so I pray that he doesn't find out that I booked this room. Don't add any additional charges."

"Do you want me to keep the baby with me until you finish at the front desk?" I asked.

"No, I have her," she said, gripping the car seat tight.

"Deja, you don't have to do that because I would never take your baby without your permission. Yes, I'm guilty of taking my cousin's baby, but what happened was unfortunate but not my doing. I would never hurt a baby, and that is on my dead father," I lied.

"It has nothing to do with what you have going on, Samantha, I just feel comfortable with her being with me," she said, walking toward the front desk.

I couldn't help but wonder again who put a ring on her finger when she didn't know how to be faithful to any man she'd ever been with. That baby probably didn't even belong to his ass. I was sure she still slept around. I tried my best not to tell how I really felt. I needed her stink ass right now.

"I don't know why you picked this expensive-ass hotel," she said, handing me the receipt.

I went into my bag and handed her the money, thanking her for helping me and saying that I appreciated her. She handed me the key and went about her business, so I took my ass up to the room to take a shower. After getting out of the shower I saw that I had a missed call from Rashad, so I listened to the voicemail. He was just asking me what time I was coming back to the house, so his ass was still oblivious. I was never coming back to his fucking house because I was getting back with my real man. I stomped on the phone until it broke, hoping he got the message when I didn't answer. He would figure out soon enough that I was not coming back and how I took his money and car. I picked up my burner phone and decided to call Jahiem just to hear his voice before going to bed.

"Hello," he answered. "Yo, who the fuck is this?" he barked into the phone.

"I love you," I whispered, hoping he heard me before ending the call and happy that I got to hear the voice that I missed so much.

Chapter Forty

Reign

"Jahiem, are you sure that it was her on the other end of the phone?" I asked for the third time after he told me that Samantha called him.

"I mean, what other female would call just to hear my voice and tell me that they love me before ending the call?"

"Did you try calling the number back?" I asked him.

"She called from a private number, but trust me, I know that it was her calling," he stressed.

I didn't know if I was more upset about her calling him or the fact that she said that she loved him. I didn't want to believe that it was Samantha, so I asked him if he thought that maybe the voice belonged to Monica.

"I haven't spoken to Monica since the day that you put her out of my house. If she wanted to express to me that she loved me, she wouldn't have been whispering on the other end of the phone."

"I just hope that Samantha isn't back here to cause havoc, because I don't have time for the bullshit. I start this job tomorrow, so I'm just trying to get back to living my life without all the bullshit. I think that we should go to the police to let them know that she may be lurking, and they need to put a car outside of my mom's place," I suggested.

"If it would make you feel any better, I could get someone to sit outside of your mother's house to make sure she'll be okay. I still wish that you would reconsider taking that job working for that nigga, because I don't trust his ass."

"Jahiem, how many times do I have to tell you that Dame and I are only friends and I'm not checking for his ass? I needed to be doing something other than sitting in the house all day, so when he offered me the job, I accepted it. I love you, so I need for you to trust me and let me do this to get some sort of normalcy back in my life."

He was stuck on thinking that Dame and I had feelings for each other, and that may have been true, but I wasn't going to act on them. I was going to respect that he was in a relationship, and he was going to do the same. I needed to get home so that I could get some rest and be at his trucking company in the morning by nine. Jahiem wanted me to spend the night, but I told him that I needed to get home. I told him not to answer any more calls from a private number because if it was her, she probably was getting off on hearing his voice.

He walked me to the door, telling me to call him when I made it home. He also told me to let him know if I wanted him to put someone outside my mother's house. I honestly didn't know if I believed it to be Samantha on the other end of his phone. It was most likely that bitch Monica with her thirsty ass, even though he said she would have said something.

When I got home, my mother was sitting on the porch smoking a cigarette and talking to Ms. Trina. I didn't know that she started speaking to her again, but if she was good, I was good, so I wasn't going to sweat it. I just wished that she would stay her ass in the house and stop being so damn hard-headed.

"Hey, Mom," I greeted her.

"I know you see my fat ass sitting here in all this damn purple." Ms. Trina laughed.

"I'm sorry. How are you doing, Ms. Trina?"

"I'm doing much better now that your mother is speaking to me again." She smiled, showing off her missing tooth.

"I don't have a problem with the two of you speaking again as long as she doesn't start drinking again," I let it be known.

"Reign, I keep telling you that I'm grown, so you don't have to keep feeling like you're checking me. I told you that I was done with drinking, and I meant it, and if you must know, me and Trina already had that conversation. I respect that she still drinks, and she will respect me by not doing it around me."

"Can the two of you come inside and get off this porch?" I said, opening the screen door.

Once in my room, I went into my closet trying to find something to wear tomorrow for my new job. I didn't really have a lot of casual dress clothes, so I had to settle on a pair of black slacks and an off-white blouse. I needed to take my ass shopping as soon as I found the time to do so because I needed a few things. After getting out of the shower I fixed me a plate, taking it in my room with me. I turned on the television to watch my shows that were recorded, being that I didn't have time to watch any of them. I wanted to watch *The Act* on Hulu, but after watching the first recorded episode of *My 600-lb Life* I was tired, so I took my butt to bed.

I woke up the next morning excited and nervous at the same time, being that this would be my first real job. I worked at my college's campus bookstore my first semester, but that was a work-study program. Dame didn't speak on how much the job paid, so I hoped that would be our first conversation when I arrived. I didn't want him treating me as a friend, because I was his employee now and I was here to make my coins.

I took one last look at myself in the mirror before grabbing my phone and keys before heading out. I let my mother know that I was leaving and to be safe and aware of her surroundings if she decided to go out. I knew that she was probably going to be walking to the store for another pack of cigarettes. I pulled up to Dame's trucking company about thirty minutes later, feeling nervous again now that I was here. As I walked into the building all eyes were on me, adding to my nervousness because they were all men. Fine-ass men, might I add, but I had a man, so I knew I would have to remind myself daily that I was off the market.

"Good morning, Mr. Black," I greeted Dame, being professional, but all he did was chuckle.

"Come into my office with your crazy behind," he said.

"Dame, I want you to treat me the same way that you would treat your other employees," I said to him.

"I told you that I would," he said, handing me a breakfast bag from Starbucks and causing me to shake my head at his ass. "It's a habit that my mother started by having me bring her breakfast every morning, so sit back and enjoy it while I get the paperwork ready for you to fill out. I mean, unless you want me to pay you off the books." He laughed.

"Hell no, I don't want you to pay me off the books. I just told your ass to treat me the same as your other employees," I said, before talking a sip of my tea. "Did you tell Deja that I'm going to be working for you yet?" I asked him.

"No, I didn't tell her because I'm not speaking to her ass right now." He sighed deeply.

"What happened now?" I asked, pulling my bagel from the bag.

"I got an alert to my phone of a charge on my company card for a hotel in Midtown that I know belonged to her. She doesn't know that I get alerts to my phone, so she probably figured that I would never find out. I hardly ever check the statements for any of my business accounts to be honest with you, unless I'm called about a discrepancy," he said.

"Why would you give her access to the company credit card? That was stupid on your part, because that was a business account for your business. Correct?" I questioned to make sure.

"Yes, it's for business, and I gave her the card to handle some business for me and have yet to get it back from her. She had never used it before on anything personal, so I have no idea what this charge is about."

"Well, you need to question her about the shit and dispute the charge instead of just saying you're not speaking to her."

"Trust me, I'm going to have a conversation with her about it, but I couldn't do it in the state I was in when I received the alert," he said, handing me the hire packet that I quickly filled out. I started my day.

My first day went well once Dame left the office, no longer catering to me and not listening to a word I said to him. His mother came in to "train me," as she called it, but she ended up doing most of the work. She started talking about how she wished it was me who Dame was dating, saying how much easier his life would be. She also expressed how she would have loved for me to be her grandchild's mother. I told her that Dame chose who he wanted to be with and how Deja must be doing something right, being that they had been together for over a decade. He was always complaining about her, but he loved that girl whether he admitted it or not, so his mother needed to respect their relationship.

After work I stopped at the mall to pick up a few things for work and to get me a new pair of shoes. I was leaving the aisle after picking up a pencil skirt that I thought was cute when I saw Deja pushing her stroller. I wanted so bad to turn and go back the other way, but she already spotted me, so I took a deep breath before heading in her direction.

"How are you doing, Deja?" I asked.

"I would be doing better if you stay the hell away from my fiancé," she spat.

"I see that you still don't believe that we are just friends, so I'm not going to even bother anymore." I rolled my eyes.

"So, if the two of you are just friends, what the hell was you doing having dinner with him and his mother without me?"

"Deja, that is something that you would have to ask him. His mother invited me and my grandmother to dinner, so it wasn't just an invite for me," I told her.

"An invitation that you should have declined knowing that you had no business having dinner with him and his mother."

"And why the hell not?" I asked, getting pissed off.

"It's disrespectful, especially when you know that his mother is playing matchmaker just because she doesn't like me. He didn't choose you back then, so trust he will not choose you this time and probably only wants to fuck anyway. Stay the hell away from him, because trust when I say you don't want these problems."

"I would tell you that I'm going to stay away from him, but it's not going to happen, being that he's my new boss," I said with a smirk on my face.

She was so pissed she stormed off, not saying another word to me, so I knew that Dame was going to be up arguing all night. I didn't even call him to give him the heads-up that his insecure girlfriend knew that I worked for him now. I paid for my things, so I was on my way to get me a hot pretzel and a peach-and-banana smoothie before leaving the mall.

Chapter Forty-one

Jahiem

I sat in my car outside of the home that I once shared with my sister, trying to find the strength to go inside. I hadn't been back since learning that her life was taken, so this was a hard pill to swallow. I made the hard decision to put the home up for sale, so today I was going to attempt to take on the task of packing her things. I took a deep breath before getting out of the car to go inside the house. We shared a lot of great memories in this house, but I knew that it was going to be hard keeping it. I was only in the house for about ten minutes trying to get my emotions in check when I heard the front door open. I walked into the foyer and saw Reign, Ms. Peggy, and Kelsey walking inside trying to make a thug cry. I told her that I was good to do this by myself, but I should have known she was going to come through.

"Don't even look at me like that, because you should have known that I wasn't going to let you do this alone." She teared up.

"We family, so trust that we got you." Ms. Peggy sniffed.

Kelsey was in tears, so I pulled her in for a hug, praying that we got through this, being that there were a few of us. I already had the moving company come by and drop off boxes in all the rooms, so the ladies started upstairs. I started in the living room, where I was supposed to be packing up the pictures but found myself just staring at them.

"You good?" Reign asked, hugging me from behind.

"To be honest, I don't think that I will ever be good. I miss that mouth of hers so much that I would give anything to hear it again." I chuckled at the thought of how she always acted like she was the older sibling.

I grabbed a box and started to remove the pictures off the wall and mantle, being careful not to break them. I knew that I should have wrapped them, but I didn't because I didn't know shit about packing. I got choked up looking at the picture of my mom, pops, and Jamila at one of my mother's church functions. I took a deep breath and continued putting the pictures in the box and taped it shut. I decided to donate all the furniture and all her things that Reign or Kelsey didn't take for themselves. I knew that this was extremely hard on Kelsey, so I really appreciated her being here with me. She and Jamila always had a tight bond that couldn't be broken if you tried.

About an hour later we took a break and were now enjoying the food that we ordered, sitting at the table reminiscing about her. When it was all said and done, I just stood looking around, wondering when the time came if I would be able to sell. Her car was still parked in the driveway where she left it parked crooked. She couldn't park for shit, but you couldn't tell her ass that because she swore up and down that she could. The mood shifted when Kelsey asked Reign about her job because I wasn't feeling that shit. I didn't want her working so closely with him but knew that I needed to trust her. I thought I was worried, being that it was so easy for me to sleep with Monica and figuring she would do the same.

"I love it, and I'm even thinking about getting my own place soon," she said, which was news to me and apparently to her mother too.

"You never said that you had plans on moving out," Ms. Peggy said to her.

"Exactly," I added.

"Well, I didn't say anything because the key word is 'thinking.' I said I'm thinking, so I haven't made any decisions yet," she spat.

I was confused as to why she would want her own place when she could move in with me, being that we were together. I wasn't going to say anything about it right now because it would only cause an argument. My cell rang, so I excused myself, taking the call in the kitchen. It was my homegirl. I saw Reign roll her eyes, but I wasn't about to address that shit after she just admitted she was thinking about getting her own place.

"What's up?" I answered.

"I was calling to tell you that I think that girl Samantha you were looking for was staying with my cousin. My cousin said that her name was Danielle, so even though she looked like the girl on the picture you showed me, I figured it was just someone who looked like her. Anyway, the reason I got to see her is because my grandmother passed away and we were all at his house. She didn't interact with any of the family while we were discussing arrangements, so I can honestly say I saw her in passing. I called my cousin up to find out where she was from, and he told me that she left, taking his cash and his car. Still, I didn't think nothing of it until we just found out that my grandmother's death was ruled a homicide. My cousin is now convinced that she had something to do with it. I sent him the picture of her that you sent me just to get his opinion, and he said that it's her. He wants to meet with you, so I told him that I would call you to ask you if you would be willing to meet with him. I'm sorry that I didn't call you when she looked like the picture, but I didn't want you to come all this way if I was wrong," she apologized.

"First, let me extend my condolences to you and your family. I also want you to know that I appreciate you for looking out. Let your cousin know that whenever he wants to meet, he can give the info to you, and I'll be there."

"Thank you, Jahiem. This shit is crazy, and if this bitch is responsible for killing my grandmother, she done fucked with the wrong family. I will hit you up as soon as I let him know you down to meet up," she said, voice cracking.

When I walked back into the living room, Reign was giving me the mean mug thinking I was talking to a shorty. Well, I was talking to a shorty, but it wasn't what she was thinking with her jealous ass.

"That was my homegirl on the phone, and check this shit out. Samantha's ass was staying with her cousin on some dating shit. Her grandmother passed away, and they just found out that she was killed. Her cousin said that Samantha disappeared, taking cash and his car, so they think that she had something to do with the grandmother's death. He wants to meet up to talk, so I told her to get back to me to let me know where he wants to meet."

"Are you serious? So, her ass is just going around killing motherfuckers," Reign spat.

"I'm serious, and I'm sure she's no longer in Middletown, so this bitch could be back here, so I need for you all to be careful. Kelsey, I know that you're leaving tomorrow, but I need for you to be careful too," I told them.

Ms. Peggy had this distant look on her face like she was in deep thought, most likely on that bullshit of thinking of Samantha as her daughter again. She needed to let go of whatever guilt she was holding on to and realize that Samantha wasn't Reign.

"Mom, you good?" Reign asked her.

"I'm good, Reign," she lied.

She was in her feelings about the situation, and I understood she wanted to spare Samantha's life, but it wasn't going to happen. She killed my sister, my friend, and an innocent baby so her punishment was death. I should have shot that bitch in her fucking back and not cared about the fucking consequences of being seen. Ms. Peggy needed to understand that Samantha would kill her ass too without a second thought. She had no love for her, and she needed to stop thinking of her as the child she birthed. I didn't know that Samantha was this fucked-up in the head, and to think my sister cared about her. She was upset about Samantha turning Anthony in, but she wouldn't have stayed mad for long.

"Well, when you go to meet with him, I'm going with you," Reign said, probably still stuck on that jealousy shit.

"I don't have a problem with you going with me, Reign, but trust me when I say that nothing is going on with me and that girl."

"I notice that you always say 'my homegirl' or 'my friend' and now 'that girl.' What the hell is her name? When you introduced me to her you said, 'Reign, this is my friend,' but you still didn't say her name. Why is that?" she asked.

"Why you always accusing me of some shit and constantly trying to make something out of nothing?" I had to remind her once again because she did that shit a lot.

"And you still didn't say her name. Mom, let's go," she said, now in her damn feelings again about nothing.

I let her ass go because I wasn't about to keep doing the same shit with her when I told her that she was just a friend. There was a reason why I never called her by her name, but it had nothing to do with what she was thinking.

"What?" I asked Kelsey, who was shaking her head at me.

"Please don't tell me that the female is Amani," she stressed.

"It's Amani," I admitted.

"You know I love you, cousin, but you wrong as shit for not telling Reign the truth."

"I couldn't tell her the truth because me and Amani agreed to take it to our grave, and the only reason I reached out was to find Samantha. If I tell her the truth, I can possibly jeopardize Amani's life, and I'm not willing to do that."

"So, why the hell couldn't you just answer the question? You men make females think the worst, and I promise you, had you said any name, she would have left it alone."

"Well, I'm sorry if we don't think quick on our feet the way that you females do," I said to her ass.

"Whatever. Are you ready? I'm staying with you tonight, but I'm going to need a ride to the airport in the morning."

"Let's go," I told her after grabbing my cell.

When I got home, I tried to call Reign, but she sent me to voicemail, so I left a message telling her to give me a call back. I couldn't tell her the truth, but I was going to make something up to make her feel as if I weren't hiding something. Now wasn't the time for her not to be answering her phone when Samantha was out there somewhere. I called Ms. Peggy's phone, and she answered, telling me that they were okay, so I told her to tell Reign that I loved her. My cell rang as soon as I hung up with Ms. Peggy, so I thought it was Reign. When I heard Monica's voice on the other end, I hung the phone up because I was already in the doghouse.

Chapter Forty-two

Reign

I was so tired of being pissed at Jahiem, but it was because he was always lying to me like the shit was okay. I didn't know who this female was, but I did remember Jamila telling me about a female named Amani. She didn't have any idea that me and her brother would end up dating when she used to talk about shit that concerned him. He didn't know that she said anything to me about this girl, and that was the reason I was stressing her name. Jamila just told me about how he was in love with this girl named Amani, but she was in a situation. Her dude and Jahiem weren't best friends, but they were cool, and he knew that she was his girl. Supposedly it only happened one time before she told him that she couldn't see him anymore. My thing was, if it only happened one time, how the hell was he in love with her? If he wanted me to speak to his ass again, he'd better tell me this female's name. If he fixed his face to say,

"Amani," I was going to tell him what I was told about the two of them. He was going to tell me the truth or it was going to be curtains for his ass, and I was serious this time.

I wasn't even in the mood to go to work today because Dame was tripping, getting on my damn nerves. He was upset that I mentioned to Deja that I was working for him, but he said he was going to tell her. He was supposed to be tight with her ass about a charge on his business card, so how the fuck did he allow her to flip the shit on him? She had his ass whipped, because he was acting like a real bitch right now, so I wasn't in the mood for him to take it out on me. When I walked in, I didn't see him, so I clocked in and took a seat at my desk, praying he didn't bring his ass in here today. I started my work, and he walked in about an hour later with a cute mug on his face, trying to intimidate me as if he were still mad. He couldn't stay mad at me for too long and he knew it, but his ass sure was trying.

"Good afternoon," I joked, being that it was still morning.

"Good morning. Do you have those numbers ready?" he said, trying to keep it work related.

Maybe his ass was still mad at me, and if that was the case, Deja's ass might have left him if he told her that he wasn't going to fire me. He needed to put his foot down and show her ass who wore the fucking pants, unless it was she who wore them.

"So, we really doing this?" I asked him.

"Doing what? I thought we were handling business," he said, not looking at me.

"Okay, if that is how you want to play it," I said, handing him the paperwork.

I wasn't going to play this game with Dame's ass, and if he continued to stress me, I would quit on his ass. In all honesty, I didn't have to work because of my nest egg that I chose not to use but could use. I was doing him a favor, not the other way around, so he needed to get some act right before I walked up out of here. I usually sat at my desk on my lunch hour, but being that he was mad, I left the building to go out to pick something up. As soon as I walked outside, I saw Jahiem standing by my car looking like a damn snack.

"What are you doing here?" I asked him with a smile on my face.

I was tired of arguing with him because, truth be told, I missed talking to his ass, and no, that didn't mean that I was letting him slide. He still had some explaining to do, so nope, he wasn't out of the doghouse yet.

"I came to see you since you keep sending me to voicemail," he said.

"Are you going to answer my question?" I asked him.

"Yes, but can we do that shit when you get off work? I'm trying to take you to lunch," he said, pulling me in for a hug.

After we had lunch, he dropped me off at work, saying he would see me after work so that we could talk. I could see the stress lines on his face, but I didn't care. I needed him to tell me the truth.

"Did you enjoy your lunch date?" Dame asked me as soon as I walked into the building.

"I don't think what I did on my lunch break is considered handling business about work," I said with a roll of my eyes.

"No, but I was just asking because you walked up in here with a smile on your face."

"I always smile after seeing my man," I spat.

"Yeah, okay. Did my mom teach you how to do the truck driver's log-in sheet for all the local drivers?" he asked me.

"She did," I responded, keeping it short.

"I need you to enter them into the system so that the payroll clerk can have access to that information before Wednesday."

"I believe your mother told me that the only time I would have to enter that information is when Ms. Harris is off. If I'm not mistaken, isn't that her sitting in the office across the way?" I said, pointing toward the office.

"That would be correct, but I'm asking you to handle it because I have Ms. Harris doing something else," he lied.

I knew that he was just fucking with me because he was in his damn feelings, so I decided not to sweat it. I had to remind myself that whether he was being petty or not, he was still my boss, so I was just going to do the shit. I was going to call his mother on his black ass, though, so she could get in his ass. She told me to call her whenever I encountered a problem, and he was being a problem right now.

My fingers were hurting by the time I left the office because he had my ass entering data all damn day. I spoke to Jahiem about an hour before it was time for me to get off work, so he told me to come by his place. I knew that I had to give myself the pep talk to hear him out and not get in my feelings. I was going to be upset if he told me that this female was Amani because he could have told me the truth about her. He wasn't my man before if he did sleep with this girl, so why not just be honest to avoid all of this?

Taking a deep breath, I stepped out of the car, going up to the front of the house and knocking on the door lightly. He opened the door wearing some basketball shorts with no shirt, and I was thinking his ass was trying to entice me. Nope, I wasn't having sex no matter how fucking good his ass was looking right now. I walked inside, nervous about the conversation we were about to have and trying to calm myself.

"So, what's her name, and why was it a problem telling me her name?" I asked.

"Her name is Amani, and the reason I didn't tell you her name was because I didn't want to admit to my history with her. I know it doesn't make sense, but that was how I was thinking at the time."

"So, you're admitting that you do have history with her? You told me that she is just a friend of yours."

"She's just a friend now, but she wasn't always just a friend to me. She was dating a dude I was hustling with who I became friends with. Well, I didn't know that she was dating him when I met her because she didn't share that she was seeing someone. We started hanging out, but it was always on her time, but I never questioned her. I mean, I was in the streets, so I figured that was the reason it was always on some late-night shit with her. When I expressed to her that I had feelings for her and I wanted us to be in a relationship, that was when she told me she was seeing someone. So, when I found out that it was my friend she was seeing, I wanted to tell him, but she begged me not to. We continued seeing each other because, like I said, I had feelings for her, so it wasn't easy to stop seeing her. Long story short, she found out that she was pregnant and didn't know who the father was. I asked her for a DNA test whenever the baby was born, but she told me that she was in love with him and that was who she wanted to be with. I was upset, but I respected the fact that she wanted to be with him, so I walked away. A few months later, I saw her in passing and she told me that she lost the baby and they moved to Middletown. I heard that she had his daughter and he asked her to marry him. I swear that I hadn't spoken to her until I hit her up about Samantha, remembering that was where she moved. I also remember her telling me that her family lived there, too, so that was why I reached out to her."

I already knew that Jahiem messed around with a lot of females, so that wasn't my issue with his ass. My issue was the lying and not keeping it real with me when I asked him about things, so I felt that he must still have feelings for her. He just admitted that they moved to Middletown, so why not hit up dude to be on the lookout? I knew that, being that this was her cousin, she was going to be at this meeting, so I was going to make sure to have my ass with him.

"If he's your friend, why did you hit her up and not him? I mean, I'm sure he's still in the game, so wouldn't it make more sense for him to be on the lookout for Samantha?" I asked.

"I never said anything to him about smashing his girl, but I think that he knows because he stopped fucking with me. Trust me, I hit him up a few times over the years, and he always acted like he wasn't fucking with me. I reached out to him before I reached out to her after he refused to return my calls. If he found out about me smashing his girl, he should be a man and speak to me about it."

"So, you didn't feel that it was wrong to contact her and show up to the house she shares with him without him knowing? I mean, if you couldn't reach him for whatever reason, why not have her relay the message?" I asked him, still not fully understanding.

"She's the one who told me that he said that he wasn't fucking with me like that, so I said fuck that nigga," he said, saying something completely different from what he just said.

I still felt like Jahiem wasn't telling me the truth about what really went down and why he reached out to her. If her man told her that he wasn't fucking with Jahiem, any real man would have told her he didn't want her fucking with him either. It was all good because what was done in the dark always came to light, so he could keep telling half the truth.

Chapter Forty-three

Jahiem

I really didn't want to take Reign with me to meet up with this dude because she stayed in her damn feelings. I was sure Amani was going to be present, being that I didn't know dude and dude didn't know me. I just didn't want no bullshit because it wasn't necessary when I wasn't checking for Amani. We were almost there, and I wanted to tell Reign to not start any unnecessary bullshit now that she knew the history. She was playing *Words with Friends* on her phone, so I didn't know if she was still somewhat heated at me or what. I pulled up to the address and called Amani to let her know that I was out front, so when she came out, she was all smiles. She went to hug me, but Reign stepped in front of her, stopping her in her tracks. I knew she was going to show her ass, but Amani kept it classy and told us to follow her inside. I gave Reign a look, but she just rolled her eyes at me, letting me know not to even say anything to her.

"Jahiem, this is my cousin Rashad, and, Rashad, this is Jahiem and his friend. I'm sorry. I don't know your name," Amani said.

"My name is Reign, and I'm Jahiem's girlfriend. Nice to meet you, Rashad," Reign said, extending her hand.

I just took her hand and walked into the living room and took a seat on the couch so we could get to the reason we were here.

"My cousin told me about your ex-girlfriend Samantha. I met Samantha about a year ago at a club and we exchanged numbers. She would give me excuses as to why we couldn't link up, so we would just talk from time to time. Anyway, she called me out of the blue saying that she needed somewhere to stay for a few weeks. She didn't go into details on the phone, but when she got here, she said that she left her abusive relationship. I felt bad for her, and being that I was feeling her, I didn't have a problem letting her stay here. Samantha and my grandmother didn't get along because when she met Samantha, she just felt that something wasn't right about her. She had no problem expressing it to Samantha, so they stayed getting into it, so I asked my grandmother not to visit as much. The day before my grandmother passed away, she told me Samantha was at her building pretending to be her granddaughter. I don't know exactly how it went down, but my grandmother said she even lied about her name. This would be the second time, being that she told me that her name was Danielle. Anyway, she is now a suspect in the murder of my grandmother because the cameras place her in the building. The only reason that I know it's her on the camera is because she came home wearing my hat and all black, same as the person on the video. I'm so mad at myself because I didn't listen to my grandmother, and the last thing I said to her was to stop visiting so much."

He was getting choked up the same way I got choked up when I found out my sister was dead at the hands of this bitch. He trusted her the same way I trusted her because she just didn't look like the type of person to kill someone. He was blaming himself the same way I was blaming myself, so I understood what he was feeling.

"Rashad, she knew that you loved her, and it's not your fault because you didn't know that girl was capable of something like this," Amani said to him.

"She took the car I lent her, but I didn't let the authorities know that it has a GPS locater in the car. I tracked the car to a street in Midtown. It was parked on a side block accumulating tickets, but there was no sign of her. I got someone sitting in the area right now because it's murder on sight, and that is on my grandmother," he said, getting upset.

"If you found the car in Midtown, there are like a hundred damn hotels in that area, so she could be in any one of them. We already know that she isn't going by her real name, so she could have had someone get the room for her," I said to him.

"Does she still have family in the city? I don't know nothing about her other than what she told me, and that was all lies," Rashad said.

"She does have family, according to her, but she only dealt with her cousin Emily, so I have no idea who the others are. This family is on her father's side, and she never spoke in detail about who she was related to. Like I said, her ass could be in any one of those hotels, and unless she leaves and is out in the open, we have no idea which one."

"Mommy, can I have juice?" a little girl came running down the stairs.

I couldn't take my eyes off the little girl because she looked just like Jamila, and she even had the same birthmark as mine on her cheek.

"Mariah, didn't I tell you to stay upstairs until Mommy called you?" Amani said to her.

"Yes, but I'm thirsty," she whined.

Reign was in tears with her hand over her mouth, staring after the little girl, until Amani disappeared into the kitchen.

"Why the fuck does that little girl look just like Jamila and have the same fucking birthmark that you and Jamila have?" she cried.

"She doesn't look like my sister, and her having a birthmark that resembles the one we got don't mean anything. I know a few people who have a birthmark on their face, but that doesn't tie them to my ass," I said.

"Nah, when you walked up in here, I was looking at the same shit, but my sister told me that you were just friends. I mean, there's really no reason to argue or speculate when my cousin is right there in the kitchen," Rashad said with a chuckle, but Reign was fuming.

Amani probably told her daughter to stay upstairs because of her birthmark, being that I mentioned to her that my sister and I got it from my mother. I really didn't want to have this conversation in front of her cousin, but Reign wanted answers. She was acting like I didn't just tell her what happened between us. If Amani lied to me about losing the baby, how was I supposed to know that she didn't? If she was my baby, she would be 3, not 4, so when she told me her daughter with Kason was 4, I didn't question it.

"Amani, bring your ass on in here because you got some explaining to do," Rashad called out to her.

I believed she was stalling in the kitchen to avoid the conversation, but she needed to come say this little girl wasn't mine. I loved Reign to death, but I hated how she let her emotions take over when she had no reason to be upset with me. I told her the truth, so that was all that should matter when I wasn't at fault for a lie that I didn't know about. I knew I should have left her ass at the house and come here on my own. Her mother wanted to come with us too, but I told her no because Reign was enough. If Ms. Peggy were here, she probably would have been cursing me out for making her daughter cry once again.

"Amani, will you tell my girlfriend that your four-year-old daughter isn't my child?" I said to Amani when she finally walked back into the living room.

"Mariah is three years old," Rashad corrected me. "Amani, please don't tell me that was the reason Kason left," he said to her.

She was just filled with lies, because she told me that she was happily married and they had a 4-year-old daughter. This fucking visit went left, and I was ready to go because I was already lied to about a kid not being mine.

"Why you not saying anything? Is she his daughter or not?" Reign spat.

"Jahiem, can we please talk in private?" she asked me.

"No, the fuck you can't speak to him in private. Your time to speak to him in private was when I wasn't in the picture. So, whatever you have to say to him, you're going to have to say it in front of me and your cousin," Reign responded.

"I was speaking to Jahiem."

"You're right. Jahiem, go ahead and tell her the same shit that I just told her so we could get this shit going," she snapped at me.

"Amani, whatever you need to say that you didn't say back then will have to be said in front of my girl. So, what's good?" I said to her.

"Are you serious, Jahiem? You can't give me ten minutes of your time so that I can talk to you?"

"Listen, just say what the fuck you need to say," I said, getting pissed the fuck off.

I was sick of these females playing with me, so she needed to start talking before I spazzed on her ass. I didn't give a fuck about being in her family's house, because she had me fucked up when she could have kept it real with me.

"She's yours," she blurted out, and I swear on everything I love, it took everything in me not to slap the shit out of her.

Chapter Forty-four

Samantha

I left the hotel with my head down until I got into the awaiting car service that was waiting at the curb for the hotel guests. I quickly gave him the address that I was going to so that he could leave from in front of the hotel. I was so damn paranoid, and I knew that it was only a matter of time before my shit caught up to me. I was going to make sure that if I wasn't the last man standing, a few motherfuckers were going to fall with me. I called Peggy last night and guilt tripped her ass to meet up with me, which she agreed to, but she wanted me to come to her. She told me that Reign was at work and wouldn't be home until after six, so I was trusting her ass. I was going to pay the dude to do her dirty, but that was how I got in the mess I was in now—by involving weak motherfuckers. I had the driver drop me off in front of her house after I scoped the block and didn't notice anything. I pulled the fitted down over my face but not enough to draw attention to myself. I knocked on the door, and she opened it, and I hesitated until she told me that she was alone.

"I'm sorry I was conflicted, but I promise you that it will never happen again. They told me that they were going to just turn you in so that you could get some help," she said.

"Why would I need help when I told you that I didn't kill anyone and that it was my cousin Emily?" I said to her.

"Samantha, honey, I didn't know what to believe. I'm just happy that you decided to trust me again."

"Do you trust me? Do you believe me when I tell you that I'm innocent?" I asked her.

"I'm not going to sit here and lie to you, Samantha. The truth is that I don't know what to believe anymore. What I do know is that I'm willing to support you, because if I didn't, I wouldn't have agreed for you to come to my home. I know that you don't believe me, but I love you, and I will always love you no matter what. I'm not going to stand around and allow anyone to hurt you, so I promise I will not lie to you again."

"All I wanted to do was to come here and tell you that I was hurt when you set me up to be killed, because you had to know he would have killed me. I don't want to die for something that I didn't do, Mom," I cried.

"You're not going to die, Samantha, but you do need to clear your name if you're innocent like you say. You can't keep hiding, so you need to do the right thing so that we can clear your name."

"That is why I came here, because I wanted to spend time with you just in case my turning myself in didn't work in my favor," I lied.

"I made a pan of lasagna last night. Would you like to have lunch with me before you leave?" she asked me.

"I would love to have lunch with you, Mom, and thanks for being honest with me. I love you."

"Do you know how long I waited for you to say those words to me?" She sniffed, pulling me into her and hugging me tight. "You have me up in here crying my eyes out. Let me warm this food up so that we could have lun—" Her words got caught in her throat from the hit she just took to her head.

Her eyes were wide, not believing that I hit her, but she was in for a rude awakening when I hit her ass again. She fell to the floor, and she was still moving, so I hit her ass one more time, waiting for her to move again, but she didn't. I didn't even bother to wipe my prints off the statue because if Jahiem was gunning for me, I was going to take a few of them with me. I gave Peggy's ass a few red flags and she missed them all, and that was why she was lying on the floor leaking. She should have known that I didn't love her ass when I was just pissed at her for lying to me with her dumb ass. I had no plans on going back to the hotel, so I called Deja because I needed another favor from her ass. She was bitching on the phone about how she told me that the hotel was the last favor, but I lied and told her this would be the last time. I told her that I would meet her in about an hour, praying that she still had her boyfriend's credit card. I felt a light drizzle, praying that it didn't start raining before I made it across town. I was worried about taking public transportation but quickly got over it because I knew how lazy the NYPD was. If it were white people who were killed, they would have been all over this case, tracking me down without a problem.

When I got off the train it was raining lightly, but as soon as I exited the train station, Deja was parked at the curb, so I got inside.

"What do you need now? I can't keep dragging my baby out every time you need me to do you a damn favor."

"I told you that this is the last time and I mean it. I need you to rent me a car, and just like with the hotel, I will give you the money," I said to her.

"I can't rent you a car, Samantha, because he took his credit card from me when he saw the hotel charge. I had to lie and tell him that the hotel was for my mother because her house had a flood, and I promise you he didn't believe me. I can't do anything for you that is going to cause a paper trail and risk me losing my man," she whined.

"Well, can you let me borrow your car? I'm only going to be a few hours, and I will return it to you," I lied.

"Girl, you must have fallen and bumped your damn head if you think that I'm going to lend you my car. You must have forgotten the last time we were together you crashed my mother's car and left me to take the blame. So, that would be a stiff no."

"Why are you bringing up shit that happened a decade ago? I didn't have a driver's license, and I didn't know how to drive. I'm legit now, and I can drive my ass off, and I promise to bring your car back the same way you gave it to me."

"How the hell will I explain my car not being in the driveway when my man gets home, Samantha?"

"What time does he get home?" I asked her.

"He gets home after six. Why?"

"I'm not going to be more than an hour, so that means I will be back way before he finds out, so can you please just trust me?"

"I swear, I shouldn't have ever agreed to help you to begin with because I already know you're going to fuck me over."

"Didn't I just say to trust me? I'm not going to do anything to get you in trouble with your boyfriend."

"If this was years ago, I would have no problem trusting you, but I haven't seen or spoken to you in forever. I went out of my way to come to Midtown and get you a hotel, so why isn't that enough for you? You got here on the train to meet me, so why can't you take the train for wherever you need to go with my car?"

"Why you being a fucking bitch right now like I'm asking you for a million fucking dollars? I'm just asking to use your piece-of-shit car to run an errand and have it back to you before the nigga get home," I spat.

"You know my car isn't a piece of shit, and even if it were, it's my piece of shit that you're begging to use. I'm going to take you to the nearest train station, and you figure the shit out from there."

"Are you fucking serious? I understand that you haven't seen me in like forever, but don't act like a bitch never looked out for you. If you want to drop me off at the train station, do what you have to do, because I'm not about to beg you."

"I'm not asking you to beg me. I just want you to understand that I'm not lending you my car, so where do you want me to drop you off?"

"You can pull the car over now and I'll get out," I told her.

I didn't think that she would call my bluff, but she pulled over, and it pissed me off, so when I opened the door, I reached over and grabbed her by her braids. I started beating the shit out of her, taking all my frustration out on her. She couldn't even defend herself because the seat belt prevented her from swinging, so I continued beating her ass until the baby started crying. I looked at the blood on my hands and the damage to her face, not believing that I just snapped like that. I swear I didn't mean to do that shit to her, but she just got me so tight by talking to me like that. I hauled ass, stopping at the first fast-food restaurant I saw, and I went into the bathroom to wash my hands. I looked out the door before leaving and making my way to the nearest train station with no destination in mind right now.

After traveling on the train for about an hour, I was now walking up on a porch that I thought I would never step foot on again. I knocked on the shabby-looking white door, waiting for someone to answer and praying someone was home. I wasn't trying to travel on the train again knowing I had nowhere else to go.

"Oh, hell no. I know you didn't bring your ass to my house knowing that the law is looking for you. How could you leave your cousin in jail knowing that she's not capable of hurting a damn fly?"

"God, Mommy, don't do me like that," I stressed because I had nowhere else to go.

"Don't 'God, Mommy' me, because the last time I saw your ass, you had a temper tantrum tearing my damn living room up. I'm going to tell you something, and you'd better receive it. If I let you in my house and you pull that bullshit again, you're not going to have to worry about the law. The coroner is going to be coming up in here and picking your dead body up off my floor," she said seriously.

I hadn't seen my godmother since I was about 18 because of the falling out that we had, and I tore her living room up like she said. I didn't remember what triggered it, but I did remember losing it that day. I was surprised that she let me back into her home because she was pissed at the time and told me I was never welcome back. I knew that I hurt her that day because she always treated me with so much love. I should have never disrespected her that day because if I didn't know if I was loved by anyone, I knew for a fact that she loved me.

"So, what's your plan?" she asked me.

"I don't know, but I do know that I'm going to have to face the music sooner or later," I lied because I had no plans on turning myself in.

"I don't know what happened that day, but what they are saying that you did doesn't sound like you, but someone did the shit. I know for a fact that Emily didn't kill anybody, but with the way you just snap for no reason, I really hope you didn't do this. If you're innocent, it doesn't look that way, because what reason would you have to keep running? I can allow you to stay here for a few days, but I can't risk having you here knowing that you

have a warrant out for your arrest. Also, I have two
foster children who live here, so you already know
that I could get into trouble. I love you and you
know that, but I can't harbor a fugitive. Now if you
turn yourself in, I would be with you through the
entire process, and I mean that."

"Have you spoken to my grandmother?" I asked
her.

"I haven't spoken to her since the day she called
asking me if you reached out to me, but I told her
that you didn't. I was told that your cousin isn't
doing too well mentally after the death of her
daughter."

She looked at me to see my reaction, but I didn't
have one, because my cousin wasn't all that stable
before losing her daughter. I didn't want to lie to
her by saying I didn't do this, but I didn't want to
tell her the truth either. I just needed to stay with
her until I figured out what my next move was
going to be, being that turning myself in wasn't an
option.

Her phone rang, and my paranoia started to
kick in, making me think that she was setting me
up, so I listened to her call. It sounded like she was
speaking about one of the kids who lived in her
home, so I calmed down just a bit.

"Are you hungry?" she asked me after she ended
the call.

I wasn't hungry, but I was going to eat so that I could ask her if I could borrow her car for a few hours. She probably was going to say no, but if she did say no, I was just going to wait until she went to sleep. Wouldn't be the first time taking her car without permission. I used to do it all the time. Only difference would be that I would not be returning her car to her driveway as if it were never moved.

Chapter Forty-five

Reign

I was upset that Samantha did this to my mother, leaving her unconscious and bleeding from her head and left to die. I was upset with myself because I should have let Jahiem get someone to watch the house when he offered. They had her in a medically induced coma to allow the brain to rest, to decrease the swelling. My heart was so heavy right now having to see my mother in this state with a ventilator helping her breathe again. I had a migraine that I couldn't get rid of because I was dealing with so much right now. I was trying hard not to even think about what Jahiem had going on because my mother was more important, but it was hard. It just seemed that shit never got better and was always going from sugar to shit within a matter of seconds. I was upset. Because we just went through this bullshit with Samantha, he was being cautious this time, so he told Amani he wanted a DNA test done on the little girl.

She looked just like him, but I thought I said the same thing about the baby Samantha said belonged to him. He was pissed at her for lying to him when she told him that she lost the baby, but again, he brought that shit on himself. He was the one who kept lying up with these bird bitches, and I wouldn't be surprised if Monica said she was pregnant next.

The police were saying that they didn't have any information to give, but just based on the fact that there was no forced entry, I knew it was Samantha. My mother let her ass in that house, trusting her again after I told her a million times she couldn't be trusted. That bitch was mental, and had she just listened to me, she probably wouldn't be in this hospital. Samantha was doing the most and mad at the wrong fucking people when she should be mad at her fucking self. If she was feeling a way about my mother giving her up, she had the choice to stay the fuck away.

What the fuck did she want an addict to do? Had she stuck around and tried to raise a baby in her state at the time, trust me, Samantha's ass would have been neglected.

"Reign, why don't you go home to get some rest? I will stay with your mother until you get back here sometime tomorrow," my aunt Cherie said.

I was surprised she was here, since when I called her last time my mom was in the hospital she was in and out. I needed to leave the hospital to at least shower. I'd been here in the same clothes for two days. I still had her blood on the shirt that I was wearing. I refused to leave, but it was time. I wasn't going to stay at my house just because Jahiem didn't trust me to be there, so I was staying with him. He had an alarm system, so if she even tried to enter his home, we would know about it. Ms. Trina left about an hour ago, but she sat with me all night the first day my mom was in the hospital. I asked her if she saw or heard anything, but she said that she didn't, which meant she was probably drunk. She never missed a beat on the block, so I knew it was for that reason.

I thanked my aunt, telling her that I would be back in the morning, before leaving the hospital. I called Jahiem to tell him that I was on the way to his house so he would be looking out for me. We didn't know if this bitch was stalking or what. He didn't want her running up on me, so he made me stay on the phone until I was in the car. I was so tired and couldn't wait to take a shower and try to get some rest. I spoke to Dame earlier when he called to check up on me and to tell me to take as much time as I needed. I wanted to speak to him about something that he said and something that Amani's cousin Rashad said. It would have to wait right now because my mother was who I needed to focus on, at least for now. I was tired of talking to the police, too, because they were starting to get on my damn nerves.

I couldn't help but smile when I pulled up to see Jahiem sitting on the porch, waiting on me and looking like he was ready for war.

"You so stupid. Why are you sitting on the porch with a damn bat with your crazy ass?" I asked him.

"If that bitch tried to run up on you, I was going to beat the shit out of her with this bat until she stopped fucking moving. My gun is licensed, but shooting her ass after all that she's done would be too easy," he said seriously before pulling me into his arms. "How are you feeling?"

"I'm feeling okay. I just want to take a shower and try to get some rest so that I can get back to the hospital."

"Well, get a shower, and I will order you some food so that you can eat something before going to get some rest. I know you probably didn't eat shit since this happened, and the reason I know is because I been trying to get you to eat something."

"I know, but I just haven't been hungry." I sighed.

"Well, just try to eat something for me. Okay?"

"Okay," I said before going to take a shower.

When I got out of the shower, Jahiem was just coming into the room with the food from Uber Eats. It smelled so good, but I swear my eyes were closing, but since he was nice enough to order, the least I could do was eat with him.

"When your mom gets better, I want to take you away because you deserve it. I'm sorry for all the stress that you have been going through because of me. This will be my way of trying to relieve some of that stress."

"I don't think that I will feel comfortable going anywhere until Samantha's ass is behind bars or in the ground taking a dirt nap," I told him.

Enough was enough, and it was time to get the police involved and tell them everything that we knew. They needed to know that she was wanted in the murder of Rashad's grandmother so they could put more effort into finding her.

The next morning, I walked into the hospital, and my aunt was sleeping so uncomfortably in the chair. I tapped her to let her know that I was back and that she could leave to go home to her pregnant daughter. Yes, Kami decided to keep Anthony's baby, so she was about to be a teenage mom with the father still in jail. My aunt tried to get her to get rid of the baby, but Kami wouldn't budge, telling her she would run away. I didn't think that Kami was old enough to be having a baby only because of how naive she still was. My aunt was going to be the one raising the baby, because Kami talked as if the baby was going to be her new doll.

The doctor interrupted my thoughts, letting me know that the CT scan showed that the swelling on her brain went down. He said that they were going to remove her from the induced coma and take her off the ventilator. I was thanking God for sparing her life for a second time when I thought I was going to lose her. I called my grandmother to let her know the good news before calling everyone else. I saw Dame walking toward the room while I was standing out in the hallway, causing me to smile.

"Hey, you, how are you feeling?" he asked, giving me a hug.

"I just got some good news, so I'm feeling good right now. The swelling on my mother's brain has gone down and there's no bleeding. They are going to wake her up and take her off the ventilator, so I'm on cloud nine right now."

"That is good news, and I promise you I been praying for her and you," he said.

"Can you come into the waiting area for a second? I want to talk to you about something if you have time," I said to him.

"I have time, being that I came here to visit you and your mom, so what's up?"

"Listen, remember when you got the alert to your phone about Deja using the business card for a hotel in Midtown?"

"I remember. Why?"

"Jahiem got a call from a friend who said that she saw Samantha at her cousin's house, but she stole his car and disappeared. Anyway, when Jahiem spoke to the cousin, he said he tracked the car and it was in Midtown. Do you think that Deja may know Samantha and that was who she got the room for? I know it's a stretch, but at this point I'm willing to chase anything that may lead us to her ass."

"I don't know if she knows Deja. She told me that she got the room for her mother whose place was flooded."

"Did you confirm it with her mother?" I asked him, already knowing that he took her word.

"No, but if it would make you feel any better, I could give her mom a call to keep you from going crazy not knowing," he said before making the call.

I waited impatiently while he was on the phone talking to her, wishing he would wrap it up and tell me something. When he ended the call, I was thinking, *about time,* but I didn't express it to him.

"Her mother had no idea what I was talking about, so that means Deja lied to me, but it doesn't mean that she got the room for Samantha or even knows her," he said.

"You're right, but my mother is in this hospital because of Samantha, so I don't care if I'm wrong. I just need to know."

"I will say that something happened that Deja isn't being honest with me about. I came home and her face was bruised, and she told me that the cabinet hit her in the face. I knew that she was lying because if it had been the cabinet, the bruise would have been in one spot. I begged her to tell me who put their fucking hands on her, but she kept saying the cabinet, so I left it alone."

"I'm going to see if my aunt can come back later to sit with my mother because I need to speak to Deja. My gut is telling me that she knows Samantha and that was who she booked that hotel room for. If Samantha asked Deja to do something else for her and Deja told her no, Samantha could be responsible for what happened to her face."

"I don't think that she knows Samantha, because we been together for a long time, and I never met Samantha. I would have recognized her if I saw her before, so I really think that you're about to waste your time. I'm thinking that some nigga she's messing with did that shit to her face, and that is the reason she's lying."

"That might be true, but I still want to ask her if she knows Samantha," I said, not backing down about my gut feeling.

My aunt couldn't come back to the hospital, so my uncle Tommy came to sit with my mother until I got back. I told him that I wasn't going to be long, but he told me to take my time, but I still had no plans on being long. I left my car in the parking lot and got into the car with Dame, praying that I got the answers I needed. I wasn't going to call Jahiem until I knew for sure that Deja got that hotel room for Samantha. Dame didn't call to let Deja know that we were coming, so when we walked through the door, she was pissed.

"What is she doing here?" she asked him.

"She came here to talk to you, so calm the fuck down," he barked.

"What could she possibly want to speak to me about? It's no secret that I don't like her ass, so I don't appreciate you bringing her here. If she wanted to ask me something, you could have called me on the phone, so don't tell me to calm down."

"Listen, I didn't come here to cause an argument between you two. I just want to know if that room you booked at the hotel was for someone named Samantha?" I asked her.

"What?" she asked, trying to act as if she didn't hear me.

"I said, did you book the room in Midtown for someone named Samantha?" I repeated.

"I don't know anybody named Samantha, so you can leave now," she said, but her body language told me she was lying.

"It's all good, but let me just tell you that once the police have the hotel submit the video for that day, if were there, we will know. If you are on that video showing that you helped her when she has a warrant for her arrest, you will be going to jail too. Now if you just tell me what room she's in, we will handle it without the police," I bluffed, hoping that the shit worked, because I knew that she was lying about not knowing her.

"Deja, if you know that bitch, you better say something now before you get locked up and never see me or your daughter again," Dame added.

"I booked the room, but that was it, so I don't know nothing about anything that was going on, and I want no part," she admitted.

"Are you fucking serious? Why the fuck would you book a room with my card for someone you had to know was in some shit? So fucking stupid," he shouted at her, but I needed him to fall back so that she wouldn't shut down.

"I don't know nothing about her being in some shit, so don't call me fucking stupid. She called me up, telling me that she needed my help to book her a room, nothing more, nothing less. I didn't think nothing of it because her aunt and my mother were friends, so we were play cousins. She always had my back, so all I was doing was returning the favor."

"Well, she has a warrant for her arrest, so I'm sure the police won't care if you knew her or not, so that excuse is not going to cut it. They will look at it as you helping to harbor a fugitive and charge you because it's a crime. So, like I said, you need to tell me where I can find her," I stressed.

"I only booked the room for a week, so she's not at the hotel anymore, but she did call me to pick her up. Once I picked her up, she wanted to borrow my car, but I told her no, and that was when she attacked me, and I haven't seen her since."

"So, you looked me right in my face and told me a fucking lie," Dame said to her.

"You were already upset when I told you that it was for my mother, so imagine what you would have said if I told you it was for a fake cousin. All I did was try to help her out, and it backfired on me, so I'm not trying to get in trouble behind her ass."

"Does she have any other family in New York that you know of? Samantha is dangerous, so she needs to be put in jail before she hurts someone else. My mother is in the hospital because Samantha attacked her, so please put your feelings for me aside and tell me something," I pleaded, not caring about my pride at this point.

"Her godmother lives in the Bronx, but like I said, this was a long time ago, so I have no idea if she still lives there. I can give you the address that I remember, but that is all I know," she stated.

Chapter Forty-six

Reign

I didn't care what Deja was saying about not knowing shit, because that stuff about not asking any questions was bullshit. Who would be good booking a room for someone with them giving them no explanation? Now if she said that Samantha told her something, then maybe I would believe what she was saying. Jahiem didn't want to involve the police, but it was time to get them involved. I wasn't willing to risk her ass hurting someone else, and clearly, she kept being two steps ahead of us. I was outside waiting for Dame to take me back to the hospital because he and Deja was arguing. She tried to justify her actions, but he was pissed because she had their daughter with her when Samantha attacked her. Dame came out a few minutes later wearing a pissed-off expression on his face and walking to the car. I left him in his feelings as I sent Jahiem a message to meet me at the hospital as soon as he was done handling business.

After getting back to the hospital, I told Dame that I was going to call the detective and give him the address. He told me not to let Jahiem talk me out of calling the detective, so I told him that I was calling and didn't care who didn't agree. That was my mother laid up in the hospital when the shit probably could have been prevented. As soon as he pulled off, I called the detective and told him that she was staying in the Bronx. I just prayed that Deja didn't give her the heads-up, being that I had no idea what the relationship really was. I didn't know if she felt she needed to warn her, but I was going to keep the faith that she didn't. A text message came in from my uncle telling me that my mother was awake, so I rushed inside, almost falling.

"Did you fly here?" He laughed.

"No, I was downstairs when I received your text message."

"She's not talking, but she can hear you if you want to talk to her. She nods her head yes or no, but she hasn't spoken."

"Hey, Mom," I said, taking her hand into mine.

My heart broke seeing the tears fall from her eyes, causing my tears to fall because I hated seeing her like this. She was probably hurt that Samantha did this to her, being that she was positive that she wouldn't hurt her. I knew better. That was the reason I kept stressing it to her, but she just wasn't trying to hear me. I didn't want her feeling bad for trusting her, being that she might have seen something in Samantha that I didn't see that gave her that hope.

"Mom, it's okay. I don't blame you for trusting her," I said, kissing her on her cheek.

I swore that if I got the chance to put my hands around Samantha's neck, I would choke her ass to death. I prayed that the detective had her ass in custody before the fucking night was over, and he probably would if he got on it. My mom fell asleep, so I was sitting in the chair, reading a book on my phone. I downloaded the Kindle app a few days ago to make it easier to read at work on my break. I hadn't had the chance to use it until now, being that I hadn't been back to work yet. Now that she was doing better, I thought I'd go back to work if my uncle Tommy could sit with her during the day. I would offer to pay him because his favorite line was, "Money talks and bullshit walks," with his crazy ass. I was surprised he agreed to come today without me offering him anything, but I did slip him a twenty before he left.

I forgot to put my phone on vibrate, so when it started ringing, I had to rush out of the room to avoid waking my mother up. It was the detective calling, so I answered just knowing he was about to tell me that Samantha was in custody. I was so ready for this entire ordeal to be over so we'd never had to worry about this bitch again.

"Hello," I answered.

"This is Detective Oates, and I'm just calling to let you know that we went to the address that you gave me. We found a woman unconscious in the living room but no signs of forced entry, so if this was Samantha's doing, she was nowhere in sight."

I swore this bitch was unbelievable, and I was getting pissed at the fact that she was able to run around and do whatever the fuck she wanted. I didn't tell him the woman was her godmother because I didn't see it to be relevant.

"This is starting to be too much, and I'm tired of looking over my shoulder," I stressed to him.

"I understand your frustration, and if it will make you feel any better, I could put an officer outside of your mother's hospital room. When she leaves the hospital, I could have a car sit outside of her home until we have her in custody," he offered.

He didn't understand what I was feeling right now as the tears fell from my eyes because the stress of it all was too much. Almost losing my mother again was killing me inside, so like I said, I needed her to be in custody or a casket. It really didn't make a difference to me which one because either one would serve the purpose for me. She wasn't going to stop gunning for any of us, and that was what I needed the detective to understand. I told him that he could put an officer on my mother's door just to be on the safe side. After getting off the phone with him, I peeped into my mother's room, and she was still sleeping peacefully, so I stepped away. I wasn't hungry, but I was thirsty, so I was going to go to the hospital's cafeteria to get a drink. I was wondering what was keeping Jahiem. He still hadn't made it to the hospital. I called Dame to tell him to be careful, letting him know that she attacked her godmother and was ghost again.

He said that Deja was mad at him, so she took the baby and went to her mother's house. I thought that she should stay there until this shit was over, being that she was already attacked. It was safe to say that Samantha didn't give a shit about anyone probably because she didn't give a shit about herself.

When I got off the elevator, I saw Jahiem standing outside my mother's room holding some flowers and a "Get Well Soon" balloon.

"Hey, you," I greeted him with a smile.

"What's up? You didn't tell me that your mother was no longer in a coma," he said.

"I sent you a message telling you that my mother was no longer in a coma and off the ventilator, but you didn't respond."

"I didn't get the message, but it was good seeing her off the ventilator. I told you that your mother is strong and that was where you get it from. What did you need to holla at me about?"

"When we were at Amani's cousin house, he mentioned Samantha being in Midtown, so I remembered something Dame said. He said that his girl ran a charge on his business card for a hotel in Midtown. Why would that make me think that it was for Samantha? I don't know, but come to find out that it was."

"How do you know it was for Samantha?" he questioned with that look on his face.

I should have known that as soon as I said Dame's name, he was going to get that accusatory tone in his voice. The shit was getting old now when I done told his ass that nothing was going on with me and Dame.

"I had Dame take me to his place so that I could question his girl about the hotel and who she booked the room for. I told her that if she didn't tell me the truth, I was going to get the police to look at the tapes for that day at the hotel. I told her if they saw her on the tapes, she would be charged for harboring a fugitive. She admitted that she booked the room for Samantha, stating that she had no idea why she needed the room. She said a week later she met up with Samantha, and that was when she wanted to borrow her car. Once she told Samantha that she couldn't borrow her car, Samantha attacked her. She admitted to not seeing her after that, so I asked her if Samantha had any other family in New York. Samantha's godmother lived in the Bronx, she said, but she didn't know if she still lived there. She gave me the address that she remembered, so I called the detective and gave him the information. He called and said that they found a woman unconscious, same as my mother, but no signs of Samantha. He said that he was going to put a police officer outside of my mother's room and at our house when she gets released," I told him, but he didn't look to happy, so I knew he was about to be in his feelings.

"So, you were running around playing detective and not confiding in me? But you got that nigga with you every step of the way," he said, getting upset and making the shit about Dame once again when this didn't have shit to do with him.

"Jahiem, are you serious? It was his girlfriend who I had to question, so why wouldn't he be with me every step of the way?" I spat.

"You should have called me to let me know what the fuck was going on. I told you how I felt about you getting the police involved," he said, getting loud.

"I understand how you feel about the police, but had we involved them to begin with, she would be in jail and my mother wouldn't be in the hospital."

"So, you blaming me for your mother being in the hospital? We told your mother not to trust that bitch, so don't blame me."

Jahiem was blowing my mind right now because he was saying all this shit because he was mad about Dame. He knew just like I did that had we involved the police when I wanted to, she would have been arrested that day. I didn't care if he was upset when all I was trying to do was prevent her from hurting anyone else.

"I didn't say that I blame you. All I'm saying is that we should have involved them and we wouldn't be having this conversation right now. I don't want her to come after my mother again and succeed at taking her life. I'm not willing to risk my mother's life or anyone else's life just because you don't fuck with the police," I told him, being honest.

"Listen, I'm not trying to argue with you. I just want you to understand that if I'm your man, you need to confide in me. That nigga Dame isn't your nigga, so start treating his ass accordingly, because I'm sick of this friend shit. All that nigga is trying to do is fuck, but you don't see that shit, but it's all good. When he shows his true colors, don't come to me, telling me that I was right, because I know what I'm talking about."

I was in utter disbelief at the words that were coming out of his mouth and his acting like I was so naive. Dame had never been the type to pretend just to get something that he wanted, so Dame could miss me with all this shit he fixated on in his head.

"Why is Dame an issue for you? Have I given you any reason to believe that he was more to me than a friend? You dismissed me and slept with someone else, and I still haven't cheated on you, so I don't know where all of this is coming from. Is it because you know that you did me wrong, so you believe that I'm capable of doing the same? I'm grown, and I will never degrade myself because of your actions. All I want is for this girl to be behind bars so that we can go back to our lives without having to look over our shoulders. I'm trying to block every obstacle that keeps trying to break us, but I need you to understand that you caused those obstacles. I'm here and I'm not going anywhere, so stop making Dame an issue." I teared up.

He just didn't understand all the stress I was dealing with, but if he kept adding to the shit, I'd be at my breaking point. I loved him, but he was not going to have me out here acting like I had to put up with his bullshit, because I didn't.

Chapter Forty-seven

Reign

Jahiem left the hospital, and that was the best thing for him because I was about to show my natural black ass. He had a lot of fucking nerve to even fix his mouth to say some off-the-wall shit to me. He was waiting for a DNA test, but he had all his focus on a man I hadn't so much as kissed. I didn't care if Amani lied to him, and he had no idea, because it didn't make me feel any better. I needed him to grasp the fact that the shit still hurt whether he knew about it or not, but he wasn't getting it. He had continued to hurt me, and I had yet to do shit but be loyal to him when it was my right to do him dirty. He had me so mad that I was sitting in the bathroom trying to calm down before going back to my mother's room.

After washing my hands and leaving the bathroom, I walked to the elevator to get back upstairs. I'd been gone too long. I could have used her bathroom or the one on her floor, but I needed to blow off some steam without upsetting her. When I walked back into my mother's room, I saw an image that didn't belong to the nurse. My mother had a frightened look on her face that sent me into protective mode.

"Sir, what are you doing in this room?" I asked, going to stand next to my mother's bed.

I had no idea who this man was, and if I needed to press the nurse's button, I wanted to be close enough to do it. He might have had the wrong room, but I was wondering why he was still in the room when he noticed my mom lying in the bed. I was sure he realized that she wasn't the person he was looking for, so I needed him to leave. He walked over to the bed, and I started to panic, thinking he was going to do something to my mother.

"Sir, you need to leave now. Right now," I shouted.

"Raul," my mom said in a shaky voice.

I looked at her, and I could see the pain etched on her face from talking, but what I was stuck on was the fact that she called him Raul. The only Raul I knew was the boyfriend she was with before marrying my father, but she said he was dead.

"I thought you were dead," she cried.

"I wasn't dead, just dead to you. I returned to the house that night, and I heard you tell them where to find me. I'm the one who had my mother tell you that I was dead because I knew if they found me, they would kill me. I wasn't trying to lose my life, so I found a way to get my mother and daughter out of New York. I heard that you didn't even wait until my body was cold before you started seeing another man. Why the fuck would you just abandon our daughter? I waited for you to get clean, taking that time to get clean too so that we could raise our daughter together. You told my mother that after you got yourself together you was going to come back for our daughter, but you never did. You started a family and went about your life as if she never existed, not giving a shit about her. I was hurt, and I promise you that I wanted to confront you, but after a while my hurt turned into anger. I wanted you to hurt the same way that you hurt me and my daughter. Did your husband tell you that my daughter came to him and asked him if she could talk to you? Do you know what that man who you put on a pedestal told my daughter? He told her that now wasn't the time for her to come into your life. So, he was okay with your daughter not getting to know the mother who birthed her. When she came to me, she was hurt, so I told my baby girl that I was going to make sure that you hurt the same way she was hurting. Your husband's death wasn't an accident, and you getting hit over your fucking head was supposed to reunite you with his ass. I never wanted you to know that I was still alive, but you know the saying: 'When you want something done right, you have to do it yourself,'" he said, pulling a gun from his waist and causing me to freeze where I stood.

I could see that he had a silencer on the gun, and my body started to tremble, so I couldn't even focus enough to press the nurse's button. The button was at arm's length, but he would shoot me if I reached for it, so I wasn't willing to risk it. I knew that my mom couldn't talk him down, so I was going to pray that the officer who was supposed to be here would show up. I didn't want to say anything to his ass, being that he just admitted that my father's death wasn't an accident. I tried to tell my mother that Samantha was responsible for his death. If only she had listened to me.

"Listen, I don't know what you think you heard, but my mother loved you, and she would have never told them where you were. That was the reason they beat her to a pulp, leaving her for dead because she refused to tell them anything. The reason that she was unable to come back for your daughter is because she relapsed time and time again, grieving your death. My father saved her life, so in the beginning, it wasn't a love affair for her. That came much later. You were the one who decided to fake your death, so if that didn't happen, her falling in love with my father wouldn't have happened. I know that you're looking for someone to blame, but my mother is not to blame. You are," I said, getting pissed that he was really standing there pointing a gun at my mother for the decision that he made.

"And how the fuck do you know what happened when you weren't even born? I know what I heard come from her mouth. If she loved me, she would have loved my daughter and not left my mother to raise her. She didn't even come for her when she was well enough to care for her, but I guess she replaced my daughter the same way she replaced me," he shouted as he cocked the gun, making my heart rate speed up.

"You don't have to do this," I said to him, moving closer to him with my hands up in surrender.

I was willing to protect my mother at all costs, even if that meant taking a bullet for her because I wasn't about to let him kill her. He wanted her dead, blaming her for his decision, when he was the reason she continued the liquor and drugs all those years. Depression over his death was what kept her using and was the reason she couldn't care for their daughter. Samantha guilt tripped my mother by using the loss of her father, knowing his ass was still alive. I hoped that my mother now saw that she wasn't responsible for how Samantha turned out. It was this piece of shit standing here holding the gun and trying to take her life.

"Don't think that I won't kill your ass, so move the fuck out of my face."

Fear pumped throughout my body, but I wasn't about to let this man kill my mother because of his hurt feelings. I had no idea where the fuck the officer was who the detective was supposed to send to protect my mom.

"Listen, there is going to be a police officer outside of that door any second now, so if you don't leave now, you will be arrested," I tried.

He chuckled, pissing me off, but he underestimated me when he lowered the gun, continuing to chuckle. I knew that it was now or never, and being that I said that I would take a bullet for my mother, I rushed his ass. I was praying that my mother pressed the button for help because he was beating the shit out of me. He punched me so hard in my mouth that I could taste the blood. He grabbed me by my hair, holding on tight while he grabbed the gun that fell on the floor, causing me to scream out when he pointed it at me.

"Put down your weapon and step away," I heard, causing me to breathe a sigh of relief when he let go of my hair.

He was still holding the gun in his hand, so the officer repeated for him to put the gun down and to step away. When he raised the gun, I knew that he must have had a death wish when he pointed the gun. That was when the shots rang out. His body fell on top of mine, causing me to scream at the top of my lungs. I pushed him off me and ran over to my mother's bed, hugging her so tight as the tears streamed down my face. Hospital security said that they needed to move my mother to another room. He handed me my phone before escorting me out of the room, stating that the staff was going to transport my mother. I stood in the hallway until they got my mother situated into another room. My hands shook so bad when I took my phone out of my pocket, realizing that the phone security gave me wasn't my phone. It must have been Raul's phone, so I stuck it back into my pocket. I walked over to the nurse's station to inform them that I left my phone in the room. She told me to give her a few minutes and she would go see if she could locate the phone. In the meantime, I used the hospital phone to call Jahiem to tell him what happened, so he was on his way.

The phone that belonged to Raul vibrated in my pocket, so I removed it and saw that it was a text message. I opened the message, and it was Samantha asking her father to let her know where he wanted to meet. Jahiem made it to the hospital in record time, forgetting that he was upset with me when he heard me crying over the phone.

"Are you good?" he asked me.

I wasn't good, because my head was banging, and my lip was still stinging from the vicious punch

Raul's punk ass hit me with. I didn't need stitches, but the shit hurt like hell, but I wasn't going to let it deter me from what I had in my pocket. I took the phone out of my pocket and handed it to Jahiem.

"What is this?" he asked.

"This is Samantha's father's phone that security gave me thinking that it belonged to me. Look at the last text message," I said to him.

"We got this bitch. All we have to do is pretend like it's him responding to her ass and get her to meet us somewhere."

"Well, we need to do that shit as soon as possible before she finds out that her father was killed here at the hospital."

I was asked not to leave the hospital because the officer said that he was going to have to take my statement. He would have to get my statement about what happened another time because we weren't about to let this bitch slip through the cracks again. The hospital had the entire floor on lockdown, but we were able to leave through one of the stairwells.

"Where did you tell her to meet you?" I asked him once we were in his truck.

"Going through the messages between the two of them, it seems as if he just got to New York a few hours ago. I was thinking that we could have her meet us somewhere secluded so that I can snatch the bitch up."

"I thought when you was texting on the phone you already told her where you wanted her to meet him."

"Nah, I told the bitch that I was going to hit her back to tell her where the meet-up spot was going to be."

"Well, text her now, because I'm not trying to let this bitch find out about what happened at the hospital and run."

Chapter Forty-eight

Reign

Jahiem and I sat outside of the Motor Inn Motel in the cut waiting for her to approach the parking lot, but we had no idea what car she was driving. We picked the Motor Inn because it was one of the worst motels in New York. You didn't have to worry about cameras because there were none because of the high-crime activities that went on in this area. She didn't even question the motel of choice with her shady ass. We were sitting in the parking lot for about forty-five minutes before she pulled up. Jahiem pulled his cap down on his head, followed by his hoodie, and stepped out of the car. I watched as he hit her over the head with the gun and dragged her to the car, putting her in the back seat. He grabbed the duct tape and tied her feet and hands before getting back inside the car. He was out of breath and sweating like his ass just ran a marathon, so I asked him if he was okay.

"That was like a fucking workout." He laughed.

He pulled up to a spooky-looking wooded area about an hour later, and that was when I started having second thoughts. I knew she deserved to die, but it just wasn't in me to take a life or condone someone taking a life. I knew that no matter how I felt I couldn't back out now because I told Jahiem that I would have his back. Killing her really made us no better than her, but he wasn't going to want to hear it. He parked near a tree and told me to stay in the car before getting out and walking toward the other side of the gate. I saw someone emerge from the other side of the gate who was now talking to Jahiem. It was dark, so I really couldn't see who that person was, but looking closer I realized we were outside of a graveyard. I hoped Jahiem wasn't about to do what I thought he was because that would be a horrible way to die. I saw him walking back to the car, so I rolled my window down, stopping him before he got to the back door.

"What are you about to do?" I asked him.

"I'm about to punish this bitch for all of her sins." He chuckled, but I didn't think it was funny.

"Jahiem, please tell me that you're not about to bury that girl alive," I said, waiting for him to tell me that he wasn't.

"Yes, I'm going to make sure this bitch is buried alive."

"Jahiem, that is a terrible way for anyone to die."
I started tearing up.

"How the fuck do you think my sister, Ginger,
and the baby felt when she killed them? She
smothered a fucking baby with no remorse, so I'm
not going to show none for her ass," he barked.

I couldn't believe that I was crying after all
she did, but I guessed that only meant that I was
human and didn't want anyone else to die. I didn't
know who the guy was, but he was in a green
jumpsuit, so it made me think that maybe he was
the yard keeper. He helped Jahiem get her body
out of the car, and he was now carrying her over
his shoulder like she weighed nothing. Jahiem
followed him while I sat in the car playing tug of
war with my feelings. I knew the right thing to do
was stop him, so I jumped out of the car, not even
knowing what direction they went in. It was dark
and I couldn't see anything, so I started freaking
out as I felt myself walking on other people's plots.
I didn't want to call out Jahiem's name, but I was
going to have to because I was lost and I had no
idea which way I came from. I took my phone from
my pocket, turning on the flashlight so that I could
try to find my way back to the car. I swear I didn't
want to fall into an open grave because I would
really be fucked. I saw some lighting, but it wasn't
toward the side of the gate where we were parked.
I only knew that because this side was surrounded

by trees, so I decided to call Jahiem. Calling him would have been my first choice, but I didn't want him to know that I got out of the car and got lost when he told me not to get out.

"I should leave your ass out here because I told your ass not to get out of the fucking car," he said, going off on me.

"I came to look for you because I can't let you bury her alive, Jahiem," I cried.

"Trust me when I say she wasn't buried alive because the bitch woke up and was still talking shit knowing she was going to die. I shot the bitch, so I hope that makes you feel better, but if it doesn't, I don't know what to tell you," he said, walking ahead of me.

I cried the entire ride back to the hospital because I couldn't believe that I was a part of taking someone's life. He didn't understand why I gave a fuck about her dying after what she did to my mother. Knowing that she was dead didn't make me feel any better because my mother was still in the hospital and my best friend was still gone. What I'm trying to say is that I didn't get no satisfaction out of her losing her life when nothing changed. I couldn't speak for Jahiem, but he shouldn't have been feeling any satisfaction either, and to be honest, I probably would have felt better if she spent the rest of her life in jail. I ignored the voice in my head telling me to say something to him, and I rested my head against the headrest.

When he pulled up to the hospital, he asked me if I was okay, and I honestly didn't know how to answer without blaming him for how I was feeling. I knew that it wasn't his fault because I was with the bullshit, and when I decided that I wasn't, I didn't speak up until it was too late. I just wanted to get back upstairs to make sure that my mother was good before taking my ass home.

"I'm okay. I'm just going to make sure that my mother is good before going home and taking a shower."

"I'm going to go to the crib to shower too, so give me a call when you get home," he said, pecking me on the cheek.

I didn't know if he was upset with me, but at this point, I could honestly say that I didn't give a fuck and wasn't going to stress it. Nobody could tell me how to feel, so I wasn't going to allow him to make me feel bad for feeling sorry for her. When I got off the elevator, walking to my mother's room, I saw that there was an officer outside of her door. I had to show him my ID to enter the room, which I knew wasn't needed. Samantha wasn't coming back, so my mother was safe and didn't need him, but I couldn't tell him that.

She was sleeping, so I walked over to her bed and kissed her on the forehead, leaving to go home once I saw that she was good. I had a lot of emotions running through me right now, so hopefully a nice hot shower would relax my mind, body, and soul.

My aunt was going to be with my mother at the hospital today, so I decided to go into work, which I now regretted. I couldn't get anything done because I couldn't stop thinking about what we did to Samantha. So much for getting her out of my life and starting to live mine, because she had invaded my thoughts since the shit happened. Jahiem got the DNA results back, so he had a daughter and a baby mother who was already starting to show her ass. *How the fuck you lie to this man and now you need him to be at your daughter's beck and call?* I told him to tell that bitch to do what she'd been doing because if she wanted him involved, she shouldn't have lied. I was so over the bullshit that I decided to let her be his headache, being that I was already dealing with so much.

"Hey, how are you feeling today? I told you to take as much time as you needed," Dame said, interrupting my thoughts.

"I appreciate you being so patient with me, but I needed to get back to work to distract me from all that I have going on. I also told you to treat me like you treat your other employees, so I don't want any special treatment."

"I've been trying to treat you like all the others, but you're not just an employee to me, so it's hard to treat you like the rest," he admitted.

I didn't know what the hell was going on with me, but the tears just fell from my eyes, causing him to pull me in for a hug.

"Is something going on with you? You do know that you can talk to me, right?"

"I know that I should be feeling a lot better now that Samantha's father was killed and she disappeared, but I'm still stressed. Jahiem just found out that he's the father of a four-year-old little girl."

"Damn, it's always something with this nigga. You don't deserve this from him, and I'm not just saying this shit to say it. You're a good person, and you shouldn't allow anyone to take advantage of that," he said, causing my tears again.

I was an emotional mess and needed to get myself together because at the end of the day this was a workplace, not a therapy session. As soon as I got up to go back to my desk, my cell was ringing, and it was Jahiem calling. I didn't want to talk to him because I was stressed enough. I knew if I didn't answer he would keep calling, fixating on it in his mind that I was somewhere having sex.

"Yes, Jahiem." I sighed.

"Hey, Reign, this is Trigger. I'm calling from Jah's phone to let you know that he just got shot out here on the boulevard. They just rushed him to the hospital, but I couldn't stick around because I laid the nigga down who shot him."

My heart stopped, and I just wasn't comprehending what he was trying to tell me because to
me it didn't make sense. I felt sick, but I knew I
needed to get it together so that I could find out
what hospital they took him to. After he told me
what hospital, he ended the call after telling to get
there because he took a bad hit.

"I need to get to the hospital. Jahiem was shot."
My voice trembled as the tears fell.

"I got you," he said, walking me out to his car.

After I told him what hospital, I closed my eyes
and prayed that Jahiem's life was spared because I
couldn't lose him. I didn't want what I said to him
earlier to be the last words he got to hear from me.
My chest felt so tight from the fear I was feeling
right now, so I tried to take deep breaths, but they
weren't helping. Dame was driving past the speed
limit, and under normal circumstances I would
have asked him to slow down.

He kept asking me if I was okay, but I wasn't
going to be okay until we made it to the hospital
and they told me that he was okay. I couldn't even
imagine losing him when I still had so much to
tell him that I didn't get to tell him because of my
being angry. I needed to explain to him why I was
so upset finding out that Amani's daughter was his.
I just continued to pray that I was going to get a
second chance with him to tell him everything.

Chapter Forty-nine

Reign

When we finally made it to the hospital, I saw a few of the guys I recognized from the block wilding out. I heard one of them say that he couldn't believe that they took his nigga, and I swear all the life left from my body. My body slumped to the floor because I didn't want to believe that he was gone. I started questioning if I heard him right as I rocked back and forth on the dirty floor.

"What did I do to God for Him to keep taking everyone from me?" I cried out.

Dame helped me up off the floor, trying his best to comfort me, but I didn't want to hear anything he was saying right now.

"I need to see him," I said just above a whisper.

I wasn't going to accept him being gone unless they showed him to me because this had to be a cruel joke. My father, Jamila, and now Jahiem all being taken from me was unreal, and I was utterly confused right now. I walked over to the security guard, telling him that I needed to see him, and he told me to give him a minute. When the nurse emerged seconds later, she told me that his fiancée was in with him and asked for privacy.

"What do you mean, his fiancée? He doesn't have a fiancée, and if he did, it would be me," I shouted, getting angry that Amani was here at the hospital claiming to be his fiancée. "I'm his family, the only family he has, so whoever is in that room is lying, and I want to see him now," I shouted.

Everything that I was feeling moments ago turned into rage as I saw Samantha standing over his body with his hand in hers. How was it even possible for her to walk in this hospital, claiming to be his fiancée?

"Get the fuck away from him," I shouted.

"How about you get the fuck out of here and let me have my last moments with my fiancé," this bitch said, holding her left hand up and showing an engagement ring on her finger.

I didn't know what happened, but something took over me as I rushed her and started beating the life out of her. She was screaming for me to get off her, but I wasn't trying to hear her as I slammed her head into the floor. I didn't want this bitch to die. I needed her ass to die, and I damn sure tried with all that I had in me. I was mad that all the bad people got to live and the good people all died. If I could just take one of the bad seeds out of the equation, it would make me feel a little better. I didn't stop banging her head into the floor until I was being pulled off her ass hoping that the bitch was brain-dead.

The officers were trying to put me under arrest, but I told them that she wasn't supposed to be in

here with him. I told them that she had a warrant
for her arrest and that the officer on the fifth floor
would tell him the same thing. After I gave them
her name and my mother's room number to speak
to the officer, Samantha was arrested. Don't ask
me how or why she was still alive because I had no
idea, and the person who could explain was now
dead. I had so many questions but knew that all
the answers to those questions died with him.

I just knew that she was the devil because as
many times as I slammed her head against the floor,
her ass was still breathing. The nurse told me that
I could go in to say goodbye to Jahiem if that was
still something I wanted to do. I wanted to curse her
the fuck out because my love for him didn't change
just because that bitch told a lie. He wasn't engaged
to that crazy bitch, and that was one question that
I didn't need him to answer. I would have never let
the words leave my mouth to ask him if he proposed
to the bitch who killed his sister.

When my father died, I couldn't go into the room
to see him because I was scared, but I regretted it. I
didn't want that same regret, so I walked back into
the room, taking a deep breath before walking over
to the bed. Nervousness started to set in that was
followed by sadness that I was never going to see him
again. I took his hand and just decided to speak from
the heart and hope that his spirit was still in the room.

"Jahiem, I don't know why Samantha is still
breathing when you told me that you took care of
it that day. I'm not upset with you, being that you

probably had those same second thoughts that I was having. It hurts me to see you lying here in this bed like this when you didn't deserve to die this way. I know the last conversation that we had went left, but it was only because how passionate our love was for each other. You were jealous of Dame because you felt that I deserved better, and he might have been the better man, being that you kept fucking up. No, you didn't say it, but trust me, I knew that was the reason. I blamed you when you found out that Amani's daughter was in fact your daughter, and I apologize. I was mad only because I wanted to give you that child you wanted so bad. I wanted the baby I'm carrying to be your firstborn. That was the gift that I wanted to give to you, but now it's too late. I didn't get to express to you that I was no longer upset that she was your firstborn. I want you to know that I love you, and I will always love you and nothing is going to change that. I know that your baby and I are going to be fine because we will have three angels watching over us. Jahiem, continue to sleep in peace."

I kissed him one last time, telling him I loved him before walking out of his room feeling lost and brokenhearted. Dame was still waiting for me in the waiting area, telling me that my mother wanted me to come see her. I asked him if he could just call my aunt back to tell her to tell my mother that I would be back to see her tomorrow. I just wanted to go home to be alone, so I also gave him Kelsey's number and asked him if he could give her a call. I didn't have it in me to deliver any bad news. To be honest, I wanted to go to sleep just to wake up to find out that this was all just a bad dream. Dame asked me if I needed him to stay with me tonight, but I told him that I was going to be okay. I asked him if he could take me back to the job so that I could pick up my car because I wanted to drive to Jahiem's place. I was going to sleep in his bed tonight just to feel close to him, even if that meant pretending he was in bed with me.

It'd been two months since Jahiem was killed, and I would be lying if I said that I was feeling any better. Not a day went by when I didn't think about him, and my protruding belly was one of the reasons he was thought of every day. I made sure to talk to my baby about his father every day, letting him know how much he loved him. No, I didn't get the chance to tell him about the baby in the flesh, but I knew that he would have loved him with everything in him. I didn't know if Samantha went crazy after Jahiem's death, but she confessed to everything, something that she refused to do before. I couldn't believe that she was only sentenced to twenty-five years with the possibility of parole after twenty years. Emily was sentenced to ten years for her involvement, but I felt she should have gotten more time. If she had called the authorities, she could have prevented it from happening, but she waited days before saying anything.

My mother and I decided that there were too many bad memories in New York, so we were moving to Fort Worth, Texas. I didn't know why I agreed to move to Texas when I knew good and well I didn't want to move there. It might have had to do with me being pregnant and needing to be wherever my mom was going to be. I was frightened to be having my first baby, so if she wanted to move to Texas, so be it. We couldn't leave my grandmother, so she was going with us because I knew that my aunt Brenda wasn't going to care for her. Dame wasn't too happy about me moving away, but I promised him that I would visit, and he could do the same.

I sat on the porch watching the movers load all the things that my mother decided to take with her. I was wondering if I was ready for that Texas heat, being that my ass was four months pregnant and already having morning, noon, and night sickness. I knew that my life wasn't going to be the same without the love of my life or my best friend. All I could do was try to continue to live my life to the fullest until we all met again.